Finding
Katrina

Deb Kemper

Charlie Dawg

Press

This book is a work of fiction. Any resemblance of the characters to real people is unintentional. I chose the Ozark Mountain area for its beauty. The people there were always kind when I was a displaced Southerner amongst them. The subject of the book is, in no way, a poor reflection of the friendship, love, and hospitality I've found in those lovely hills. Bigotry and anti-Semitism are everywhere, often hidden.

Sonata for Katrina is not an existing piece of music. I don't write music but credit the many hours of comfort and delight that instrumentals inspire, not the least of these being almost everything Jeff Victor has recorded.

ISBN:
978-1-944979-15-7

Dedication

This book is dedicated to grandchildren. I wish we left you a kinder world. Bigotry and antisemitism are dangerous traits. Without them, the world would be a much better place.

The Beginning

Katrina stepped out of her rental car, adjusted her sunglasses and took a deep breath. The sunshine was bright and the warmth welcomed. She stretched, bending back and eyed the walking trail ahead, cut through a nature preserve. She tucked her dark braided hair on top of her head and clipped it, stretching a few more times, leaning forward to touch her toes and retie her Keen walking shoes.

Anxiously, she took long strides toward the trail set in a deep forest. The trees were tall, meeting overhead to make a living tunnel. It was a beautiful fall day in San Antonio and Kate was determined to unload all her stress on that trail. She was not alone.

The first half mile went quickly.

She stepped to one side to check her phone message that pinged 10 minutes into her hike. Her mom texted;

All is well, Asher is having a well-deserved nap. He and Uncle Leroy checked all the fence lines this morning and mended several. I called the Kleins to see about Isaac, earlier, to find him playing chess with his grandpa. Of course, your son was winning. We want you to relax and take your time coming home. We'll take care of everything here. Your boys will be fine, except missing mom's hugs. I love you so much, Katie.

Kate's eyes teared. She sniffed. Someone approached her, at a brisk pace, from her left. She glanced up, over her sunglasses. He slowed, then stopped about 2 feet away and whispered "Freeze! Don't move!"

Her first reaction was defiance, but she watched him and checked people nearby who stood still, moving only her eyes.

He whispered again, "There's a rattlesnake about a foot from your right shoe. If you move, it'll notice you. Be still and don't be alarmed. I can get you out of the way, if it appears to be life-threatening."

When Kate met his green-eyed gaze, he smiled and winked. He whispered, "I'll tell you when it's passed."

That three minutes on the trail felt like an hour. The trees blocked the sun overhead and kept the breezes at bay. And a wild poison critter had 10 human adults spellbound.

A woman approached from the carpark, toward the group, with her headset on, while scrolling her phone messages. She didn't look up. She approached the gathering quickly.

"Oh, hell." The green-eyed man whispered, as the new path walker appeared, a few feet away, in his peripheral vision. He reached for Kate's arm, snatching her back down the trail at least 3 yards. She made it easy.

Everything unfolded at once; an elderly woman, on the returning side of the path, had eased her backpack off and tossed it toward the wooded area behind the snake, thinking it would move away quicker.

Hell broke loose when the rattlesnake jerked itself into a striking position.

A few people ran back the way they'd come. Folks backpedaled to put more distance between themselves and the snake in front of them.

Someone alerted the bewildered newcomer, yelling, "Get back!"

She turned her gaze toward Kate, who mouthed SNAKE, knowing the woman couldn't hear past the music on her headset.

The newcomer spotted the snake, screamed, flailed her arms a few times and turned back to the carpark, running directly to her vehicle.

The snake struck without making contact, then recoiled tighter.

Again, the captives waited.

After fifteen more minutes passed, there was no obvious threat. The rattler relaxed and turned toward the opposite side of the woods. Everyone on the returning path let out a sigh of relief and moved at a quickened pace when it cleared.

Kate's savior chuckled. He said "You're trembling. Come on, I'll take you for a coffee." He intertwined her arm with his. "The cafe here makes really great coffee."

"Is that your introduction?" She asked, taking a deep breath and releasing it slowly.

"I feel like I've known you for a long time already." His amusement returned.

She countered, inspecting his lean build, short graying hair and absence off facial hair. *Looks vaguely familiar.* "Name, rank, etcetera would be appreciated."

A runner approached them from behind, breathing heavily and said, "Fletch, you still got some moves, buddy." His voice changed to tease, "*Saving your lady.*" He slapped his open palm on Fletch's back and returned to his run, laughing.

"Yeah, at least I found one to save, Sully!" Fletch boomed good-naturedly.

He turned to Kate, "Sorry. We used to be friends. Played Little League together a life time ago."

Kate unpinned her hair and adjusted her sunglasses. They stepped onto the patio behind the café. Fletch pulled out Kate's chair and seated himself beside her. A waitress appeared. They ordered iced coffees.

He sat back in the painted iron chair, studying Kate, who openly studied him. He pulled out his wallet, producing his Texas driver's license, sliding it across for Kate's perusal.

"That's who I am." He declared with a smile. "It's bonified. Even the Gold Star."

She read 'Lt. Commander Camden B. Fletcher'. Kate glanced up at his smug demeanor. *So familiar.* She dug out her identification and business card from her fanny pack, sliding both toward him.

She asked, "What do you do in the Navy?"

"Fighter pilot, flew F-18s for umpteen years. Military Intel for the last year and a half. Left Corpus Christie this morning for a few days leave." Sarcastically he added, "I'm off to Germany after—oops, that's classified,"

Fletch read her business card aloud. "*Telulah Jane's Catering Chef Kate Bishop Kosher/Hallal Parties/Banquets up to 600.* You own a catering company." He seemed surprised. "Who's Telulah Jane?"

Kate replied, "Telulah was my maternal grandmother, who died at 45 and Jane was my paternal grandmother, who kept me while Mom worked. Both mountain women. I use some of their recipes and they passed on the DNA to turn my passion into a living."

"How long have you been in business?"

She answered, "Sixteen years in December."

He checked her driver's license. "Katrina. That's lovely." He returned her license, but tucked her business card into his wallet. "What brings you to San Antonio?"

Kate sighed, wondering how much to tell the handsome stranger. "There was a conference here for chefs, booked last spring. Mom stepped up and volunteered to take care of my boys, who are teenagers. Conference is done, but I wanted a few more days here."

"Married?" He asked.

She shook her head, "Widowed."

He replied. "Sorry. So, you're alone?" He crossed his arms and leaned back.

She smiled and said, "A friend offered to come along, but I need the time. My staff is fantastic. They can run the show without me. So, I can relax."

"Do you *dance*?" He asked, his brow wrinkled.

"Yes, but not professionally." She quipped.

He chuckled. "Yeah, I need a dance partner tonight. You up for it?"

She nodded, "I'll make time for that, considering you saved my life today."

Seven hours later

Kate used her pass card to open the motel room door.

Cam Fletcher, standing behind her, spoke in a teasing tone, "Quite a coincidence, being in the same motel and neighboring suites."

Kate glanced back as she stepped through the doorway. "I thought you planned it that way." Her look was sober.

He laughed and said, "Above my paygrade, darlin'. I just asked for something near you when I checked in here." He stood in the hallway, leaning on the doorframe, his foot propping the heavy door open. "Could be handy to use the connecting door."

She didn't respond.

"I have a key?" He suggested.

Kate asked, "Do you wanna come in?" She'd removed her wrap and folded it, laying it in her open suitcase.

"Yes, ma'am, I do. Just don't know if I should."

She kicked off her ballet flats and unbelted her coral silk tunic. A hint of softness peeked out from her cleavage. Kate sighed and said, "Suit yourself."

"Give me fifteen minutes." He replied, closing her door.

After brushing her teeth and changing into her silky nightshirt, Kate linked her phone to her speaker, chose her nighttime favorite and plopped onto the love seat, propping her feet on the coffee table. She laid her head back and closed her eyes as *Luther* gently lullabied her tension away.

The connecting door opened, as her neighbor stuck his head inside. He asked, "May I come in?"

Kate nodded.

"That *Luther*?" Fletch asked hopefully.

Kate answered, "Yup."

"Sweet." He dropped onto the small sofa beside her, touching her thigh.

She smiled, checking out his plaid pajama pants and Texas A&M tee shirt.

She asked, "A&M your school?"

He responded, "Nah, my nephew and brother had me along with them when we toured campus the other day. Jimmy's trying to decide where to go to college. He bought the t-shirt for me as a joke."

"Annapolis doesn't have t-shirts?" She asked.

He jerked around to face her, "How do you know where I went to college?"

She smiled, "You must have mentioned it earlier."

"That's odd. I don't usually tell my personal story." He eyed her suspiciously, then relaxed and went quiet

After a while, Fletch yawned and looked longingly toward the connecting door. He turned back to Katrina and said, "I'm going to bed now. I'll leave the door unlocked if you decide to join me. Don't worry about waking me up, I'm awake every 3 hours anyway. Pilot training."

She smiled, "Thank you, I may take you up on that." She watched him walk into the next room and leave the door cracked. She stretched, turned off the music and climbed into her bed. She felt more relaxed than she had in a long time. Sleep came quickly.

At 3:00 am Kate heard her neighbor stirring and deserted the solitary warmth and comfort of her bed for his.

He sat in bed with an e-book propped open in his hand. He smiled at the sight of her, half asleep, tousled hair, the tail of her nightshirt caught on one side, in the waist of her bikini panties. He flipped the covers back.

She stretched like a cat, before climbing in on the opposite side of his bed and said, "I hope you don't snore."

He replied, "I don't *think* so." He put his e-book away and slipped between the sheets, after turning off the beside lamp.

Springfield, Missouri
2 years, 8 months later

In the foyer of her uncle's favorite restaurant, Kate Klein waited for her family to arrive. It was Uncle Leroy's 80th birthday.

Her long, braided salt and pepper hair hung to her midback. Her snug black dress slacks and red v-necked sweater kept one's eyes moving, exploring the curves.

She'd worn her black leather rubber soled shoes, that she worked in, because of the nasty weather.

She glanced up when the restaurant's main door opened with a blast of wet frigid air. An attractive bearded man entered. He scrubbed his shoes on the rug and shucked his wet raincoat, hanging it up on the crowded coat hooks. His longish dark, graying hair was slicked back from handsome features. His green gaze landed on Kate.

He hurried toward her with a familiar smile; his hand extended. A Texan accent warmed his words, "Kate? Cam Fletcher. Ruth's not here yet?" He didn't bother searching beyond her.

Kate recalled her friend, Tere's remark about Camden Fletcher, '*Handsome, dreamy eyes, like Neil Diamond dreamy*'. She was right.

Kate raised her voice to be heard over the echo of diners in the next room and smiled. "She's late. It's nice to finally see you. Mom talks about you all the time."

He leaned closer and said, "Your family makes the area palatable for me." He found himself grinning, at a glimpse of earrings with tiny triple diamonds in her earlobes, a diamond for each award her catering company had received. (He'd sketched the design of the Celtic knot for her mother.) He asked, "Wanna wait in the bar?"

Before Kate could answer, a petite blonde woman, sashaying toward them, stopped when she neared Cam. She flipped her long blonde hair over her shoulder and smirked. "*Fancy* meeting you here, stranger! I was just talking about you. Come on over and sit with us." She reached out to grasp Cam's arm. He warded off her hand and stepped toward Kate.

Kate turned to him, taking his arm, gazed into his dreamy eyes and said, "I'll understand if it's business, honey." She squeezed his arm when he didn't respond immediately.

Cam couldn't look away from the mystique of her dark gaze, long lashes, no makeup. Her right breast pressed against his bicep. He shook his head slowly.

His voice turned husky, "No, it isn't business, baby." He took her hand in his and turned to the blonde, who simmered. "*Mrs. Petersen*, I'm not here alone and even if I was, we've had *that* conversation."

Adele Petersen stumbled back a step, her hand at her throat, "Hah!" She exclaimed dramatically. She tried to smile.

A mob of revelers, preparing to leave, swarmed the small space, vying for spots nearest the coat racks. Finally, the tallest man among them held up jackets for identification.

Adele Petersen attempted to step between the couple, who were locked together. Her exit was thwarted. Awkwardly, she pushed past Camden.

Once she left, Kate asked, "Was that out of line?"

Cam looked down at her hand that he still held. "No, ma'am. She's a client's wife who won't leave me alone. Thank you for the rescue. Do I need to give you your hand back?"

Kate responded, "No, I'm good. Glad to be of service."

Another large group of diners made their exit.

Kate and Cam sidled closer to the front desk.

The hostess, at the back of that crowd, caught Kate's eye and mouthed, signaling with her hands, 'Your table, give me ten minutes.'

Kate nodded affirmation.

Seconds after the throng cleared out, another damp, cold blast accompanied Ruth and Evangeline inside.

"It's about time you got here, Mom." Kate shot her mother a conspiratorial look.

Ruth was all smiles, her voice pure Southern Highlands, "Sorry, darlin', traffic was horrible. Leroy's parking the car." She kissed Kate's cheek and bussed Cam's, whispering, "We've been waiting for you to arrive."

Cam chuckled and replied, "Yes ma'am, I suspected as much."

Ruth turned toward the lady's room. "I *must* powder my nose." She strode away with her usual regal composure.

Evie, Ruth's younger sister, stayed back to meet her husband at the door. Once inside, Leroy placed his umbrella in a large stand.

A bolt of lightning split the sky, followed by a roll of thunder that shook the place. Lights flickered for a moment. The guests quieted. A generator kicked on and lights followed.

Kate's aunt ambled over for a hug. Her nose wrinkled, as she grinned, and said, "Law! I have missed *you*, child." Kate kissed Evie's flawless mocha cheek. Evie turned to Cam and said, "Camden, you *do* look handsome tonight."

Cam responded, "Thank you, Miss Evie."

Leroy, dressed to the nines in black leather, leaned his dark, lanky frame toward his niece's cheek for a kiss. "Lookin' gorgeous as evah!" His Mississippi accent still fresh and smooth, 66 years after he left the Delta behind.

"Get it from Aunt Evie and Mom." Kate smiled.

Leroy nodded, his voice deep and mellow, "Speakin' the truth, baby girl."

He shook hands with Cam and shoulder-bumped him. "Man, I'm starvin' let's go!"

The hostess, who waited at the entrance to the dining area, smiled and led the patrons to their table.

Chapter One
Bishop's Bailiwick

The three-story Victorian quivered as roofers tossed bundles of asphalt shingles up to the second story. Kate turned on the shower.

The doorbell chimed over the uproar.

All three dogs raged. She redressed in discarded sweats and a tee shirt.

Peals rang out again.

Kate muttered to herself, "Who on earth? I have to answer. I left the blasted car out."

She dashed down the grand staircase of her family home, in southeastern Missouri.

She flew past the landing's window-seat, crowned by a six-by-eight-foot-stained glass meadow.

The silhouette framed in the oval frosted glass of the ancient oak front door was familiar.

Dang! It's the roofer! and I look like.... A glance down revealed dust and paint stains on her clothes. *He hasn't seen me cleaned up in a month.* She flipped her long salt and pepper braid over her shoulder and threw the door wide, smiling. "Mr. Fletcher, there's a newfangled invention called a telephone."

Cam chuckled. "Yes ma'am. I left two messages on your house phone, one on your cell." Honey iced his deep Texan drawl, his green eyes bright with amusement.

Mmm, I do like the beard and mustache, wonder what it would be like to kiss him. Kate bit her lip and replied, "I'm sorry, the shop vac's loud. I didn't hear the phones. Have on girl pants today—no pockets." Her crooked smile robbed her words of acidity.

He nodded. "Third story roof's about done." He held her eyes, still smiling. "I'm pulling the crew off for a job in town until your carpenter replaces the siding, that he tore off the second-floor bathroom."

"He's not been here in two days and I can't raise him on his cell phone." Her bare foot pushed her mom's two rowdy Wirehaired Dachshunds back from the door. Her Border collie stood guard at her knee, following the conversation.

"I want it done before we tear off the second story roof. We have to flash the siding prior to laying the shingles. I have a man." He pressed his lips together and studied her with a warming green stare.

"Does he show up and finish what he starts?" Kate frowned; hands propped on her hips.

"Yes, ma'am." Cam's eyes held hers.

"By all means, call him." *Your regard is engrossing, sir.*

"I will. How's Ruth doin'?" Camden asked.

"Very well, thank you. I'm headed to see her within the hour." She yanked her hot pink, holey, paint-stained tee-shirt down.

Silence fell amid staccato blows of air hammers and the rattle of men's voices.

Kate's voice softened, "Was there anything else? I'm in dire need of a shower."

"You ever ridden a motorcycle? I'm riding a charity poker run this Sunday, for Breast Cancer Research...."

Crap, I'm not wearing a bra! She looked away, recovered her smile, and met his attention returning from a quick frontal scan.

He continued, "...mother beat it ten years ago. Ride every year in her honor."

"How can you play poker on a motorcycle?" A chilly breeze drifted through the open door. Kate fought the urge to cross her arms.

"We stop at participating businesses along the trail and pick up a card. At the last stop, best hand wins."

"Well...I had no idea." Kate said.

"You don't know what you've missed." Camden backed across the deep front porch. "Tell you what, I'll run out later. We can take a spin and see how you like it. I'll be here at 4:30." He turned to the steps.

"I haven't proper attire." She shouted, envisioning buxom blondes covered in leather, that she'd seen on billboards.

"Jeans work with a heavy jacket. Got a lady's helmet I'll bring." He pulled on Ray-Ban sunglasses as his long strides put distance between them.

"I'll bet you do." Kate muttered, admiring his broad shoulders and snug Levis.

The Rehab Center

"How's our roof coming, darlin'?" Ruth Bishop stood for a few moments, with the aid of a walker. Her wavy silver hair was bobbed to frame her classic features. Even without her usual lipstick, blush and powder, she was a handsome woman.

"Mr. Fletcher came by. They've completed the third story." Kate answered.

"Call him by his given name, Katrina." Ruth scolded her daughter. "He's only a few years older than you are. He's also single and, in case you haven't noticed, very handsome." She caught her breath, "It's been three years since Reggie's death, honey. Time for you to move on. You're young and vital. Don't let this love pass you by."

Kate inhaled the fragrance of a rose and lily bouquet in a fine crystal vase on the armoire. "These are lovely."

"They're from our roofer." Ruth grinned.

"He's coming over later with his motorcycle. He asked me to ride a poker run with him on Sunday."

"He finally got up the nerve to ask you!" Ruth straightened, stretching her back. "He has a sidecar he bought for his nephews. I've ridden the past two years with him." She laughed at her daughter's expression. "Yes, your mother's been riding around with a man young enough to be her son, on a motorcycle *and* gets flowers from him." She stood a bit straighter, amused at her only child's consternation.

"Mmm, it's like *that* is it?" Kate twirled a strand of hair that slipped from her braid.

"If my son had lived, he'd be like Cam. He reminds me so much of your father—the good parts, at least." Ruth paused. "Take him up on his offer. You'll have a blast—and high time you did."

With a somber face, Kate said, "I resolved to never date again. Men are too much trouble."

Ruth stopped to study her daughter; one eyebrow raised, and sighed deeply. "Not all men are like Reggie, Kate. Give Cam a whirl, for your mother's sake, please. There's so much more to life than work. You've always been a *good girl*, who works too hard. It's time to loosen your inhibitions…and let your hair *all* the way down."

The Bailiwick

The low rumble of the Harley vibrated the kitchen windows. Kate watched Cam Fletcher dismount the black beast, remove his helmet, and sweep his hand through his hair.

She met him at the backdoor.

He grinned. "Miss Kate, you ready?"

"Yes, Mom sends regrets she won't be able to accompany you on the poker run Sunday." She passed through and locked the door behind her.

"You'll do nicely." He turned toward the yard, staying in step with her. "Let's go over basics, how to sit, where to put your feet. Then we'll head down the road. There's a pub a few miles away. I thought we'd have a bite to eat, if that suits you."

"Thank you, dinner would be lovely." Kate replied.

She pulled on the helmet he handed over. He reached to secure the strap, saying, "Let me do that. You don't want it to blow off."

His breath smelled mildly of tobacco smoke and mint; the tip of his tongue teased the corner of his mouth. Kate averted her eyes, relishing the clean scent of his soap.

"You sit here." Cam stepped back and patted the raised leather seat on the rear of the bike. "Your feet go there." He pointed at the footstep. Be cautious of the exhaust. It gets super-hot, so stay clear. Leather boots were a good choice." He climbed on the bike. "Now, come on." He raised his arm to give her a boost.

Kate mounted the seat behind him to slide snuggly against him. *This can't be right. We're way too close!*

Cam reached back and pulled her knees against his hips. "Hang on and move with my body. It's kind of like…dancing. When I lean, you lean with me. Got it?"

Kate felt her dignity turned to dust as she decided to obey. "I hope so." She glanced at his sideview mirror and caught him grinning at her discomfort.

He started the bike and moved slowly to give her time to adjust to the noise and momentum. They reached the gate to the property, a quarter mile from the house. Cam leaned a little to the right, Kate moved with him. When he accelerated at the blacktop, she grabbed him and held on.

What on earth am I doing? I'm too old for shenanigans! Her resolve to refuse his Sunday ride held for the first few minutes.

As she grew accustomed to the racket and vibration of the machine, she began to notice the fields they passed. The shield on her helmet kept the wind from taking her breath.

The scenery was lovely, shadowed in the deep dusk of early autumn in the Ozark Mountains. Waning sunlight set the ash trees' orange and yellow flames flashing through the dark eastern cedar.

Trees shedding for the art of all seasons. How like their cycle is this life? She mused.

Five miles from home, Cam parked the bike in front of Homer's Saloon, a rough cedar-sided building with a low green metal roof and few windows.

"Did I do it right?" Kate asked as she dismounted, using Cam's arm as leverage.

He grinned. "Any day we don't lay her down's a good day, darlin'."

Okay, positive affirmation, she thought.

Country music boomed from a jukebox when Cam opened the wooden cross-hatched door for her. His hand fit the small of her back. He steered her to a booth on the right then slipped onto the bench opposite her.

Cam explained the menu, "They have great steaks here, chicken too. Grilled over a wood fire. The owner's brother grows all the food on his organic farm down the road."

A young woman with curly shoulder length red hair arrived at the table wearing short shorts and a tank top. "Hey, Cam." She laid menus in front of them.

"Hey, Lucy." He glanced up. "This is Kate. We'll need a few minutes. Wanna bring me a beer? Miss Kate, what'll you have?"

"Club soda with lemon, please." She responded.

"Good." He pushed the menu away, tapping his knuckles on the tabletop and exhaled noisily.

"What are you ordering?" Kate leaned toward him, studying his hands.

He stopped knocking on the table and rubbed both palms down the front of his jeans. "Beef, rare. Salads are acceptable and Homer does an old fashioned twice-baked potato that's nirvana."

He waited a few minutes, watching while she perused the menu. "So, Miss Kate, what'll it be?"

When she smiled, one eye almost closed, long lashes framing her dark eyes. "Can you just call me Kate? I like the way it sounds in your mouth. It keeps me from feeling like your elder."

"My pleasure. Will you stop calling me Mr. Fletcher?" He asked.

She beamed and said, "I can do that. I'll have the salad and baked potato." She closed the menu and handed it to him. "Tell me what brought you to Missouri from Texas."

Lucy appeared with drinks and took the order from Cam. He rolled up the long sleeves of his denim shirt, and crossed his solid arms on the table.

"Came up here after bad weather to help a buddy of mine do a few jobs and decided to stay. Like the scenery…," he paused and glanced around, "and business was good. There's a lot of new construction goin' on, so we have steady work, between tornadoes." He shrugged. "It's a short trip to visit Texas. I built a house here a year ago, thinking I'd sell soon and go back. He shrugged.

She noticed several couples left their tables for a dance floor on the other side of the room. Cam watched her glance their way.

"Now tell me why you decided to move back." He'd regained her attention.

"My youngest son left for college. I came for a visit, before Uncle Leroy's birthday and realized Mom's health wasn't superb. She asked me to get the house into livable shape. So, I sold my catering business in Kansas City and rented out the condo, I bought after my husband was killed. It's near a major hospital, so I left it furnished for visiting nurses to let."

He nodded and replied, "Glad you're here. Can't believe I've known Ruth for more than two years and *we've not met until*…what a month ago? Guess that was the right time. What are the two of you goin' to do? There's eight bedrooms in the place."

She laughed. "Yes, and six baths, all needing work. Mom envisions **Bishop's Bailiwick Bed and Breakfast**. I'll cook, we'll hire help to clean, and she'll run it." Kate pondered the future for a moment. "My grandmother kept an old-fashioned boarding house when I was a child. I could go for that, a communal house with ladies in residence. We'll see how Mom fares when she gets over these surgeries."

"Think we need to build a ramp so you can get her in and out when I…," he cleared his throat; "…you don't have help?" His cheeks burned.

Her voice softened. "That's a good idea."

"I'll see to it then." Cam nodded.

Lucy arrived with their dinner. "Can I get you anything else right now?" Her darkly outlined blue eyes sparkled in the dim light.

"I want a glass of tea, please ma'am. Kate?"

"The same, thank you." She noticed the look Lucy passed her and wondered if she'd invaded territory.

After dinner, Cam left the table for several minutes and stopped by the jukebox, which had fallen silent. He fed in quarters and made selections. When the first song began, he was back at their table, extended his hand, and waved his fingers, saying, "C'mon."

Kate slid out. He caught her hand in his and headed for the dance floor.

The slow song drew them close. Kate felt a little breathless. *This man mmm.... He probably has a harem—or two.* She inhaled his scent. *So familiar!*

Cam leaned to her ear, the heat of his whispered words on her neck sending shivers through her. "You feel good in my arms, Kate." He smiled into her dark eyes.

She asked, "Feels wonderful to me, too. I'm starved for human touch. My crew started and ended the days with hugs."

"Happy to oblige anytime." Cam smiled.

They lingered for the next song. He pulled her close again. "There's a woman comin' this way. She's Homer's sister. Play along with me, please."

When the next song began Kate felt a tap on her shoulder. She glanced over to find Raggedy Ann had turned seventy years old. She stood a few inches shorter than Kate and wore a ruffled red dress with a white pinafore.

"Excuse me, this is my dance." The doll frowned through heavy makeup and tossed one unnaturally red braid over her shoulder.

Kate, surprised, turned to Cam who smiled. His arm stretched around to rest his hand on her hip, pulling her against him.

"Ruby, darlin', meet the love of my life, Kate Klein. Honey, this is Ruby. Remember I told you about her, we're...friends." He winked so Kate nodded affirmation. "Miss Ruby, I'm afraid I'm spoken for. Kate holds the keys to my heart."

Ruby stomped her foot like a mad four-year-old and crossed her arms, "Well!" She stormed away.

"Thanks. That's one of the drawbacks to comin' out here. If Homer gets busy, and doesn't keep a close eye on her, she can get outta hand." He pulled Kate back to face him. "You see, I'm not her only boyfriend. There're twenty or more of us." He grinned. "Any port in a storm's the way it is with gals like our Ruby."

"I see." Kate was amused at the encounter.

Cam smiled and wrapped his arm behind her. "Will you dance with me anyway?" He took her hand in his and moved to the music.

Kate whispered into his ear. "Why does she dress up like a doll?" Her knees went weak at his nearness.

Strong arms pulled her into his firm body. "I have no idea. Trying to start a trend I suppose." He chuckled at Kate's bewilderment.

Kate asked, smiling, "Do you have a woman queued up everywhere you go?"

Cam laughed and shook his head, "I swear, no. It's purely coincidence. Nobody ever sees me with anybody, but Mark or one of the crew."

She smiled and said, "Just checking. I'd hate to be with a man who was already spoken for."

He shot her a sidelong glance and shook his head. "Not yet."

***

The ride home was slow. She fought the urge to lean into him. The night air held a damp chill.

There'll be fog in a little while. A gloaming mist settling over the damp places, lit by the full moon. She raised her eyes to the brilliant light fighting for showmanship.

What'll happen when we get back? If I invite him in, he might get the wrong impression, or maybe the right idea. I'll thank him for dinner, say goodnight and hope he doesn't rush off.

Cam rolled through the gate to the property. He stopped in the driveway and turned off the ignition. They sat motionless, as silence settled around them. Cicadas chirping intensified as the dark stillness deepened. Off in a distant pasture, a coyote howled, joined by three more, as they ran rabbits to ground.

Cam reached back and squeezed Kate's knees. They moved at the same time, almost tipping over. He caught himself, the bike, and her.

His deep laughter resonated in the still night. The dogs barked wildly at the breakfast room window.

"Come on, girl. Let's bring the dogs out, for their nightly run and get you inside." He still held her arm and wound it into his. He stole a glance to find her studying him as they climbed the steps of the back porch.

She dug her key out of her pocket and unlocked the kitchen deadbolt. He reached past her to open the door. Three dogs shot through to the yard. Cam watched Kate's dog, Dixie, run along the path on the outer edge of the yard that she had recently started.

Cam said, "She's quite a gal. Border collies will work a herd until they drop dead. Did you know that?"

Kate nodded before she answered. "Yes. Their hearts burst. They don't know when to stop. They need responsible people to love them."

"Mmm…. They're really smart too. I read an article awhile back, in *National Geographic.* They're the smartest animals in the world."

"I believe that. She understands me better than my sons do." Kate glanced up at the handsome man.

Cam laughed. "That may be a gender issue, too." He took a step closer. "Thanks for the evening. Think you can help me with the ride Sunday?"

"I'll look forward to it." She smiled up into his gaze.

He glanced down at the few inches between them. "I caught the look Lucy threw your way. I've never plowed that ground and don't intend to. Don't waste time wonderin' about those kinda things, Kate. I'm not like that. Some girls have odd ideas. Pardon my verbiage, but they want a penis with a paycheck and that's all they're looking for."

"Mmm, yeah. Two young ladies who worked part-time for me were determined to marry money, so they'd never have to work again. One wound up raped, by an attorney, she took a shine to and the other was severely beaten right before marrying *that* perfect man."

Cam nodded and studied her mouth for a moment in the light from the kitchen window, sighed, and turned away. He whistled sharply; all three dogs raced past them into the house. "Well, I'll see you Sunday about 8:30. That's a.m., *Katrina.*"

She watched him, as he walked back to the bike, pulling on his leather gloves. He quickly mounted the machine and rode away.

Chapter Two

Sunday's weather was delightful. The day was cool to start, but warmed after noon. Kate enjoyed the scenery and the ride. They pulled into the drive at Bishop's Bailiwick an hour before sunset.

Stiffly, she climbed off the bike, stretching to relieve the kinks.

Cam dismounted, watching her from the opposite side.

"I have to be out of town for a few days. Cracker will have the crew here tomorrow morning." He accepted the helmet, securing it on the seat she'd vacated.

"Alright, thank you for telling me." She yanked her shirt down and unhooked her braided hair to drop down her back.

"Do we have dinner waiting?" He asked, with a smile.

Kate grinned. "I thought perhaps you'd forgotten."

"No ma'am. Not a chance." He followed her to the door. "So, what do you think about the ride?" He placed his hand in the hollow of her back.

She glanced over. "I'll let you know in a few days. See if I'm able to climb the stairs to my room tonight *and* brush my teeth. Sorry you didn't win with that full house. I thought for sure you would."

He took the key from Kate and opened the door, saying, "Trust me. It was a very good day."

Cam opened a bottle of red wine and half-filled large goblets while Kate dished up fagioli. He swirled the glass and savored the bouquet of the merlot.

"Local winery?" He took a sip.

"I brought a few bottles down from a vintner I used outside Kansas City."

"When did you have time to cook all this?" Cam gathered silverware and water glasses to set the table.

"Last night, after I visited Mom, who sends her regards." She removed the olive focaccia bread from the oven, covered it with a cloth, and set the pan on hot pads. "Aunt Evie came over to put it in the oven and set the timer to start 45 minutes ago and voila."

He grinned as he placed bowls of chopped Greek salad on the table. "Great timing." He ran his fingertips along a newly painted cabinet door. "Your kitchen's comin' along." He filled a water pitcher, picked up two glasses, and delivered them to the round kitchen table.

"Thank you. I like light and bright. Mom likes traditional dark wood. She told me to change what I wanted, so I aimed for medium and went with this green. You're pretty handy to have in here." Kate admired his progress.

"No sister 'til I was fifteen." He popped a radish in his mouth, crunched in the quiet. "My father was a Methodist preacher. Momma organized dinners for parishioners, council, and the rest of the righteous. With no daughters, the help fell to my brother Cooper, and me."

"Are your parents still in Texas?"

Cam gazed her direction for a moment. "You could say that. The Preacher died in a wreck thirty-six years ago and Momma remarried. She taught music at the local high school 'til she retired. She and Pop live outside Austin on his family's ranch.

"I should be back in town before Saturday night. How about dinner?" He watched her closely. "Somewhere that's not a bubba bar or that I *have* to wear a tie and jacket to get in? Maybe dancing afterward?"

She turned away to dish up bowls of Italian soup and set them on the table at their placemats. "We'll see." A shy blush singed her complexion.

"What has to happen in the next few minutes to make that a 'sure, I'd love to'?"

She propped her hand on her hip, cocked her head to one side. "You're awful bossy. Can I think about it? Maybe I have other plans."

"No, I checked your calendar by the fridge. Next Saturday's clear." He flashed a brilliant smile and winked.

Kate went quiet, turning away to hide her smile.

Cam held her chair and waited until she was comfortable before taking his own. He reached for her hand and they closed their eyes. "Thank you for a lovely day and a beautiful woman to spend it with."

Kate peeked up at him. "Sometimes I go to…worship on Saturdays then spend the afternoon with Mom. They give her a day off from physical therapy, so we can walk in the gardens at the rehab center and have dinner together. She should be home before long. She's passed the halfway mark."

Cam scooped up the fagioli. "Mmm…fantastic! You're good, woman." He broke a piece of focaccia and laid it on her bread plate, broke a larger piece for his own.

"Thank you." She smiled, enjoying his pleasure as she tasted her soup.

"We've talked about you a lot. Ruth does go on about her lovely Katrina and grandsons. I forget you don't know as much about me as I know about you."

He paused. "About a year after your husband died, I met Ruth at church. My partner and his wife are always trying to save me. I'm tolerant to their loving efforts. Ruth and I had lunch occasionally with the group we all attended. After a while she invited me out here for dinner. She cooked and found a willing audience for her stories." He sat back and studied Kate.

She met his eyes for a moment, then looked away with a smile. Her response was tender. "Cam, someone can seem familiar through their mother's praise but, *knowing* them is totally different."

"You're faithful, persevering, and true. You err on the side of mercy. You champion the underdog. The other stuff's important, but not nearly so much as a strong character."

She beamed as she met his gaze. "I don't know what to say."

He gave her a moment. "You don't have to say anything. Just know I'm not killing time with you."

He thumped the antique oak table with his knuckle. Cinnamon and Shuga, the wirehaired Dachshunds, rallied to bark and dance.

"I've gotta learn not to do that around here." He chuckled. "These two clowns make you laugh, don't they?" Both dogs stood with their front paws on his thigh. They jostled each other for position, tails wagging their whole back ends. He rubbed their bearded chins.

Kate nodded. "There's something about their grumpy old man faces and crazy antics that keep you from taking them too seriously." Kate sipped wine and watched Cam tease the dogs. Dixie sat beside her chair, always vigilant, golden eyes taking note of every movement in the room.

Cam looked serious for a moment and asked, "Tell me what kind of music you like?"

Kate grinned and studied the ceiling, "Everything, I think. Some freeform Jazz is irritating, Asian music is not always for me." She explained, "When we started a job, and we did three or four large orders at a time, I'd put on soft Jazz or another instrumental composition. Concentrating music. When we needed motivation, I'd put on something feisty, like R&B. But when we needed more encouragement or were exhausted, but plodding on, I put on *Santana*. The ladies who worked with me were mostly Mexican and Central American, or African immigrants. Sometimes they brought their own music in and we danced!" She smiled at the memory.

Cam grinned and said, "That's fantastic! Who taught *you* to dance?"

"Aunt Evie loves R&B. She taught me to groove with that, from a tender age. When Uncle Leroy joined our family— yeah, *that* was when I got an education. He loves Funk. He's smooth too." She paused for a moment, "It's hard to believe he's passed his 80th birthday. They still go out clubbing."

Cam nodded, "I love that. Just hope I have a few moves at that point."

Kate smiled, dreamily. Then she leaned forward, grasped his hand and asked, "Your turn?"

Cam lost his train of thought at her abrupt nearness. He sat back in the chair and began, "Um, Momma was a high school music teacher. We all had piano lessons. Cooper is really good with any stringed instrument. Lindy is superb on piano and percussion. I like everything, even rap, and that's saying something. Mostly I love ballads, jazz and classical music. We were reared on the classics." He shrugged. "Country's okay too."

"Where'd you learn to dance?" She sat back, realizing his discomfort.

"Momma insisted. She taught us the old standbys and my uncle, her brother, took us in hand. We always have a blast with Han. He taught us whatever was in vogue at the time *and* took us clubbing."

They fell quiet for a few seconds before Cam said, "Come on, I'll help you clean up. Gotta get to bed."

"Go ahead I'll get this." Kate replied.

"I don't want to leave just yet," Cam frowned. "If that's okay?

"Then stay as long as you want. I enjoy your company." She smiled encouragingly.

"Yeah, me too. Um, did you go out much with Reggie?" Cam asked.

It was Kate's turn to be quiet for a moment and think through an answer. She sighed and said, "No, not...I can't think of a time that we left the boys with a sitter and went out. I worked *a lot.*

"We had a deal. I made the money, Reggie worked on his tenure and publications. Eventually he'd have salary increases, but it was up to me, if we were to have a house, two cars and a babysitter.

Cam's frown stayed in place, "Not even like...anniversaries and birthdays?"

"No. After Isaac was born, with all his difficulties, there was no *spare* time for anything. I waited tables before and after we married, saving what I could for the business I wanted."

She took a sip of wine, then continued, "When I had enough money stashed, to buy an old, rundown house in a questionable area, I began looking and found a neighborhood full of new immigrants. Uncle Leroy and Daddy came up and looked at the house, didn't like a few major problems. We looked at another house, down the same street that suited their requirements and met code. We three ripped into it. It took a few trips for them and all my savings to get it ready *to become* 2 kitchens. I doubled down on work and made it happen a year later. They still came up and helped by painting and laying tile and such.

"They both pitched in cash to cover those costs. There were 2 bedrooms and a bath upstairs that I waited several years to finish. The time came later that I needed the space, had to hire that renovation out."

"How did Reggie feel about you making a business move to the slums?" Cam crossed his arms.

"Wasn't *his* business." Kate crossed her arms, still smiling. "He agreed to stay out of my business if I stayed away from campus. He didn't want his...associates to know what I did. He saw it more as a step up from waiting tables, but I was still a servant."

Cam shook his head. "I don't get that. Seems he should have encouraged his...associates to employ your services."

Kate smiled. "Not the way he worked. He aspired to a lofty place because he came from acquired wealth. His father didn't behave like that, but his mother was superior to the rest of the world.

"I love cooking and feeding people. My job was to have sons and provide capital. I did my best. There were people from the university who frequented my clients' soirées, but I avoided them to keep from embarrassing Reggie. It never occurred to me, until after his death, that there was much wrong with our set up.

"Mom and Aunt Evie worked hard, at nursing, to support the Bailiwick. I don't know that Daddy ever sent money home. Grandma, Mom and Evie did everything or paid for it to be done."

Cam still frowned and said, "You've *never* been a princess?"

Kate burst out laughing, then said, "Hell, no!"

Cam grinned at her amusement and shook his head.

Kate said, "I need to move around and loosen things up before I shower." She grimaced when she stood. "Let's get busy."

Cam picked up the dishes and stacked them on the counter. He ran water and rinsed the dishes, while Kate loaded the dishwasher.

"What do you want me to do with the soup?" He asked.

"I'll let it cool and come back down later to stick it in the back fridge."

"Okay, I'll set it back there on the counter. Hand me a trivet." He picked up the pot and carried it to the laundry room counter and returned to the kitchen.

"Thank you for everything." Kate moved closer to him, stretched upward and kissed his cheek.

He caught her hands and nodded. "The privilege is mine, Katrina. Walk me out?" He asked.

"My pleasure." Kate followed him through the mudroom and out the backdoor.

Chapter Three
Kendal Ranch

The small twin-engine plane circled a white Greek revival house, situated in the middle of two hundred acres of lush Texas pasture, and orchards. By the time Cam was ready to land, his mother, Elaine Kendal, arrived at the runway, to pick him up. She stood at the front of an ancient Jeep and waved a white hankie.

It's always a surprise to see you older. Your dark hair turning gray, new wrinkles, a little more stooped. But your eyes sparkle and you'll always be 36 in my mind, Momma. He mumbled, "None are immune to the ravages of time."

Cam taxied to within sixty feet of her.

He waited for the system to shut down and reached behind his seat for a duffle and garment bags. He hauled his clothes out and dropped the duffle at her feet for a full arm hug.

"How you doin', pretty lady?" He asked.

"Glad to see you. Harry's driving me crazy waiting for you to get here. Coop will be over later, without the boys." She inhaled noisily, coughed and cleared her throat. "I don't understand avoiding the subject of death with kids. They *have* to learn. Lindy won't try to make the trip."

"It'd take her a couple of days to get here from England if she could get a flight." Her son reminded her.

"Yes, it's so much trouble and her children are in school. I doubt her husband could do without her, for even a week." She mumbled, "The imbecile."

"How's Pop taking it?" Cam asked.

"Honey, Grandma's been dying for the last twenty years. In a way he's relieved. He's mostly disappointed not to get to spend a day or two with our daughter, but you know, that's life." Elaine snagged Cam's duffle and tossed it in the backseat.

Cam hung his garment bag behind the passenger's seat and climbed in for a bumpy ride across the pasture.

"Tell me how you're doing." She gave him a brief sidelong look.

"Good. Business is good." Cam nodded.

Elaine cut a green-eyed glance at her son. "How's your heart?"

Cam choked a laugh. "Get right to the point, don't you?"

"You're different. The scowl's missing. What's that about?" His mother probed, as she poked him in his ribs.

"Ah...Ruth fell, broke her hip a few weeks ago...."

"Is she alright?" Elaine asked.

"Yes ma'am. She had surgery, they replaced her knee, same side, while they had her in the hospital. She's in rehab." His voice turned wistful. "Kate's there now. She takes care of everything."

"Has she moved back?" His mother asked.

"Yes ma'am, sold her catering business, rented her condo out, and came back to the Ozarks. She's working on the house. Ruth wants to turn it into a B&B. They'll decide when she's released how much she can handle." He swallowed the rest of what he was dying to share.

"And...you're seeing Kate? For real, you've taken her out and all that?" Elaine parked in the driveway between the house and garage.

He nodded. "She's intimidating— totally open." He chuckled. "Momma, there's so much...I don't think I know how to do this right, you know? Once burned, twice shy..." He swiped his hand over his beard. "I don't want to screw it up."

Elaine's voice fell flat. "Then don't. She isn't Jackie."

"I can think of a thousand reasons she won't be as crazy about me as I am about her." He stared out the windshield at ancient oaks swagging Spanish moss. The deep shade sheltered the house from intense Texas heat.

"None of them are valid." Elaine patted her son's arm. "Be yourself. Trust your heart. If it's right, it'll be the best thing to ever happen to you." She parked and opened her door to head for the sunporch. Once inside, Elaine had a coughing fit. She grabbed a few tissues out of a nearby box.

Cam had followed her in, stowing his bags at the rear stairs. He turned, "Momma, that cough's nasty."

She waved him off, nodding her head. "Been to the doctor, have meds. Taking them. Now, go find Harry."

He tromped through the butler's pantry, dining room, front entry, formal parlor, and music room.

Classical music cleansed the atmosphere. He stopped to savor Harry's favorite composer, Frederic Chopin, before opening the massive old library door. His stepfather lay back in his favorite brown leather recliner, eyes closed. Thick short gray hair brushed straight back, framed his well-lined square face. A black Lab sat beside his chair. She lifted her head at Cam's intrusion and turned to check on Harry. She rose, put a paw on her master's leg, and whined.

Harry opened fading blue eyes and smiled. "You're here then?" He fumbled for the remote and turned the stereo down.

Cam slid through the door. "Yes sir, just now walked in the house. How're you doin'?"

"Very fine, son. How 'bout you?" Harry reached for the halter on the dog's back. She moved forward slowly, as he stood, hesitantly straightening himself.

Cam caught his hand to shake it. "Better now, seein' you, Pop. Heard you have a helper. What's her name?"

"This is Zelda. Say 'hi' to Cam, Zelda."

She yipped and wagged her tail.

"She's fine, isn't she?" Harry leaned over to rub her. "Remember the Lab we had when you were a kid? Finest bird dog I ever owned."

"Yes sir, I do. Old Samson was a sweet friend. Let's go to the kitchen. I'm pretty sure Momma's making coffee and I think I spotted a pound cake on the table." He followed the duo to the opposite side of the house.

***

Elaine poured coffee around and sat between her husband and son.

Harry looked her way. "Did you tell him yet?"

"No, that's your job, darlin'." She sat, lifting the coffee cup to blow across the surface of the rich black brew.

Harry scratched his day-old white scruffy beard and smiled. "Grandma made you executor of her estate. You'll need to be here Thursday, for the reading of the will. I wanted you to know now, so you could make arrangements to stay longer if needs be."

Cam's mouth dropped open. "What? Why me?"

Harry responded, "Well, I'm in the fix I'm in and your mother's busy takin' care of me."

"Why not Lindy? She's blood kin." Cam asked.

"Lindy's all over the world with a husband, a career and kids to tend. Coop's got a business, a princess for a wife, and two boys. You're the only one who's not tied down. Besides, she favored you most." Harry lifted his cup slowly and sipped, then continued, "Mother had a lot of admiration for your service record and the way you built a business out of nothing, in a place you weren't known."

"It wasn't exactly out of nothin', Pop. You fronted me money." Cam replied.

"We did the same for Lindy and Coop. You're the only one to pay me back. Coop's doing well, in a place he's been known most of his life. Lindy's playing the stock market; some days are diamonds, some just stones. No, you're the one Mother chose, *and* you're the eldest. Blood has nothing to do with it."

Harry's tone was final. The discussion was closed. He moved on to his favorite jibe. "Have you gotten a girlfriend yet? I'm beginnin' to worry about you. You haven't taken to battin' for the other team, have you?"

Elaine laughed.

Her son blushed to the roots of his graying black hair. "I'm seeing somebody and she's all girl, if that makes you feel better. You've met her before, in Kansas City, but that's been years ago." Cam replied.

The old man chuckled. "When're you bringing her home?"

"Kinda pushy, aren't you? I'm not sure she'd come this far with me yet."

"Does she ride?" Harry leaned forward.

Cam's memory flashed to his fourteenth birthday when Harry introduced him to a Harley-Davidson motorcycle. Momma invited her 'friend' for dinner. Harry arrived in full leathers. Cam had been in awe, from the first moment, of the man who would be his father.

"She does now." Cam grinned. "She rode the poker run with me yesterday."

Harry reached for Cam's arm to squeeze. "Trust me. She needs to see where you come from, son. She'll be a lot more impressed. It speeds up the process, too. You don't buy a race horse without lookin' at the bloodline."

"I love being compared to stock, Pop." Cam hid the smile in his voice.

Harry sipped more coffee. "Hah! I thought we had cake. Where is it?"

Cam shifted the plates and server. "I've got it covered. Keep your shirt on, old fellow."

***

Elaine hadn't changed a thing in the music room at the Kendal Ranch, since she and Harry married thirty-two years earlier. What had once seemed too fussy to Cam, as a teenager, now felt comfortable. The calm patina of ecru silk-covered walls lured him into the inviting space. He opened the keyboard of the Grand piano and eased himself down on its antique bench. He ran through chords a few times, found a sour note, and winced. He began to play.

Elaine stood in the doorway eavesdropping on her son. He caught her reflection in a mirror over the fireplace.

Cam addressed the mirror. "Come on in. I need professional help."

Elaine entered the room and joined her son in a nearby chair. "What's that?"

"I call it 'Sonata for Katrina' but I haven't gotten far. As I get to know her better, I add to the song. I hope to have it finished soon."

"It'll make a nice wedding present." His mother responded.

Cam paused. "I'm not sure how to answer to that, Momma." He rubbed his hands together. "Gotta have this tuned. I'll call in the morning."

"What do you foresee in your relationship?" Elaine probed with a hint of amusement.

"I'm in for the long haul. It's just…don't know if she'll have me. I'm pretty rough stuff compared to what she's accustomed to—a genius and all that." He turned to face her.

Elaine laughed. "You're my most intelligent child. But, she knows very little about you because you don't talk. Have you played for her?"

"Lord, no! I struggle to make coherent sentences. My mind gets so muddled; I stumble all over myself. Stupid seems to boil out my mouth every time I open it."

She shook her head. "Try mundane subjects: music, art, poetry."

"Yeah…I have trouble with the weather and asking her to dance. I squeeze out 'c'mon' as though that's enough. It's hell trying to fill quiet lulls when your mind's a blank. I want to sit and gaze into her dark eyes for an hour or two, and never leave. She prefers conversation."

"You don't have trouble talking to Ruth." Elaine said.

"Ruth's almost your age, and my Missouri mother. I'm not trying to impress her. She's the only reason Kate's gone out with me. What can a man do with that?"

Harry and Zelda loitered at the door. "You bring her home, son. Your mother will fill her in. Worked for me. I flipped over this gorgeous widow with two teenage boys. I couldn't put 'boo' together, so I made time with you and Coop and brought her home to meet Grandma. She saw the ranch and was hooked."

Elaine laughed and shook her head. "I was hooked before the ranch, Harry Kendal, *long* before the ranch."

"That's another thing, Pop, I don't have two *boys* to impress." Dread flavored Cam's tone. "Somehow, I have to pass muster with young men. We haven't even talked about them yet."

Chapter Four

Kate heard the familiar diesel truck in the driveway. She didn't hurry to see if it was Cam. Cracker drove a truck nearly like his. But, when the doorbell chimed, she felt giddy.

He's back. She dashed to the door, drying her hands on her jeans, and turned the knob to find him waiting. He looked down into her dark eyes with a grin.

"Hello, Katrina."

"Hello, Camden." She smiled and leaned on the door. "Wanna come in?"

"What I'd love is a walk. I'm stiff from sitting too much the past few days. A stroll to the apple orchard might prove profitable. Saw you had a few left, on the trees, when I drove past."

"That's true. Come on through. I'll get baskets to take along and put my shoes on."

He followed her. "I know a lady who's a chef. Hope to talk her into something involving apples and pie crust."

"Is that right? Is she ordinarily compliant to your wishes?" Kate stopped in the kitchen and removed two flat frozen bundles from the freezer. She placed them on a metal rack over the sink, then continued to the mudroom for baskets and slipped into her gardening shoes. She glanced back at Cam when he didn't answer immediately.

He replied, "No ma'am, she's not. For instance, I asked her out to dinner for Saturday night and she never did answer me. Hasn't called me. That's been five days ago."

"Shame on her, she doesn't appreciate you." Kate's eyes narrowed, as he approached.

"Come here a minute." Cam's hand covered the nape of her neck to hold her still. "Something's in your hair—scraps of wallpaper." He plucked them out, flicking them into the wastebasket behind her.

He examined her eyes for a moment, then kissed her slowly.

She shook her head.

Cam pulled back, chuckling and said, "Un-uh be quiet, woman."

He kissed her again.

I have coffee breath! She thought. *Why can't this man call and warn me he's coming?* Then Kate relaxed in his arms, molding to his body.

Cam released her and stepped back. He said, "I've wanted to do that since the night we met at Leroy's party."

Kate was nodding. "Me, too."

"It didn't feel right. Not kissing you didn't feel right. I've fought it every time we're together." Cam said.

Kate responded, "You didn't have to. I was about to take things into my own hands and make a serious pass at you."

"Really?"

She stepped into him and kissed him soundly, then whispered, "Really."

The orchard was near the road, a decent hike from the house. They arrived out of breath from the brisk walk.

"That feels good, so much better than climbing up and down the ladder." Kate stretched and pushed her fist into a spot on her mid back.

Cam reached behind her. "Let me do that." His strong fingers found the tense muscle and massaged until it relaxed. "Better?" At her blush and nod, he stepped back and turned away.

"Thank you, that's heaven." Kate watched as he took a deep breath and exhaled quietly, broad shoulders shrugging. Kate said, "Well, let's get to it. The Jonathan apples are in the farthest row. Only a few are left. I like those for pies. There are Granny Smiths and Winesaps too. We can mix them up. Are you okay, Cam?"

He nodded. "Yes ma'am, just need a minute to admire the view." He paused for a breath. "Sometimes wish I was an artist."

"Have you tried it?" She asked.

He glanced back. "Occasionally. Maybe watercolors would be a forgiving medium. Charcoal, at least on my drawings, looks best smudged."

Kate laughed. "Mine too. I get an artistic effect plating food, but no one, who isn't a chef, understands what I see as an art form."

"Hey, come 'ere." He motioned her to his side, his eyes trained on a distant target, on the north side of the highway.

Kate stepped in front of him. He drew close behind her, dropped his face beside hers, and pointed up past the trees in the distance, to the top of a rocky crag.

He whispered, "Right there, see it?"

She laid her cheek against his. "It's a nest, isn't it?"

"Aerie, watch for the eagles." His hand rested on her hip. He caught sight of an eagle toward the west. "Ah, there's one skimming the treetops, see him?"

"I do. Cool, I didn't know they nested around here."

Cam said, "See 'em more now, than when I first came up here. Don't know if the population is increasing or I'm paying more attention." He straightened.

Kate turned to face him with her crooked smile. "Thank you. Sighting eagles is enough to make your day, isn't it?"

He gazed into her eyes. "My day was made when I pulled into your driveway." He handed her a basket. "I'll pick the apples and you fill the baskets. How about that?"

"It's a deal. The crusts should be thawed when we get back. You can roll them out. My arms are tired from pulling paper. While the pie's in the oven, I'm taking a shower."

Cam thought, *I'd love to share that shower with you.* But he said, "I'll scramble eggs and make toast for supper." He grimaced. "Breakfast's what I do."

"Suits me." Kate responded.

***

Kate reappeared, in a dark blue velour pantsuit and barefoot, on the backstairs to the kitchen. She found Cam slicing bread for toast. Her hair was damp on the ends, pulled into a high ponytail.

His gaze swept over her, taking note of her pretty toes, sans nail polish. "Hope this is okay. I found the loaf in the fridge."

"It's fine, thank you. With only me here, a loaf lasts two weeks."

"Have you always baked your own bread?" He peeked up from buttering bread for the toaster oven.

"Yes. I'm not a fan of preservatives. My youngest son has an autoimmune disorder. He can't eat processed or chemically preserved food. Gluten deals us fits as well." She poured a glass of juice, held it up. He nodded. She filled another glass and the water carafe.

"Is he sick a lot?" He slid the tray of bread into the toaster oven.

"Only if he strays from his diet. Being away at school, he has to be cautious where he gets prepared food. Isaac learned to read labels at an early age."

"Do the boys visit often?" Cam asked.

"Holidays and vacations, sometimes long weekends. Whenever there's a break, they'll be around. Asher has a job at a bike shop that keeps him busy between business classes at the University of Alabama in Tuscaloosa. Isaac opted to double his classes so he can finish college sooner. He's at Iowa State. We'll see how long it lasts, but I expect he'll do fine."

"Really smart, then?" Cam asked.

Kate reddened, then turned away to set the kitchen table. Her voice sharpened, "He's very much like his father." *In more ways than one.*

"If you don't mind the question, how long were you married?" He looked away to check the toast.

"I don't mind. We were just shy of our twentieth anniversary when Reggie was killed by a hit and run driver. Married right after I received my bachelor's degree, in business. He was already teaching." Her thoughts drifted for a moment.

Cam dished up scrambled eggs, laying buttered toast in a cloth-lined basket. "We're ready. The pie smells good."

She smiled, as she responded, "I haven't made an apple pie in a while. I'm glad you wanted one."

Cam seated Kate, sat beside her, and took her hand. He studied her dark eyes a moment, massaging her fingers and sighed.

He sat back in his chair and said, "You know, I think maybe you need help pulling paper and repairing walls more than dinner out. What do you say? Tell me when you want me here and I'll give you a hand. My folks have an old house. I have lots of experience."

Kate smiled, tasting the eggs. "Mmm, good. I'll take you up on that. I'd love to have paper pulled, on the third floor, before Mom gets home. If I can get the plaster repaired too, it would be a bonus."

Cam nodded. "It's a standing date then. I'll be here Saturdays and Sundays, and any other time to pull paper—as long as you'll feed me. I'll bring steaks."

Kate laughed. "I rarely eat red meat, but I'll have the grill ready to go and make a salad."

Cam enjoyed her merriment. "Good enough."

The silence settled between them, for almost a minute, when Kate asked, "Will you humor me for a while?"

Cam nodded.

She carried on, "I'd like to discuss San Antonio, if you don't mind."

The look on Cam's face was surprise, followed by a touch of awe. "Um, yeah—yeah, I guess that needs to be addressed."

"How has all this," she waved her hand in the air between them, "transpired? Does the time we spent together, there, embarrass you? Are we playing a game? I need rules to participate, Commander."

Cam inhaled and began, "It feels like a lifetime ago." He brushed his hand over his beard and made eye contact. "I want this time with you to get to know you, let you get to know me. I've been waiting for you. You needed time to heal. That's all. And it *finally* just happened, Kate."

"Does this mean we can't be intimate?" She asked.

He nodded, "I don't want to hurt you or be hurt. Can sex wait just a little while? *It's killing me to say that. I want you like crazy*. Every time you touch me I feel like I've tripped into a firepit."

Kate nodded. "If those are the rules to *your* game, alright. I…"

He interrupted, "It's stupid isn't it? Can we ever be certain of anything, much less everything?" Cam leaned back and rested his hands on his upper thighs. "I don't want to admit this, but I wasn't sure you'd remember me or the three days and two nights we had together. There—I've said it!" His face flamed

Tears rolled down her cheeks. She swiped them away and responded, "You were the second man I've been with, in my whole life. I'll go to my grave, when I'm a hundred and ten, still dreaming about our whispered confidences— your hypnotic touches— the thrill of your hands on me— the taste of you in my mouth." Kate stood and picked up dishes. She scooted past Camden's chair.

On her way back to the table, he caught her hand, pulling her onto his lap. He leaned his forehead on her chest. "If I've upset you, send me home." He looked into her eyes and saw defiance.

The oven timer pinged.

Kate countered with, "You have an apple pie to eat, *buster*, you aren't going anywhere." She stood, put on oven mitts and, using a flat wooden paddle, shifted the pie plate, from the oven rack to a stone slab on the counter. The smell of ginger, cloves and cinnamon filled the breakfast room and kitchen.

She turned back to Camden and said, "This'll take at least an hour to cool enough to cut it. Wanna watch a movie with me?"

"Um, no." He stood beside his chair.

Kate responded, "No?"

"Let's go upstairs, if that's okay?" Cam smiled and sighed when she nodded. "I'll grab my kit from the truck. Take the dogs out." He whistled sharply, and opened the kitchen door, stepping out to the cold clear air and felt happy with his choice. He watched the trio run laps, then stop to take care of business and head back to the porch. Three wagging tails preceded him inside.

They lay in Kate's bed, watching the fan blades, above, turn slowly.

"Why did it take you more than 2 years to make contact?" She asked.

"I was out of the country for 9 months. Came back through Texas, spent a week with Momma and Pop. Then I flew into KC. Rented a car and drove to your place of business. Parked on the street, walked down the alley to the back, figuring that would be the way you came and went. You were standing on the stoop, at the back door. Your arms were wrapped around a man and you were crying. I left and came back later, but you'd gone to meet a client. I tried calling three times, but couldn't reach you. I stayed at the Marriot downtown and tried again the next day, but one of your staff told me you weren't feeling well and had gone home."

"What did that man look like?" Kate asked, with a frown.

"Like a wide receiver. I saw a picture of you and Asher a few weeks later, here in the music room. At that time, it was hard to get away. There were back-to-back storms and we were swamped mending, tarping and trying to keep folks dry. It was six months of 7 days a week, before we were able to come up for air. I called you again to a closed mailbox."

She cringed. Her voice softened, "Oh, my. That sounds *so* discouraging. I always cry when Asher leaves. He'd flown up to pick up Reggie's car and drove back to Alabama. He'd moved into an apartment, with a friend and had a parking place for the car. He'd been riding his bike for almost 3 years, which he did throughout high school, anyway."

"Well, I decided to let nature take its course." He responded. "Heard you were coming down three weeks before Leroy's birthday. I was in Texas for those few days you were here. Pop had major surgery and I needed to be there. P.O.A. and all that comes with it."

Kate ran her hand over his chest. "Thank you for persevering."

Cam asked, "You're welcome. Did you ever try to call me?"

"Mmm...one time. I tried your satphone and there was no answer. I didn't want to call your cell. I wasn't sure where you'd be or what time it was."

"Satphone went down the day we landed in Germany. I'm sorry. Uncle Han didn't take his, because we had mine. After a week, we had to buy one, used, at a pawnshop. I lost all my phone numbers, and yours was in it. Had to leave all our identification at home."

He rolled onto his side to face her. "Can we just have pie for breakfast?"

"Mmm, a splendid idea." She curled into his warm body, feeling his breath on her neck. She smiled and thrilled at his touch.

Chapter Five
Three weeks later

"Thank you for coming out with me today." Kate drove her Camry toward Tere's home, after a day of shopping at Branson's outlet malls. "I needed a break from the restoration project to have some girl down time."

Streetlights struggled against heavy mist in the emergent darkness. The well-treed street felt like driving through a tunnel.

"You're very welcome. I missed the daylights outta you for 22 years after you moved to Kansas City. I love that you came back home. Besides, you need to get out more." Tereza Diaz popped a piece of gum into her mouth. "You and Ruth get so caught up workin' on that house you forget there's life going on outside."

"It's consuming. We're almost finished with the third floor. I bought fabric for drapes last week. Mom can work on those when she gets home."

Crowded, by vehicles on each side of the narrow, one-way street, in Tere's neighborhood, Kate maneuvered her Camry through the maze. She stopped, to let another car pass, and turned her wipers up.

She sent Tere a quick glance. "We're beginning to see progress. Cam hooked me up with a carpenter who stays with the job. In turn he knows a guy who does plaster. It eats into my profit from the catering business, but the projects are finished sooner."

"You're seeing him, aren't you?" Tere asked, her brilliant smile and teasing tone amplified by the dashboard lights.

Kate felt her friend watching her. "Huh? Oh, you mean Cam Fletcher?"

"Yeah, I wasn't talking about the carpenter." Tere giggled.

What do I say?

"Kate?" Tere probed.

Kate exhaled. "We do things together—oft— uh frequently."

"Out here in the world we call that dating." Tere sighed. "He went out with another friend of mine for a little while. She said he was weird, never even kissed her til the last date, said 'it's been nice' and didn't call or take her calls again. She thought he could be gay, but honestly, that'd be a huge waste of a good-lookin' man. What's he like, really?"

Kate stumbled, "He's…nice, fun…comfortable."

"Is he a good kisser? I've always wondered that about him, he looks like he would be. Hey, isn't that Cam's truck?" Tere pointed straight ahead to the right side of the street.

Kate chuckled. "You're so nosy."

She stopped two car lengths behind the black truck with *Fletcher Roofing* plastered across the tailgate. She had to wait for it to move, before she could pass. She took a deep breath. *At least I'm spared answering intimate questions.*

They watched a woman turn to talk to the driver, his profile blurred by the gun rack and rain-flecked rear window. The woman reached across the divide to kiss the driver on the mouth. The passenger's door flew open, propped by a spiked heel. She stepped out under a streetlight, tall, thin with short frosted hair. She held a glowing cigarette, in one hand and a silver sequined handbag in the other, a jacket slung over her arm. A revealing lamé halter topped her black leggings.

As she closed the door, she threw him a kiss and waved "Bye, sugar, I'll see you in a little while." She turned, hopped to the sidewalk and into a small bungalow, after using her key. As soon as she closed the door, the truck pulled away.

"Don't jump to conclusions, Kate. That could be his sister." Tere whispered, her hand over her mouth.

"His sister lives in England. I wasn't jumping to anything." Kate's stomach flipped. She was thankful for the darkness.

A block farther down the street, Kate parked in Tere's driveway, popped the trunk, and joined her friend at the back of her car. They gathered packages.

Tere rambled to cover the tension, "Law! I know I bought more than you did. Look at this, two pairs of shoes and three dresses. I love that turquoise concho belt you found. That was a deal. I wish we could've found another, slightly larger one. May I borrow it sometime? I've started the grapefruit diet again."

"Sure." Kate's throat throbbed as she struggled to keep her voice steady.

They flounced up the cobblestone path to the ivy studded front stoop. The arched doorway gave Tereza Diaz' cute cottage a fairytale feeling. They huddled under the awning, out of the cold mist, while she fumbled for the key.

The door finally opened and Tere slung bags on the sofa. "Just put 'em anywhere, Kate. I've gotta pee. How about a glass of wine?"

"I'd better get home. The dogs need to be fed. Aunt Evie let 'em out a couple of hours ago, but I'm sure they'll be glad to see me. I want to beat the heavy rain to the Bailiwick or the hounds won't potty."

The toilet flushed and Tere reappeared. "Okay, well don't be a stranger. Let's plan to do this again in a week or so. At least we could have dinner. I'll be glad to let you cook for me anytime."

Kate forced a laugh. "That's a deal, a week from today." She opened the door and slipped through. "Bye!"

She eased the door shut and sprinted to the car. Once inside she inhaled deeply and sat in the silence, her eyes closed for a moment before cranking the car. "Some poker game, Camden Fletcher."

***

Fletcher Roofing's tear off crew worked on the first story, ripping up old shingles and decking. Roofers worked on the second story replacing decking and shingles. The house was rife with pounding and shook every time a laborer tossed up a bundle of shingles. The men's chatter and occasional laughter seeped into the house.

The phone rang. Kate checked caller i.d., Fletcher Roofing. She passed it by. Moments later her cell fired off with the same i.d., she let it ring. An hour dragged on before another attempt. She checked the name and kept working. When the air was free of ring tones, she went through the house to silence phones. Only the primary line would ring and her cell vibrate.

Less noise to wrack my nerves and fortitude.

Cam's truck pulled in the driveway again, for the third time. She hadn't answered the door when he rang the bell earlier.

At lunchtime she prepared a hummus wrap, tossing a few baby carrots on her plate. She pulled her laptop from the middle of the table. While she waited for her mailbox cycle to run, she glanced outside.

The scoundrel parked the truck near the kitchen window beside her. She looked away.

I will not change seats. She silently declared.

She turned back to the window to find the owner of the truck leaned against the side, ten feet away, legs crossed, lighting a cigarette. He wore Rayban sunglasses and no hat, dark hair tossing in the breeze. He scrutinized her through the window.

She checked email, took one bite of her wrap, and fought the urge to throw up. She logged off the laptop and pushed it back.

I'm crazy about this man and have no idea what to do with him. How can I trust him after what I've seen?

The knocker rapped on the back door. She sat still, covered her face with her hands, muttering, "Please go away! I don't know what to do with you, Camden Fletcher."

A key scraped in the lock, the door opened and closed and he walked into the kitchen.

"What's goin' on, Kate? Are you okay? You don't answer my calls. You won't see me. What's happened?"

Startled, Kate tried to leave the table. Sat again. She shrieked, "You have a *key*?"

"Ruth gave me one a couple of years ago in case she had an accident. Came in handy when she fell. Evie and Leroy were out of town. Now answer my question, please." Cam demanded.

"I just want to be alone for a while, Cam." She turned away, toward the butler's pantry, as he approached.

"Then tell me." He stood across the table from her. "Look at me. Tell me to get lost. Tell me why. I'll go."

Her head dropped; eyes closed. She shook her head. She pulled out a chair, dropping into it. "That isn't it. It's just, something's come up…I don't know how to process or…even discuss it."

"What is it, Katrina?" He rounded the table to pull a chair in front of her. "Talk to me. Use words."

She composed her face and looked up, to ask, "How was your poker game?"

"Changing the subject won't help." He studied her.

She sat mute, absently stroking Dixie's silky coat.

Finally, he answered, "Okay, let's see…I lost fifteen bucks. Cracker lost thirty, Greg won twenty. Larry was losing his shirt, when his girlfriend called, ready to leave work." His voice kicked into monotone. "His truck was blocked, so he took mine from the shop to fetch her. On return, his luck changed and he cleaned us out." He paused. "Oh, yeah, your hummus and pita chips were a hit. But they're all male and they figured out it's made of beans."

Her eyes filled; she bit her lower lip. She still didn't have a clue what to say or do. She squeezed out, "Larry was driving your truck?"

His plea became tender, "Kate, what's wrong?"

"Why did you leave your truck at the shop?" She asked, massaging her forehead. She closed her eyes.

Cam sighed, looking dismayed, and answered, "Because I hoped you'd call and need me for something—anything—so I could escape. I hate poker night. Mark insists it builds relationships—team-building, he calls it. I don't mind hosting people I like, but I don't like many people. Besides all that, I just wanted to be with *you*." He locked into her gaze. "Please, tell me what's wrong."

She shook her head, closed her eyes. "I don't know how to do this. Dating is foreign to me. I've been married most of my adult life. Reggie was one of two guys I went out with more than once. Daddy didn't let me date, until senior prom and Mom chaperoned that. I have no experience with men, who I'm not related to, or work for."

He left the chair and knelt between her feet. "Woman, I'm crazy about you. Look at me." Tears spilled into his hand, when he turned her face to his. "I don't care about anything but you. Whatever you want—or need, I'll do. It hurts that you think I'd screw this up, with no regard to the future we're building."

She shrugged and said, "I'm struggling with moving back here, leaving everything I worked *so* hard to build. Neither of us needs to change to suit the other. I *want* us to be who we are and can't see if that'll work." She wiped her eyes with the back of her hand, sniffing.

He considered her for a moment with a narrowed gaze. "Did somebody see Larry and his girlfriend in my truck and tell you it was me with another woman?"

Her eyes closed again, tears dripping off her chin. "No— it pulled in front of me when I was taking Tereza home."

Cam snatched tissues from a nearby box and dried her face. "That's it?"

He sat in the chair closest to her, cupping her legs with his own and leaned forward. His tone was definite, "Kate, my dad was a preacher, but he had the morals of an alley cat. When he died in the wreck, he was on his way to Albuquerque for a pastor's conference. His secretary was with him. A Ranger had just left the house, bearing the news, when the phone rang. The caller asked for Mrs. Fletcher. It was the hotel he'd booked under the names Reverend and *Mrs.* David Fletcher. I decided, at that moment, while Momma was melting down from embarrassment and a broken heart...*I could never do that to anyone.* I told you on our first date. *I'm not like that.*"

Cam shook his head. He muttered, half to himself. "It's not fair that I know way more about you than you do me." He stood, stretched, took in a lungful of air, blew it out. "You need to meet my family. See where I come from." He inhaled. "I'm not good at bein'—walls not easily breached." He pulled her up. "I wouldn't have given you a second thought, woman...but," he looked past her. "Kate, I've had a crush on you for years. Can't shake it! I *have* tried."

She glanced up at him, sniffing and squeaked, "What?"

"Honey, the first time Ruth handed me your picture, I knew you were meant to be mine. San Antonio wouldn't have happened, if we weren't meant for each other." He faced her. He rubbed his forehead and flushed. He ran his hand through his hair and shrugged. "I just know you're made for me. The day we met; I was hooked. Please don't blow up this relationship."

She shook her head, sniffing, "You did nothing wrong. I feel very vulnerable right now, but that's *my* issue."

He nodded.

Kate said, "You do, too. Tell me how to do this dating thing. Do we plow full steam ahead? Would it be wiser to take a break from each other?"

Cam answered in a whisper, "Full steam, Katrina. I've been searching for you, my whole life. Leroy's birthday? I wanted to take you home with me and close out the world."

Kate frowned and said, "Me too. I've never had that thought about anyone before that night; 'I hope he takes me home and never leaves me.' Where did that come from?"

"Probably me thinking the same." Cam answered. "Ruth told me you have," he made air quotes with his hands, "an unusual gift. Is that how you knew I was safe, when we first met?"

"It isn't on all the time." She looked away. "But, I'm glad it was that day."

"Listen a minute, then I'll get out of your way. Remember the old dial radios, with the stick antennas?"

She nodded.

"Folks figured out the best place for them was the top of the fridge so they could pick up one, maybe two stations. You're that one station for me, lady. You're my music." Cam held out his hand to Kate.

She laid hers in the center of his. He closed his hand over her soft, strong fingers.

He sighed and continued, in a rush, "Look, I'll be back in a little while. Take you out to dinner. We can go dancing." He kissed her hands. "I need to hold you."

Kate stood.

He pushed the antique oak chair under the table then leaned against it for a moment and checked his phone. "I'll pick you up in an hour and fifteen minutes." He turned toward the door, without waiting for a response.

Kate summoned her reserved moxie and kicked in her mom voice, "Fletch?"

He stopped, turning, his face etched with dread. "Yes ma'am?"

"I *don't want* to go out. We need quiet, not noise to hide the silent moments." She crossed her arms, closing her eyes in a long blink.

"Okay." Cam looked confused but nodded.

Kate's voice softened. "You may bring wine to dinner."

"If that's what…yes ma'am." He smiled, with relief, and hurried to his truck before she could change her mind.

***

Kate prepped vegetables for the grill, salting the sliced eggplant on a rack over the sink, quick thawed flounder filets on a cookie rack, and squeezed half a cup of fresh lemon juice. She stirred capers into the juice, thickened the sauce, and turned off the stove.

She dashed upstairs to dress, Dixie on her heels. For fifteen minutes she perused her closet for the perfect dress. *This is nuts! For pete's sake, I've worn paint clothes and jeans for the past five months. Anything's a step up.*

An ankle-length Dashiki dress with three-quarter sleeves and a contrasting placketed vee neckline was her final choice. The silk was painted a colorful mixture of tropical leaves. She pulled on a pair of sling-back sandals, adding silver hoops to her ears. Her hair tumbled from the bun, she'd twisted it into earlier in the day. She combed it out, drew back the sides, securing them with a silver and mother-of-pearl barrette. *I'm scared to death of what I feel for that man.*

She checked herself in the mirror again, adjusted her revealing neckline and spun toward the door.

She carefully made her way down the front staircase to find Cam, at the bottom, dressed in black cords and a dark green Guayabera shirt that made his eyes the color of pine needles in summer.

He said, "No need to act like I don't have a key." Cam held his breath when she stepped onto the landing. He met her, offering his hand. "You do clean up nicely."

She accepted his assistance, smiled, and stopped six inches shy of his belt buckle. Her eyes closed. She inhaled his scent and knew he would kiss her.

His nervousness was apparent with his opening line, "I brought white and red wines, didn't know what you'd want. Would it be okay if I kiss you now?"

She opened one eye to find him flustered. She whispered, "Please do."

At first, he brushed her lips lightly, then tilted his head, and kissed her slowly. He grasped her waist and pulled her close. She laid her head against his chest.

Mmm, I love the way he feels, caught in a testosterone wave.

Cam cleared his throat and stiffened. "Katrina, you need to feed me and send me home. We're hovering in a danger zone."

She stepped back and took his hand. "Coals in the grill should be ready. I'll don an apron and see to it. Mom gets to come home tomorrow."

"Good, it'll be nice to have her back where she belongs. For my part, we need a chaperone." Cam said.

They proceeded to the dining room. A crystal vase of dark red roses sat in the middle of the antique oak table.

Kate stopped. "Cam, these are…beautiful."

He nodded. "You're welcome. Way overdue, darlin'."

She pressed her face into the bouquet. "Mmm…divine fragrance. You have excellent taste." She cut a glance toward him.

"Thank you." He smiled and turned to look beyond her toward the butler's pantry. "I'll set the table. We have candles?"

"Yes, we do." She followed him to the kitchen.

Cam completed the table setting with folded napkins and opened the wine. He poured chilled Chardonnay into crystal goblets.

Kate grilled eggplant, zucchini, and onions from the garden. The flounder filets quickly reached perfection. She topped the fish with a lemon caper sauce.

Cam tossed baby greens Kate picked that morning, with a vinaigrette that she whipped up a minute earlier. He lit the candles on each side of the roses.

He held her chair and sat beside her. His green eyes captured her dark gaze for a long moment.

"Many blessings over this meal and the hands that prepared it."

"Omayn." Kate met Cam's quizzical regard. "Mom didn't tell you I'm Jewish?"

Chapter Six

After dinner they adjourned to the music room, with coffee and rich, delicate truffles. Cam carried a tray to a hand-carved ebony coffee table, fronting the burgundy velvet settee. He poured coffee, adding cream to Kate's, sat beside her and handed her the cup.

He said, "Thank you for dinner. I didn't know I liked eggplant."

"You're welcome. Grilled or roasted vegetables are more appealing than boiled or fried." She sent him a sidelong glance.

"You've sold me. Now explain the differences in Jews and Christians. I have Jewish relatives, but I want to hear it from your perspective. Both believe in the same God, right?"

"Not exactly. Elohim has no equal. Remember the ten commands given to Moses. No God before Me. Jews believe Jesus was a learned, gifted rabbi. We keep the Jewish traditions, celebrate Jewish festivals and use the Jewish calendar. Yashua, in Hebrew, the name Jesus would have heard his mother call him, kept his Jewishness. He was born a Jew, lived, died, and was buried as a Jew. He never forsook his heritage."

"Did you go through conversion?"

"Yes—and I birthed two Jewish children. We reared Asher and Isaac in their father's faith. Reggie grew up in an Orthodox home and he wanted the same for the boys. We mostly kept Kosher. My sons are fluent in Hebrew and the history." She stopped, prepared to answer questions.

"How'd you handle holidays?" He asked.

"Daddy loved Christmas. We tried it here, but he and Reggie didn't mesh. They were completely intolerant of each other. On the other hand, most of Reggie's family never stopped seeing me as an intruder. He celebrated holidays with his folks and the boys. Together, when they were young, we observed them at home." She paused for a drink, resetting her cup on the

China saucer. "The boys and I came here for Christian holidays. When the seasons conflicted, we took turns."

Kate stopped to take a sip of coffee, then continued, "After Daddy died, Reggie came down occasionally. We were never a cohesive family, but he and Mom were civil, as long as they avoided hot topics like social programs and state's rights. My sons and I have a foot in each world." Kate paused, then softly spoke. "Where do you stand on religion, Cam?"

He inhaled, then let out a long sigh. "Agnostic, at this point in my life. Don't think I can conjure up an image of a God who loves us. Too much suffering in the world and it's always the innocent and poor who bear the brunt of the punishment. How'd you meet Reggie?"

Kate sat quietly for a moment. "Reggie's sister, Abigail was my college roommate. Old story, she introduced us. At first, I think I felt novel dating Reggie. He worked on his doctorate while I waited tables and worked for a bachelor's degree. He was very intelligent, but also...superior. He acted *superior* to the rest of us. The fact that they were Jewish intrigued me. In hindsight, I wonder if loving Abigail was more motive to marry him than loving him."

"How would your sons feel about you seeing me? I'm not a sophisticated English professor. I'm a Texan with great hick potential." He considered the smallness of a truffle and popped it in his mouth. "Mmm...raspberry."

Kate smiled. "What I do isn't their business. I hope they respect my wishes."

"Do you make these?" He chose another dark chocolate truffle.

"I do and freeze them for special company."

Cam asked, "Is that a polite way to warn me I have competition?" He sipped the strong, rich coffee and replaced the delicate cup.

Kate laughed aloud. She fell back against the sofa cushion, studying the ceiling. "As though I have time—or energy!"

"How about inclination?" Cam scrutinized her reaction, then scanned her voluptuous form, wrapped in the silky dress, shifting his memory of her undressed, into overdrive.

She waited for a long moment and turned back to him; her eyes gleaming. "No, I think not."

Kate looked too inviting against the fluffy cushion.

Cam swiped a hand over his beard. "I have ideas, right now, but…"

She sat forward and tasted her coffee. "Me too."

Cam chuckled, reached for her hand, and kissed her fingertips. "I guess it's my turn."

She nodded, sipped cooled coffee, took a dainty bite from a truffle, and placed the remainder on her saucer.

She had to prime his pump, "What sort of life did you have when you weren't flying?"

"Um, we'd return to base, wherever that was. I was mostly stationed in Pensacola." His eyes looked dreamy, when he said, "It always felt strange to be back on dry land, so we could hardly wait to get back to normal—for us, floating in an ocean, waiting for orders and 30 seconds after alarms sound, climbing into the bucket and praying it all works out.

"After I retired, I got the ranch sorted out. Momma can't keep up with all the rental issues. Liability is a factor. I cleared out the pastures of renters. We're gonna let it go fallow for a few years and try to get back to native grasses. Then we'll see which direction our future lies. Coming up here was a no brainer. Hoped above all else you'd be here." He looked Kate squarely in the eyes.

"Have you been married?" Kate asked.

"Once, many years ago. Similar to your love story. Jackie was roommates with Jane, my sister-in-law." He looked away.

Kate waited while he searched for an explanation. "What happened, Cam?" Her tone was gentle.

"Neither of us were good at it. I was away most of the time. Then the worst thing that could happen, did."

"What's that?" She sat her coffee cup on the table.

"Lost a child. Died while Jackie was in labor. A healthy little fellow's heart stopped beating ten minutes before they delivered him." Cam took a deep breath, studied the plush pillow between them. Cinnamon and Shuga slept snugged along Kate's thighs.

He continued, "*That* wasn't on my agenda. I'd blown up. We'd been talking divorce for two months. Married a year and a half, separated three times. She showed up 6 months pregnant, having been gone longer than that. We committed ourselves to the legal bondage, for the sake of the child. Then she lost him." He shrugged, shook his head. "Too much for a fragile relationship and no reason to continue the agony."

Kate whispered, "I'm sorry." She let him sit quietly for a moment, watching him brood. Her soft voice coaxed him along. "Have you forgiven yourself for being angry with Jackie for the pregnancy?"

His jaw worked. He tensed, swallowed hard. "What?" His dark frown was foreboding.

"Have you said the words out loud or even silently?" Kate persisted.

"Help me out here?" He cut a narrowed side-long glance her way.

Kate whispered, "'I forgive Jackie for the death of our son and myself for being angry that he existed.' That's all, no pixie dust. It's not a religious thing, Camden, it's a human thing. We can't carry the burdens of our past mistakes—we can't change them—forgive and move on-try to do better." Kate studied his face.

"Just like that, it's gonna make it alright? Guilt and heartache disappear?" Cam's body tensed.

"You may have to repeat the words every hour for the next ten years, but at some point there's no longer emotion attached, just a precious memory of a beautiful baby boy."

He studied her, sighed deeply, and cleared his throat before relenting. "Okay. I forgive my—," he covered his mouth. He left the settee, turning his back to her. He inhaled through his nose, exhaled through his mouth. Static tension increased in the close warm air of the room.

"Is it always so difficult? It seems impossible!" Cam's voice teetered on the verge of angst. He walked to the French doors, sliding the curtains back to peer longingly outside and studied the dark fields beyond the fence.

Kate spoke quietly, "When we hold onto unforgiveness, we damage ourselves—inside. We don't need to forget the anguish or the child. Forgiveness releases a power of mercy for our own humanity." She gave him time to relent. Her voice dropped lower, "I can leave the room if you want."

"No, I have to be held to account by somebody. You're the one here." He scrubbed his hand through his hair, walked to her and dropped on the settee, leaning forward.

His voice shifted away from agitation. Tears dampened his face, unheeded. "I forgive myself—the *rage*—at Jackie and her child." He rubbed his forehead and mumbled, "I don't want to be angry anymore. I don't want to feel anything like that again."

Kate pressed tissues into his hand. He blew his nose and wiped his face. Silence permeated the room for a time.

The ticking of the grandfather clock became nine hollow peals.

A mantle clock in the parlor chimed.

Cuckoo, cuckoo, cuckoo…the clock in the dining room chirped nine times.

In the distance a train whistle blew, barely audible in the thick silence.

Cam sighed and regarded the Grand piano in the middle of the floor. "You play?"

"Some. Not concert quality by any means. That was Daddy's baby." She smiled; her hands folded in her lap.

"Mind if I do?" He didn't wait for her answer, but rose and opened the keyboard.

Kate wasn't sure what to expect, but it wasn't what she heard. *I'd never have dreamed this man would play Tristesse from memory.* She closed her eyes, subjected to his misery through the music.

Cam finished the piece, his eyes closed throughout the performance, his posture less rigid, marking his first sacrifice of grief.

He sat quietly for a few minutes then turned to her and patted the seat beside him. "Come here?" His voice was hoarse from unshed tears.

She joined him, her back to the piano. He kissed her cheek, stroking her hair.

"I love your hair down, it's beautiful." He ran his fingers through the sleek, wavy tresses. Light reflected off the silver woven through her jet-black hair. "Beautiful." His thumb traced the curve from her temple to her chin.

"Mmm...thank you." Kate felt her body relax at his gentle touch. She closed her eyes and indulged in the rhythm of breathing. She raised her head, met his gaze, and smiled.

Cam said, "If I'd had an ounce of sense, I'd have pursued you the first time we met, 24 years ago."

Kate looked into his smiling eyes and asked, "24 years ago?"

"Knew you wouldn't remember. You worked at the downtown Marriot waiting tables."

She nodded, with a frown.

"I was stationed in Olathe, Kansas, at the Naval Air Station. Took a course there. Had dinner one night at that restaurant and you waited on a table full of hotshot pilots so damn full of ourselves, you became *coldly* polite." He waited for her reply, still smiling.

Kate thought a moment, closing her eyes to the distraction of his attention, before replying, "Yes, I remember you. The others, no, they were jackasses. Had to flush that, sorry you went with it. You came back several times."

"Leaving the jackasses on base. I met my parents there occasionally. They'd come up to visit KC. Pop had been stationed, at the same base, doing the same course in the early 70's. He likes the area and Momma had never been there. They went sightseeing every day for 2 weeks. One night, you were working in the kitchen and had to change smocks before coming out to light a flaming dessert Momma had ordered. It was something with cherries and brandy."

Kate nodded. "The chef was out with flu, I was next up, as sous chef and wound up doing my job and his too. Yeah, a lot of the waitresses were scared of flaming the dessert. It didn't bother me, it was a beautiful presentation, but, as sous chef, I took it off the menu and subbed a 4 layer lemon and cherry torte. I can't swear anyone missed the fire."

"I'm surprised you remember that." He reached for her thigh.

She nodded, "Your parents were kind. They ate brunch every morning. I usually saw them. Your mom always waved at me."

"Yeah, Momma's like that. She's a sweetie." He inhaled, then sighed. "Thank you for a lovely evening, Kate. I'm not much at cooking dinner, except to grill flesh, but I do okay at breakfast. Will you join me in the morning, at my house—say eight?"

"I'd be honored. May I bring anything?"

"A smile and your appetite. I'll draw a map for you. It's only about four miles away." He stroked her back. "I can run over and fetch you, if you want."

"I'll find it, Cam. I'm from here you know." She smoothed her hand over his arm, completely relaxed. She whispered, "I just want to touch you."

He didn't need encouragement. He held her, kissing her tenderly. He pulled back and rested his head against hers. "I'd better go." His tone questioned the statement.

She nodded. "Mmm."

They continued in silence on the bench, for a while. Kate ran her hand over his shoulder, down his thick biceps to his hand. He caught her fingers.

"We can sit on the couch if you want. It's more comfortable." She offered.

He said, "That's kind of a problem."

"Why?" Her eyes narrowed as she met his.

He grimaced. "It's hard for me to get *too* comfortable with you."

She straightened. "Oh?" She began to rise.

He slipped an arm around her waist and held on, pulling her back, growling, "Un-huh, sit down, Kate."

She resettled and met his gaze.

"It's…you're very…sensual. It's difficult…." Cam cleared his throat, blinked and exhaled. "You could have me for a wink right now. This'll be easier when Ruth's home." He loosened his hold on her. "Please tell me to leave."

"For a wink?" She grinned that endearing crooked grin.

"Yes, ma'am." He regarded the dogs stretched out on the settee.

"I like that. I've never been told I'm *sensual*. Thank you." She marveled at the compliment.

"You're welcome. If you can turn it off, I'd appreciate it." He caressed her back and laughed, cutting a glance into her smile.

"I can't turn off something I didn't know I had. You'll have to suffer, I'm afraid." She scooted back on the bench and kicked off her shoes.

"No! No undressing!" He laughed. "How is it that you aren't aware of your power? Really, no one ever told you that you're sexy?"

She pondered his question, kicking her bare feet. "Not that I recall."

He frowned. "Kate, Reggie never told you?"

"I don't remember that he did. He wouldn't have said something like that to me. It would imply I had a special hold over him. I was tolerable because I gave him sons." She cocked her head and turned to face Cam. "Do you ever think about marrying again?"

He nodded. "Not having children though. There are too many kids who need parents. I'm godfather to my nephews. And my sister's trio. We don't allow Lindy and Cooper to even run to the store together for fear of losing them both. You want more children?"

"I feel blessed to have raised two special young men." She glanced around the room. "I wonder if we're nearing the end of life as we've known it, in America. Our freedoms seem to be melting away."

"Yeah, it's not as severe as the dark places my uncle and I visited in Europe a few years ago. Of course that was the point of the journey, but fascists are imbedded everywhere. Uncle Han retired and has a passion for keeping an eye on neo-Nazi groups here and in Europe."

Kate nodded. "You were with him, after you left San Antonio?"

Cam answered, "Yes, he was born a German Jew. Adopted by my grandparents." He shifted the subject, "May I go with you to synagogue sometime?"

Kate smiled. "There are no card checkers at the door. No one is turned away but…." She became solemn. "In the congregation I attended, one Shabbat, Rabbi said 'I need to talk about something we don't want to think about. We have to be prepared for bad things to happen. As a people, with history, we are assured that bad things *will* occur. You sit with your backs to the door. Should danger enter, you need to know it's there and be ready to drop to the floor. We have security personnel, throughout the room who'll jump into action. I'm going to give you a word that's completely out of the ordinary for me. If I say, 'daffodils', you hit the floor.'" She swung her feet and studied the carpet. "It wasn't until that moment that I realized there can and *will* be danger in my life."

"Is that a warning?" Cam questioned; eyes narrowed.

"I think—there's no going back for me." She met Cam's eyes soberly. "You don't have to live like that. The whole world smiles on you, Camden Fletcher. Mixing up with me may not be the wisest life choice you make." She smiled again. "Even, if I *am* sexy." She slipped off the bench and stretched.

Cam spun on the bench. He spoke to her back, eyeing her feline grace. "I'm already in the mix, baby."

She turned, leaning down to kiss his mouth gently. "I'll understand if you want to set your sail for a new course. My heart would shatter, but I'd understand."

He rested his hands on her ample hips and looked up. "I'm in for the duration. You can't get rid of me."

His intense green gaze seared her heart.

Chapter Seven

Kate knew she was in the right place when she bumped across the cattleguard. On each side of the road was Cam's house and the shop. She kept right, at the Y, until she pulled into the driveway and took in the view for a moment. A large cedar A-frame house was built into the hill. A two-car garage finished the right side of the structure. The curved driveway, native flagstone, ended at the base of a few stairs leading up to French doors, thrown open to the morning breeze.

She left her blue Camry, sunhat in hand, and hurried up the steps to find a brown Boxer with white boots waiting on the deck to greet her. He pranced merrily ahead through the doors and barked.

"Hello." She called out into a cavernous post and beam room with a balcony on the second floor that overlooked the living area. A double sided stone fireplace stood in the center of the first floor, open to the kitchen beyond. She stopped at the Baby Grand piano. A picture frame lay face down on top of a yellow file folder.

Cam's voice came from behind her, "Hello, yourself. That's my pal, Buddy." He held a handful of freshly picked flowers, mostly wild asters. He swept the bundle over her shoulder into her arms. "Happy Friday, Miss Kate."

She curtsied. "Happy Friday, Camden Fletcher. This place is stunning!" She twirled to catch the view; her sage green linen broomstick skirt swirling around her legs.

"Thank you. I hoped you'd like it. Breakfast is almost ready. After, we'll take a walk out back."

He strode past her to the kitchen. She followed.

Sunshine brightened heart pine cabinets from two skylights in the roof and highlighted the oak butcher block counters.

Cam filled a vase with water and set it on the island in front of her. "For you, madam. How do you like your eggs fried?"

"One, over medium is fine. What are the little orange flowers? They look so delicate." She snapped stems to get everything to a pleasing height.

"Mexican marigolds. Brought seed up from Texas. They grow wild there, last til a hard freeze. The bluebonnets and gaillardia fade at first frost."

"When I went to San Antonio for the conference, a few years ago, I fell in love with the place."

Cam grinned and turned away from her, whispering, "And I with you, lady."

"This is beautiful." She set the completed arrangement in the middle of the bar and threw stems in the trash. "What did you cook for breakfast?"

"Your biscuits, gravy, wild turkey sausage and eggs. I almost put on a pot of grits, but wasn't sure if you'd know what a grit is." He grinned. "They're so much more a Southern thing."

"I'm not only familiar with grits but fond of them as well. Someday, if you want, I'll prepare my blue grits and grillades for you." She smiled.

"Since grillades imply meat, I'd like that." His smile faded. His voice deepened, "May I kiss you good mornin'?"

"That would be wonderful." She sighed.

He gently held the nape of her neck in his hand as he stepped close. He smiled into her eyes and kissed her sweetly. "Good morning, lovely lady. I hope you have a fantastic day because it's scheduled to the last moment." He turned back to the stove.

She smiled. "What's planned?"

"After breakfast, we'll take a stroll on the back forty. We pick up Ruth at ten and take the long way home through the woods. She's missed most of the best fall color. We'll have a picnic lunch in your gazebo. I fried chicken and made potato salad. Figured you'd have tea and a tomato to slice. On the way, we'll stop at a bakery, that Ruth's nuts about, and get her favorite—caramel apple pie. Sound like a deal?"

"What about this evening?" Her tone was innocent, a smile playing at her lips.

"Oh, I've got that covered too. While we're at your house, you'll pack for Texas. We leave after Ruth gets settled. Evangeline and Leroy are spending a few days with your mom."

"What if I have a salon or doctor's appointment scheduled?" Kate asked.

"You'd've written it on your calendar." He peeked back at her and winked.

Her dark eyes rolled. "You've been busy. May I pour juice or something?"

"Everything's on the table." He plated eggs. "Right this way." He led her around a short partial wall of cabinets, over a bar, to a Mission style dining table and chairs. The windows and double doors were opened to a view of the back landscape.

He seated her, facing the large expanse of glass and glanced out at the in-ground pool. "Have to cover that soon. Water's too cool even with the heater on right now. You like to swim?"

She hesitated, nodded. "It's great exercise."

His larger hand enveloped hers. His gaze rested on her, as he gently massaged her fingers. He offered a cloth covered basket. "Have a biscuit."

***

Arm in arm, Cam showed Kate around. From the back deck she could see the roof of his shop, on the far eastern side. He carried his work phone, set on speaker, static crackled, interspersed with orders, as the crews received the day's assignments.

The sun beamed in the cloudless azure sky. Kate walked a well-trod path, through buffalo grass, beside Cam. In minutes, they came to a clearing with a firepit. A creek wound through eastern cedars and bare ash trees framed horseshoe pits. A thirty-foot travel trailer sat on one side of the clearing with chairs under the awning.

"Oh, I like it." The shade afforded her a clear view of the rock-covered creek bed, the clear water singing a path over tree roots and around boulders.

Cam replied, "Good place to unwind. When my folks come up, Pop likes to hang out here, drink beer, and smoke cigars. And we have company parties after we wrap up a huge job, like yours. Families included."

He shifted his feet and looked up as a red-tailed hawk circled overhead. "When I bought the land, Buddy and I lived in the trailer down here while the business and house were built. It was a year before I had the lower level to the point that I could move in. My brother and nephews came twice a month to lend a hand. Pop flew up a few days a month to help me, before macular degeneration stole his sight."

"How long ago was that?" She studied him watching the hawk dive and reappear with a small rabbit.

"About a year. He got around a good bit with a stick. Momma bought him a dog in August. Zelda gives him some measure of independence again."

Buddy trudged out of the grass. He stopped in front of Cam, dropped his head, and whined.

"Hawks gotta eat, Buddy. They don't live the soft life you do with dog food and a fluffy bed." Cam leaned over to rub the dog's ears. "There'll be another rabbit to chase, in a minute or so. Go to it." He clapped his hands.

The boxer dashed back into waist high grass.

"Cam," the phone crackled.

"Yeah?" He keyed the mike and turned away from her.

"We got a call from Tuttle. His dad passed away. He doesn't want us to start today."

"Call Anderson, to make sure nobody's sleeping late. Send the crew over there. We won't be able to get back, to Tuttle, for at least two weeks. Mark, be sure he knows that. Who gets to be me for the next few days?"

"We drew straws and I lost." Cracker responded.

"Bless your heart, old fellow. Make me proud, hear?" Cam grimaced.

"I don't reckon anybody'll confuse me with you. I'm not the pretty boy, but I am awful cute when I…"

"There's a lady in the vicinity." Cam snapped with a scowl.

"I'm sorry. I didn't know your momma was in town." A coarse chuckle followed.

Cam muted the phone and cut his eyes at Kate.

He waited for a moment, in case there was another interruption.

His scowl melted when he turned back to her. "Sorry, that happens a coupla times a day."

"I'm glad you're busy. That's encouraging."

He grinned and reached for a loose lock of her hair to twirl between his fingers. "Do you need a financial statement to see if I can afford you?"

"I'm easy, not cheap!" She crossed her arms and grinned. Her face flushed when she recalled their hours together, in San Antonio.

They strolled amiably along the trail toward the house. A pool shed sat on the edge of the large patio beyond the pool; a table and six chairs were nicely arranged under a cabana.

Kate admired all three stories of the back, of the house, from where she stood. She pointed to the top of the roof. "What's the room at the peak?"

"Primary bedroom. Great view, looks past the creek onto the hill beyond. You can run up and check it out if you want to."

They took the stairs up to the deck, off the dining room.

"I'd like to see it, if you don't really mind." She glanced back at him.

"Not at all. Go. I'll clean up the kitchen." He gathered dishes from the table to carry to the bar.

Kate climbed the staircase, looking back across the living area to the vista out front. *Lovely!* She turned right, along the foyer to the bedroom, pushed the door open, and stepped in. *Mmm, smells like Cam. Familiar and something else—a memory.* She walked around a platform bed, immaculately made with a hand-stitched brown and gold quilt and matching shams. The window opened to the morning sun and a light breeze. Beyond the creek, horses grazed along a hillside, tails swishing in the gentle wind.

She glanced into the bathroom; one side dedicated to a granite shower, with two entrances. Easing through the door she peeked around the corner. *Two shower heads? Huge vanity, two sinks…have a lot of company?*

She turned back to the door to find Cam walking in.

He asked hopefully, "Do you like it? I just finished the tile in the bathroom." He embraced her.

She nodded and said, "Very nice." She wrapped her arms around him and kissed him lightly. "The shower looks fun."

"If we had an hour more, I'd give you a tour of it." His mouth covered hers. He pulled back. "Ah! I do like the look of you, in here."

Kate smiled and searched for something to say. "I-um," her eyes dropped to his chest. "Look forward to it." She nodded.

He chuckled, "Me, too."

At the top of the stairs, Kate took a deep breath to clear her senses and descended. Cam grabbed his bag and followed.

Kate stole across the living room, to the piano. Curiosity won out. She lifted the picture that lay face down. It was a black and white portrait taken twelve years earlier, for her catering company's website.

"Probably should've put that away. I didn't think about it, until it was too late. Sorry." Cam stood behind her.

Kate asked, "Where did you get this?"

The frown she wore concerned him.

"Ruth gave it to me because I admired it greatly." Cam grinned. "It was in the music room on the fireplace mantel. First *picture* I saw of you—well as an adult."

She said, "I see."

He approached her with caution. "Do you?"

"No." She replaced the picture.

He stopped short of touching her and shrugged. "Does it matter? I mean in a negative way?"

Kate struggled to find words. Her hand fluttered in the air. "Why did you want it?"

"I told you yesterday, Kate—*and* I'm working-on a piece of music, as I get to know you better. It's— it's complicated."

She turned away from him, gazing out the windows for a moment. When she glanced back at him, she was still frowning. "So, I'm your Muse?"

He quickly answered, "Yes. Why is the picture a problem?"

"It felt so contrived. I only did it because my friend, who's a photographer suggested that it was a safety feature, for people using the website. When I go to meet new clients, they know it's me. And I've never taken good photos. I'm usually mid-blink or my mouth is open."

She dropped her gaze to the floor and then looked up, with a teasing grin. "I've never been a Muse before. Are there rules or something? Does this mean I'll get to hear the song someday?"

"No rules, just keep being you. You will definitely get to hear the song." He said and nodded.

She responded, "Okay, then."

Cam stepped closer, embraced her, kissed her gently. At first, she responded with ease, then passion, and emotions quickly escalated.

He stepped back, holding her shoulders, his voice husky. "I'm sorry! I let that get outta hand. We don't have that kinda time."

She focused on the third button of his crisply ironed chambray shirt. A tuft of dark curly hair peeked over the neckline of his white tee shirt. She tried to smile. She looked up to meet his beautiful green eyes and saw her heart reflected.

He pulled her close, kissing her hair.

She closed her eyes. *You know! You know I really love you!*

He muttered, "We have to leave here in fifteen minutes to pick up Ruth."

She whispered. "Yes."

"No time." He gently caressed her back.

"No." She shook her head against his shoulder.

They held each other tenderly, each wondering what the other contemplated.

Several minutes ticked past, when he stepped back. "You alright?"

She nodded; biting her lower lip and trying to smile.

He grinned and returned the nod. "Okay."

She sank onto the piano bench, his hand still at her shoulder. Buddy propped his head in her lap for a rub. Cam brushed a stray lock of hair from her face.

Buddy yipped when they heard someone climbing the front steps.

Mark wiped his feet on the coir rug at the door.

Cam said, "Kate, this is my partner, Mark Miller. Mark, Kate Klein."

Mark reached for her hand with a smile and gripped it firmly. "Glad to finally meet you, feel like I know you. Been to your house a dozen times, for one thing or another. Then, of course, he doesn't shut up about you."

Kate and Cam both reddened.

Mark chuckled. "Gotcha!" He pointed at Cam.

"Owe you." Cam pointed back.

"Got mine, bro. Janiece and I've been married thirty years next month."

"You don't look old enough to be married that long." Kate smiled the compliment.

Mark removed his ball cap and ran a hand over his short graying curls. "Thank you, ma'am, but I feel it most days." He reached down to pet the boxer. "Buddy's going home with me, for a while. Cam and I have joint custody of him."

Cam said, "Yeah, we better get outta here. Don't wanna keep Ruth waiting." He offered Kate his hand, as she rose from the piano bench. He checked with Mark. "Call me if you need to. Got the order in for the next two weeks of lunch deliveries this morning."

"Thanks, I don't like that job. I'll keep an eye on things. Don't worry. Give Elaine and Pop my love." Mark stepped out the door, Buddy at his heels.

Cam asked. "Ready, Kate?"

She looked up. "We'll take my car. It's easier for Mom to get in and out."

They went down the steps hand in hand.

"Good, you can drive. The picnic cooler's in the garage. I'll put it in the trunk." They reached the bottom. Cam took a deep breath. "What happened earlier…"

"We both had the opportunity…" She shrugged.

"I've made mistakes before—you know—when feelings are based on physical responses."

"Mmm." Kate assured him. "We're mature enough to know better."

Chapter Eight

Ruth was thrilled to be home. Kate parked close to the back door and the new ramp, in case she wanted to use it. Cam brought Ruth's luggage, out of the trunk.

The ramp eased Ruth's ascent to the porch. "I think I'll be fine, eventually, with the front staircase but the back is steeper. I'll have to work on that a while." She dropped her purse off in the mudroom and walked into the kitchen, using her walker.

"Oh, Kate, the cabinets look smashing. They brighten the room so much. I like the change." She nodded her approval.

"Good, I'm almost accustomed to it." She placed Cam's covered iron skillet of fried chicken on the island and turned on a wall oven. "I'll heat the chicken and we'll go to the gazebo. Try not to do too much, Mom. I know you're excited to be home, but this place consumes energy."

"I'll be cautious, dear. It'll be good to have some time with Evie and Leroy. It's been too long since my sister and I had a proper visit." Her voice dropped. "You have fun at Elaine and Harry's ranch. They're precious people. I'm sure you'll love them." She patted Kate's hand. "You need the break, sweetheart."

Cam met the ladies, after he deposited Ruth's luggage in her room. "How long for the chicken to heat, fifteen minutes?"

"About that," Kate replied.

"If you want to pack, I can take care of it." Cam declared.

"Deal." Kate left by the backstairs. Before she reached the top, she heard Ruth's laughter in response to something Camden said.

Dixie followed her mistress up the stairs, tail wagging slowly.

Kate considered her wardrobe. *The brown sweater goes with cream slacks or gold sweater, jeans.* She held up a coral ribbed knit sweater. *I won't have any secrets wearing this. Maybe it's a good thing Tere talked me into it.*

She settled on a burnt orange knit tunic with black jeans and quickly slid into them. She folded the rest into a suitcase with a pair of loafers and pulled on black boots. She hooked a silver concho and turquoise belt over the tunic, added silver earrings and necklace, then slipped three silver bangles on her left arm.

She checked her look. *Good!*

She rolled her suitcase down the hallway, as Cam met her to take it.

Dixie trotted behind her mistress, while she took in Kate's instructions. "Okay, girl, you need to obey Gram and be good for her. Your job is to keep the hounds inline and protect everybody. Got that?"

Dixie's tail wagged and she answered with a 'yip'.

"You look…amazing." Cam eyed her, with a smile, for a moment before descending.

"Thank you." She responded.

Kate followed a few steps behind, stopping to rub Dixie's ears near the bottom of the stairs.

Kate threw a cloth over the table in the center of the gazebo. Cam set up food and utensils. They brought chair cushions and an extra pillow for Ruth. The day was warm, bright, and a little breezy, but the gazebo offered shelter from wind gusts. The trio enjoyed their lunch together.

When Kate unveiled the caramel apple pie, Ruth nearly swooned. "Oh, my, Camden, you shouldn't have gone to the trouble. Now I'll be tempted to binge whilst the two of you are away."

"You can share. You'll have company." Kate cautioned.

"Pfui, who says I have to?" Ruth took a bite. "Mmm, as marvelous as I remember." She took another tiny bite. "I wish I was going with you. Maybe your next trip, I will. Do invite your parents up for a visit, dear. It's been almost a year since we were all together." Ruth finished her sliver of pie and helped put away the dishes.

Kate carried cushions inside. Dixie stayed close to her.

"They're doin' well." Cam's voice dropped. "Just hope Kate likes them."

Ruth patted his arm. "She will. Don't let her frighten you so much. She's a frail human like the rest of us, not the goddess you see before you. I promise, she has failings, just like all mortals."

Cam's forehead wrinkled when he grinned. "Yes ma'am." He stood and grabbed the cooler. "We'll get all this put away. We gotta leave soon."

Kate said goodbye to Dixie, before they went outside, "You be a good girl and I'll be back in a few days." She kissed the top of the pup's head, turned, and followed Cam.

***

Kate was surprised when they pulled into the county airport, after following Cam's directions.

Cam appeared uncomfortable. "I—have a plane. Pop gave me his, when his sight began to fail. He was a Top Gun, flew during the Vietnam War. He was also shot down over North Vietnam and taken captive. He spent a year and a half, in a hole in the ground. He nearly drowned every time it rained."

He sighed, looking away. "Pop was great with my brother and me. We finally found out what a father was like. We did our best to follow his footsteps." He met her eyes.

She smiled. "Okay.

***

"Is this your first time in a small plane?" Cam kept check on the controls while waiting for Kate's answer.

"Yes, it's fascinating and a little scary. In a commercial airliner, aside from the noise and crowd, you can forget you're thirty thousand feet in the air."

"We're not that high and subject to far more turbulence." Cam scanned the horizon.

"Where will you land?" Kate peered out the windshield.

"Pop built a landing strip in an upper pasture. We'll circle the house. That's the signal Momma listens for. She'll pick us up."

"Okay, then what?" Kate swallowed her anxiety.

"We take a rough ride in a beat-up old Jeep. I think the suspension failed in that buggy a decade ago and it never had shocks."

Kate laughed nervously.

Cam stole a look at the color in her cheeks, the way she flipped her hair back, over her shoulder. He shook his head and checked the control panel.

He continued, "We'll go to the house and entertain the inmates. I have no idea what to expect. They're both dying to meet you again, so the festivities may be elaborate or they may plan to spend all their time talking. It's like that more these days, with Pop not up to speed."

"Will we attend church Sunday?"

"Maybe, if they go. Mostly we don't bother. We sit around talking over breakfast dishes, until one or two in the afternoon. Does it matter to you?"

"Not at all. Will there be other people around?"

"Coop may come over, bring the boys. Is that alright? I hate to swamp you with all my kin the first trip."

"It sounds wonderful. I'm with you. That's enough." Kate smiled.

He grinned. "Thank you. Very much."

She asked, "How did you come to be partners with Mark?"

"We were in the Navy together. I was assigned as his wingman. Pop and Mark's dad served together, but we didn't know that at the time. Later Pop explained how he and Harold kept running into each other over the course of *their* careers. Used to be, men from whole regions signed up, to serve their country together. Not so after the first World War. Wiped out too many villages and small towns. It was purely chance that Pop and Harold wound up together on a dozen different missions. Turned out to be the same with Mark and me." Cam answered.

"Why is his name not on the company title?" She watched his face, but he just smiled.

"Mark's idea. He had a feel for the Ozarks, that a black man doing business, with no history in the area, would not be well received. He holds 50% of the company, Coop and I hold

25% each. It'll always be Mark's. His dad started it." Cam replied, as he glanced at the instrument panel.

Kate nodded, "He was right to feel concern. There's a lot of racial and antisemitic tension there. Is it the same in Texas?"

Cam nodded. "In places. It isn't prevalent everywhere."

Chapter Nine

Elaine waited at the landing strip when the plane stopped. Kate stayed seated, until Cam indicated that she could get out.

Cam's mother trotted out to greet them, getting to Kate first for a hug. "I am so glad to finally lay eyes on you again, girl. Cam talked our ears off, about you, when he was home a few weeks ago. Harry insisted he bring you for a visit." She reached one arm around her son as he dropped his bag on the ground. "How're you, handsome?"

"Pretty fine, Momma." He kissed her forehead. He snatched up his duffle and proceeded to load their bags into the Jeep.

"How's Ruth fairing, Kate?" Elaine kept a hand at Kate's elbow.

"She's well, glad to be home." Kate smiled. "I hated to leave her the first night back, but Aunt Evie's a better nurse than I am. She and Uncle Leroy will stay until I get home."

Cam captured Kate's hand, as he walked up behind her. "Come on." He led her to the Jeep and opened the back passenger door. "Cozy?" He asked, as she snapped her seatbelt.

"I am." She beamed.

Cam closed his mother's door, climbed in the front passenger's seat, and slapped the old metal roof. "Let's roll!" He studied his mother carefully.

She released the brake; rolled back a few yards, cranked the manual steering to her limit, and popped the clutch to start the engine. "We need a new wagon, but this one has been in the family for five decades. It's hard to give up. I keep saying when the beast dies, I'll get another one, but that may be for you kids to do."

They bounced along the pasture. Kate hung on to the leather strap, over the door and prayed her bladder would hold, until they made it to the house.

Harry awaited them in the brightly lit kitchen, with Zelda at his side. She barked a short, snappy greeting. Harry stood cautiously, when he heard the door open on the sun porch.

Cam stowed their luggage on the back staircase, and went to Harry.

He grasped his dad's shoulder to steady him and took his hand. "How're you, Pop?"

"Mighty fine, son. Where's your gal?"

"She's right behind me." Cam reached back for Kate and put her hand in Harry's. "Kate, this is my father, Harry Kendal. Pop, Kate Klein."

"Kate, we're thrilled you'll be with us a few days. Please have a seat. The teapot's on. Son, get us set for tea. Turning on the pot's all I'm allowed to do. Break way too many cups."

"I can handle it." Cam responded.

Elaine rescued Kate. "Honey, the powder room's behind these stairs." She led her down the hall at the rear of the house.

In moments, Kate rejoined them. Cam set the ancient round oak table, for tea, and seated Kate and his mother.

Harry resettled. "Honey, tell me what she looks like now."

Elaine smiled. "Kate, let me study you for a minute, since we're in the light. Harry's vision has reduced to shapes."

Elaine tilted her head back to peruse Kate's features.

"Her photographs barely do her justice. Sometimes people look different in real life. Kate's features are still handsome. She's tall, a little taller than I am."

"Five-six and a half." Cam interjected; arms crossed.

Kate looked at him, raising one eyebrow.

He glanced away.

Harry nodded.

Elaine continued. "Her hair is still long, almost to the middle of her back. It's black, but with silver embroidery. Her complexion is smooth, like Ruth's." Elaine dropped her voice to a whisper, "We've seen pictures at your home. You haven't changed since we met you in Kansas City." She continued, "Her eyes are dark as coal and luminous." Elaine mused for a moment. "Time is short, days are sweet...passion rules the arrow that flies...a million faces at my feet...but all I see are dark eyes."

Harry frowned. "You got me."

Elaine smiled, winked at Kate. "We love to quote songs and poetry, trying to guess the artist or poet. Dear, it's Bob Dylan."

They all had a good laugh.

Kate caught Elaine's glance. "Thank you."

* * *

"Camden, take Kate up to the pink bedroom, if she needs it. I'll heat a pot of soup that I fixed earlier. I made rolls this afternoon; they should be ready to bake." Elaine opened the fridge, as Cam and Kate filed out of the kitchen.

He grabbed their bags off the backstairs and nodded to Kate. "Come on up. We'll go back down the front stairs, so you get an idea of how the house is laid out."

Kate followed him. They turned left into a wide hallway on the second floor. He dropped his bag at a door as they passed. "My room," he glanced over, "in case you need to know that."

He opened the next door and stood back for her to enter. She walked into a little girl's dream, everything pink or white with pink polka dots. The full canopied bed, covered in ruffles and eyelet lace donned a wedding ring quilt and dust ruffle.

"Oh, my goodness, this is lovely. Is this your sister's room?" She asked.

"No, Lindy's favorite color was purple. Her room's across the hall from mine. You can guess...it's all purple. This is Momma's favorite room. She collects the dolls in the cabinets." Three antique curio cabinets housed about a hundred dolls. "That's maybe a third of what she owns. They're scattered all over the house." Cam set Kate's suitcase on a low bench, at the end of the bed. He stood awkwardly, in the doorway, for a moment, then said "Um, you don't have to sleep in here."

She returned to him, after switching on the bed-side table lamp. She reached for his crossed arms and made sure he was looking directly into her eyes. "How do you know exactly how tall I am, Camden?"

"Good with measurements. Know how tall I am and where you fit." He loosened her grip when his arm slid around her. "Anything else?"

"Where's the bath?"

"I'll show you on the way." He steered her toward the other end of the hallway to the fourth door on the right. "Here you go. I'll use the one across the hall. In case you need to know that."

"This house is bigger than the Bailiwick, isn't it?"

"Almost half again. The Greek revival is designed like a big box, where your Victorian charmer is large downstairs but loses square footage with the second and third stories. Third floor here sports a ballroom. At least that's what it was during prohibition. See the black buzzers at all the doorways?" He tapped the button, at the portal, to the third floor. "They alerted people when lawmen were on their way to bust up the fun. There's a fire escape off a second-floor porch roof. We'll go up tomorrow, check out the view." He kept her arm tucked into his, stroking the back of her hand as they moved.

"Now we're headed toward the front entry?" Kate asked.

"Yes, ma'am. We'll take a quick tour. The entryway opens to the parlor, then the music room and library. The first-floor bedrooms and baths are at the back." They passed a window seat on the landing, then down the wide walnut staircase.

"Did you grow up here?" Kate asked.

"Cooper and I spent our teen years here. At the turn of the 19th century, when Pop's grandparents built this house, it was intended for multi-generations. Pop's dad passed when he was overseas and he lost his brother in Vietnam. He retired a year after he married Momma. We moved in here with Grandma." He nodded. "It was good."

At the base of the stairs, they stepped into a large foyer. Leaded glass inset the front door and sidelights. The transom heralded a welcome to Kendal Ranch. Finely crafted original woodwork gleamed.

"How does your mother keep up with all this?"

"Full-time help. A lady comes in five days a week. A few times a year she brings in a crew to pull furniture out, clean baseboards, all the fun stuff."

"Quit, you're wearing me out." Kate's laughter rang like wind kissing glass chimes as she leaned into his arm. "Our old houses are lovely, but they *do* require a lot of maintenance."

He led her through the east wing of the house.

Cam turned toward her, as they came back through the music room. "This is my favorite room. We've made great music in here. Friday nights Coop and I both played football and basketball through high school. Saturday nights were for dates, if we had one, but Sunday nights were family. Everybody had their instruments for Sunday jams. We took turns leading. It was fun." His eyes brightened with the recollection.

"Sounds like it." Kate replied. "We used to have music night, when Daddy was alive—and home. Aunt Evie and Uncle Leroy would join us, for dinner, and everybody would find an instrument. Uncle Leroy can make his banjo smoke. Did you know that the banjo was an African instrument?" Cam nodded. "Aunt Evie has a voice from heaven and Daddy loved to hear her sing old gospel songs and the music brought out of the Appalachians. Mom and Aunt Evie were both born in Virginia. Their folks were hill people. My grandma Telulah, was a nurse. Mom's daddy was killed in Korea and Grandma remarried the local doctor, who, as you might have guessed was a black man. Aunt Evie was born a few years later. She's my darling."

"And you're hers. She lets everybody know you're her girl." He pulled her close and sighed. "We'd moved around a lot as kids. It was nice to belong someplace and know you can always come home."

"I agree, though all my childhood was spent at the Bailiwick." She pecked his cheek and took his hand. "Let's get back. I don't want your parents thinking we've deserted them."

"We'll go to the kitchen through the west wing." He kept her hand as they passed through a small living room, ornately furnished, large dining room, butler's pantry, and finally the kitchen. "Don't be afraid to holler if you get lost. I'll always come for you."

She smiled. "I think I have it."

Chapter Ten

After breakfast the next morning, Elaine led Kate along the rows of pictures on the ecru silk damask-covered walls of the music room. "Here's Cam when he graduated Annapolis. Did he tell you he had a full ride scholarship to Julliard?"

"Really?" Kate shook her head. "And he turned it down?"

She admired the handsome young man in the Navy's white dress uniform. His full, sensuous mouth and piercing green eyes made him almost too perfect. A scar on his chin added just the right amount of machismo.

I've traced that scar. Lying in bed with the man who saved my life. She looked away from Cam's picture, trying to focus on Elaine's voice.

"He couldn't stand being in a big city, indoors most of the time. He must be outside. Cooper, on the other hand, spends his days at a desk, on the phone. He has a construction company." She tapped a picture of Cooper in Navy blues. He resembled Cam, a little, but fairer, less like Elaine. "Camden would lose his mind if he was stuck in an elevator for an hour." Elaine muttered.

"At his house all the doors are wide open. It just seems natural." Kate replied.

"He designed that house. Coop helped. Harry pitched in to build it, but Cam did most of the work. He just recently finished the master bedroom and bath. We'll have to get up there to see it. He's very independent. I guess you've noticed that."

"I have." Kate smiled as she perused Cam's photographs.

"Sugar, you also need to know that he always gets what he wants. Harry refers to it as his 'Burger King mentality.' I want what I want *now*." She smiled to temper her words. "He'll badger the daylights outta you, until he gets his way."

"We'll see about that." Kate's posture stiffened, her chin set.

Elaine led her to a coral velvet Victorian-era sofa with cream fringe, to sit. "Cam tells me your husband was Jewish."

"Orthodox, yes." Kate steeled herself.

"I have a story to tell you. Would you like some tea or coffee?"

"No, ma'am. I'm fine, thank you." Her body tensed, perching on the edge of the seat.

"My parents were German immigrants. They left as the Third Reich came into power. My older brother, Elias, was an only child at the time." Elaine propped an additional pillow behind her back. "Mother applied to leave the country, to visit relatives, knowing there was a six-week waiting period for a visa. She interviewed with a young woman, who asked to see her home. She thought it unusual, but agreed to meet there. That woman's name was Ana. She asked my parents to take two Jewish children out with them. She'd supply paperwork. All my parents had to do was claim two more children." Elaine paused to get hold of her emotions; her eyes filled. "Anti-Semitism was rampant by that time. Ana entrusted them with a baby, Greta, and a toddler, Han. The two lived with them, while they waited for clearance to leave.

"Mother sewed information about the children's Jewish family members inside the hem of her coat. She vowed to find them after the war." Elaine blew her nose and dabbed her eyes. "I'm sorry, it still chokes me up when I think how courageous my parents were, to attempt something so dangerous. In hindsight, with what we know now, it's appalling. But truly they had no idea all they were up against.

"Greta became accustomed to my family, in a few weeks, but Han had a difficult time. He cried a lot. It was very hard on all of them. The neighbors began to ask questions. Mother told them that Papa's sister was hurt in an accident and left unable to care for her children, that they would take them into Austria to other family members."

"Did the children have anyone left after the war?" Kate choked back tears.

"No. My parents went to great lengths to look for anybody who might have known their people. Papa pursued it until his death." Elaine smiled faintly, held her handkerchief to her mouth. "He took us to a Jewish community thirty miles from home on Saturdays so Greta and Han could learn about their own culture. Several families offered to take the two of them." She shook her head. "Papa couldn't give them up, but made arrangements for extended visits. We'd go to Israel once a year when we were all old enough to travel. He spent his time looking through records, visiting nursing homes to talk to Holocaust survivors. He never found family for them."

"Where are they now?" Kate asked as she sniffed.

"Greta's married to a Presbyterian minister in Dallas and Han runs a halfway house in Laredo, since he retired. So, we already have Jewish family. I thought that may put you more at ease. There's no judgment here, Kate." Elaine patted her hand. "Though Harry's abrupt and sometimes demanding, he's less tolerant of bigotry than cattle rustling."

Kate's posture relaxed. "Thank you for sharing your story. I'd been concerned. Sometimes people have their minds made up. Until Cam and I began…I never presumed to be in this situation." She stumbled, searching for words. "It didn't occur to me that I wouldn't just grow old with Mom, at Bishop's Bailiwick and run a hostel for ladies. I had no idea I'd ever be," her voice dropped, "in love." She felt her face flame.

Elaine squeezed her hand again, smiled. "It's good, isn't it?"

Kate nodded. "Yes, very good."

***

Cam knocked on Kate's open bedroom door. "You got a few minutes? I wanna run somethin' by you."

"For you, always. Just about to put my shoes on." She grabbed a pair of loafers from her bag.

"You can go barefooted here if you want to." He winked when she glanced up, lounging in the doorway, attuned to her every move.

"Too Bohemian for my first visit." She met him with a smile.

Cam took her arm in his for the trip through the hall and stopped at the window seat, on the landing. He pulled her down with him, kissed her long, and slowly, then took a deep breath.

"Hold that thought. We'll come back to it. I have a surprise planned for Momma that involves going to town."

"I'm game." Kate nodded.

"We'll borrow her car and drive in. I have an appointment with a dealer at the Chrysler place. We're gonna get her a new Jeep. Talked to Cooper this morning and he gave me the name of a fella he trades with. I hate to spend any time, your first visit, with something like this, but she has trouble with arthritis in her arms and shoulders and watching her crank the wheel of that old jalopy...."

Kate's fingertips touched his lips. "Shh...let me grab a jacket."

***

Cam parked in front of the showroom. "You can go back if you want to. You don't have to stay through this."

Kate shook her head. "Are you kidding? I love to buy cars. Besides, you need my help." She patted his shoulder.

Cam grinned. "Come on, then. I've done research on the Wrangler. We can get a four door and it's guaranteed to climb mountains. It ought to be able to handle the cow pasture."

"I read an article a few weeks ago about the new Jeeps. I liked the fuel efficiency of the Wrangler. It's their best seller this year." Kate offered.

"Where'd you find that?" Cam took her arm.

"*Motor Trend* magazine, while I waited for Mom to get through PT."

"All righty, then." Cam responded.

The salesman met them at the door. "Hey, Cooper called me, said you were coming by. I'm Joe."

"Camden Fletcher. This is my...Kate, Joe. I want a four door, four-wheel drive Wrangler. I want to take it home today. What do you have on the lot?"

"Five of 'em. Come this way." He started ahead, then looked back. "If what you want's not here, I can order it from another dealership and have it in a day or two. You know the Wrangler's our best seller this year."

Cam eyed Kate. "I've heard that."

The trio walked across the lot to an aisle facing the street. Bright canary yellow caught Kate's attention. She strolled toward it while the men approached a gun metal gray Wrangler.

Cam realized Kate had gone another direction. He searched for her, smiled, and turned to Joe. "I think I've been overruled. Let's look at the yellow one."

"That one was special ordered by a local high school teacher." Joe explained. "Found out she was pregnant with twins the day before it was delivered. They opted for a van. I'll get the keys." Joe headed for the office.

"What do you think?" Cam studied Kate.

She climbed inside, checking the dash. "It looks fun, which is what a Jeep should be. It's automatic, power steering—for girls. And then, for the must have trip on the wild side, mrrur," she purred. "Leopard print seat covers." She grinned; her nose wrinkled. "What would your mother think?"

Cam shifted, stepping away from the door. "She'll laugh, cry, and say 'you shouldn't have, but I'm glad you did.' You want to drive it?"

Kate made wild eyes and said, "Lets! She screams 'take me' doesn't she?"

Cam laughed. "If you say so, honey."

Joe returned and handed Kate the keys. They all hopped in for a cruise around the town square. Cam helped her navigate the one-way streets. She parked back in front of the dealership. They studied each other for a moment listening to Joe extol the features of the vehicle.

Cam winked. "You want it?"

Kate nodded. "If you think your mom would like it, yes."

"She will, especially because you picked it out. You comin' in with me?"

"Absolutely, we need to see what incentives they offer. Joe, how're you going to sweeten this deal?" Kate turned to the salesman in the back seat.

"Let's go inside and barter." Joe opened his door and led the way. He waited for the couple to join him. "Go on back to my office. I'll be with you in a minute." He pointed them to a gray cubicle and left.

Kate drove the Wrangler back to the ranch. She pulled up in the front horseshoe driveway while Cam parked Elaine's car in the garage. He hurried through the house to bring his mother out. She loped all the way to where Kate propped against the side of the Wrangler, smiling.

Kate handed Elaine the keys. "It drives like Mom's Cadillac. Want to go four-wheeling?"

Elaine turned back to Cam, "You shouldn't have!" She dashed to the driver's side, climbed in, threw her head back, and crowed. She cranked the Wrangler, rolled down the window, and yelled at them. "Well, come on. Let's give her a spin through the pasture!"

Harry sat on a porch swing, Zelda at his feet, to wait for the family's return. "Ah, girl, there were days when I'd've been right beside her. Now, I find the most pleasure just to hear her excited. We raised good boys, Zelda." He reached down to rub the Lab's ears. She propped her head on his knee.

Cam listened from a few feet away. "Thanks, Pop." He climbed the steps to the porch and plopped onto a wicker chair near Harry.

"I thought you went with the girls, son."

"Are you kiddin'? They only needed me to open the gate to the pasture. Momma kicked turf goin' through it. She didn't stop for me. They were both screaming, when they hit the low water bridge at the creek. It's probably better I stay here."

"You don't sound disappointed." Harry grinned.

"I'm not." Cam admitted. "Not at all."

"Thank you for takin' care of your mother. It means the world to me." Harry pulled a hankie from his pocket and dried his eyes.

"Yes sir, I know. You did the same for us. Besides, I wasn't on my own. That gal I brought home can dicker. She saved us five grand. I was ready to write the check twenty minutes, before she got through with Joe." He chuckled. "When the salesman said 'let's barter' he had no idea who he was talking to. She wore him out, knew more about the vehicle than he did."

Harry guffawed. When he recovered, he said, "Let's take the girls out tonight. Whadaya say to the Roadhouse?"

"Sounds good." Cam leaned forward. "Better go open the gate. I hear 'em headed this way."

"Take Zelda, Cam." Harry loosened her halter. "She needs the run."

"Yes, sir!" Cam and Zelda raced for the gate.

Chapter Eleven

Cam followed his mother into her bedroom. She retrieved a black velvet box from the top drawer of the dresser and opened it. "It's a lovely setting. Gold was an excellent choice. Do you think she'll like it?" Elaine handed Cam the box.

He gazed at his maternal grandmother's engagement ring reset and sized to fit Kate. "She will. She loves old stuff." A half-carat oval diamond nestled among eight tiny oval rubies, glowing against the black velvet. "Thanks for handlin' it, Momma." He took a deep breath. "It's time."

***

"Come sit with me on the porch, Kate?" Cam asked.

He opened one of the eleven-foot double doors. They passed to the front porch, supported by twenty-four-foot columns. He led Kate to the deep swing covered with floral cushions set among a half dozen rattan tables, chairs, potted palms, and a settee.

They sat. He laid his arm over the back of the swing behind her.

"So, what do you think so far?" He inhaled deeply.

Kate laughed. "Your folks are wonderful. You were right. Elaine's given me all the fine points of your history, including your first spelling test." She caught his hand and the look in his eyes. "They are marvelous! I love that she had a blast with the Jeep."

Cam nodded. "They're nuts about you. Ruth and Momma email back and forth. They've heard all the Katrina tales from your proud mother." He shifted and took another deep breath.

Kate rested her hand on his thigh. "Are you okay?" She smiled into his eyes.

"Yeah, I need to talk to you about something. I'm trying to get the words situated so they come out right." He swiped his hand over his mustache and beard, took in a bushel of air. "I can

85

remember mission orders word for word from fifteen years ago, but I can't recall exactly how I wanna say this to you." He sighed. "I've practiced a hundred times in my head."

"Relax, I won't bite you." She smiled, watching him squirm.

He picked up her hand from his thigh, ran his fingers along hers, then placed it gently in her lap.

He left the swing and paced to the end of the sixty-five-foot porch to another arrangement of similar furniture. He returned and stopped at her feet. "You scare the daylights outta me."

"Is that what you wanted to say?" Kate questioned, her eyes narrowing.

"No, I'm just letting you know why this is hard." He knelt at her feet, reached for her face, and held it in his hand. "Kate, I love you more than life."

"Thank you. The feeling is mutual." She waited patiently.

Cam dug into his shirt pocket for the ring. "I know I come with baggage, but will you consider marrying me?" He looked doubtful.

Kate's head dropped to contemplate her lap for a moment, then looked up, with tears. "I wasn't prepared for this." She smiled.

He nodded and handed her a tissue, produced from his shirt pocket. "It can wait."

"No, you deserve an answer." She waved away his objection. "Don't make assumptions." She inhaled, closing her eyes. "I have trouble breathing when you enter a room. You make me giddy. You're familiar and–sometimes a total stranger. But I've lost my heart to you, Cam Fletcher." Tears spilled down her cheeks.

He grinned. "The feeling's mutual." He held the engagement ring between his fingers. "Katrina, will you be my wife?"

Kate nodded as she choked back tears. "Yes, yes I will."

Cam slipped the ring on her finger, a perfect fit. "This was my grandmother Bantz' ring, smuggled out of Nazi Germany in the hem of her coat. Momma had it reset on a new band, for you. Ruth gave her your ring size. It's been waiting for you for a while."

"I would have waited for you forever, Camden. There could never be another take your place." She blinked to clear her vision enough to see the ring through tears. "This is beautiful."

"Almost as lovely as you are. I told you I've had a crush on you for a while, 3 years, my dear. After we met again, I just knew you were destined to be mine." He glanced away. "We don't have to wait unless you want to. I don't."

"How do you want to…a wedding or what?"

"Our mothers expect a wedding. They've talked it to death. I think the only things they haven't ordered are flowers and cake. I hate to disappoint them, but I'm all for eloping." He rose to sit beside her. His arm rested behind her. He twirled a lock of her hair.

"Well, I guess we need to discuss it with them." She wiped her face again. "If we elope, we can have a reception. Maybe that would suit?"

He nodded. "Now to meet your boys?"

"Oh, my." Her hand fluttered to her mouth again. "Yes, I suppose it's time."

"What, no confidence in your man?" He smiled.

"It's not that, Cam. It's…well Isaac will be the bump in the road. Asher trusts my judgment." She swiped at her eyes.

"I've got two things going for me, darlin'. I'm male and I have *cool* toys." He grinned.

She had to laugh.

Chapter Twelve

Cam and Kate walked in the front door of Pappy's Roadhouse, hand in hand. They paused, once inside, to find Harry and Elaine at a glass topped wagon wheel table and a leather horseshoe shaped bench.

Kate slid in. Cam sat on the outside close enough for his thigh to rest beside Kate's.

"Still have your regular table. Come out much?" He checked his mother's discomfort with a frown.

She answered. "Not as much as we used to, occasionally for dinner, not as often to dance these days. My knees give me too much grief."

A young lady in a cowgirl outfit arrived at the table with an order pad on a tray. Her blond ponytail swished behind her. She spread cocktail napkins on the table. "Hey, Mr. Kendal, Miz Kendal. What can I get y'all to drink?"

Harry glanced toward her. "Sounds like Gloria."

"Yes, sir, it's me. I'm sorry. I forget." She whined.

"Don't fret, child." Harry turned to Elaine. "Momma, what're we having?"

"There's a bottle of champagne, in the walk-in cooler and bring the appetizers I ordered too, dear. We're all hungry."

Gloria left at a trot.

Kate studied the room, then read the fire marshal's posting. *Seating capacity a thousand-eighty-four…but it looks like a rough bunkhouse from outside.*

"Kate, there're a variety of vegetables and a petite steak that's just right for ladies." Elaine offered with a strained smile, her hand on Kate's arm.

Kate smiled and responded, "Thank you, it sounds good." *Why this feeling of imminent doom, sweet lady?*

After dinner, the Roadhouse began to fill up. A band set up and worked on tuning instruments. Seating became scarce by eight o'clock.

"Gloria, have Ron bring me a mic, please ma'am." Harry sent the waitress on her way, as she cleared the table.

Elaine laid a hand on Harry's arm. "Harry, do you...."

He patted the top of her hand. "Sweetheart, don't agonize over it. This is our place. Always has been. We came here to celebrate with Camden and Katrina. That's exactly what we'll do."

Ron appeared with the microphone. The old cowboy's once lean form, only a memory; a large silver belt buckle spanned a third of his pot belly. He reached across the table to shake hands. "Haven't seen you in a coon's age, Camden."

Cam took care of introductions, "Kate, this is Ron. He runs the place. Ron, my fiancée, Kate."

"Good to meet you, Kate. I suppose that explains this." He placed the mic in Harry's hand and switched it on. "It's hot, Harry." Ron stepped back.

"I beg your attention, for a moment." At the sound of Harry's deep voice, the busy room fell silent. "My wife and I have the pleasure of announcing our son's engagement. Camden's finally gettin' married."

The band struck a celebratory song, applause broke out across the room. Harry clicked the off the switch and chuckled.

Cam peered, with longing, at the exit. "Figured that," he said under his breath. He turned to Kate with a grin, shaking his head.

"You lived through it." Kate leaned to Cam's ear. "Are we going to be here awhile?"

"Yes, ma'am." His foot bounced a steady beat, more anxious than musical.

"I need to powder my nose." She slipped out of the booth. His hand swept over the back of her red sweater to her black velour jeans, as she passed. She crossed a narrow space, browsing pictures of celebrities and band members through the saloon's history, lining the wall of the dimly lit hallway to the restroom.

As she returned, Cam still stood at the end of the booth, arms crossed, watching for her. When Kate met his eyes, relief washed over his expression.

A woman, her back to Kate, stood at their table in conversation with Elaine, tossing an occasional remark in Cam's direction.

Kate studied her thinking, *how on earth does she walk on six-inch spike heels? I'd break my neck. There's more fabric in my sweater than her whole outfit. If she sneezes, she won't have any secrets.*

Cam turned his attention to the guest and shook his head, with a determined air, to accentuate a comment he added. Kate caught the coldness in his eyes.

She arrived at the table. Cam joined her when she sat, his thigh pressed against hers, his arm behind her.

Kate continued her study, noting that no one introduced her. *Not as young as she looked from the rear, maybe forty-five. Tanning beds make good leather. Lots of makeup, professional nails.*

Kate leaned on the table, folding her hands. *Her tone's changed, no longer assertive. My return's affected the atmosphere, thick enough to slice with a very sharp knife.*

A hand extended toward her. "I'm Jackie Fletcher. So, you're Kate."

Kate shook the woman's damp hand firmly, feeling the apprehension and anger. "Yes." She smiled, bemused at the woman's obvious discomfort.

Elaine patted Kate's thigh, tilting her head to peer up at Jackie. "I could swear Jane told me you married Skeet Keller a few years ago. Had no idea you were still using my son's surname."

Jackie's hazel eyes narrowed, regarding Elaine with fire. She let the remark pass. Her gaze returned to adhere to the engagement ring on Kate's hand.

I hope she never wanted this. Kate continued to smile graciously. *What a study in contrasts we are, almost exact opposites, like Cam and Reggie.*

Cam's ex-wife's Texan drawl was thick. "I'll let y'all get back to your *little* celebration." She grimaced and shuddered, as though she could remove the effects of the encounter, she initiated, and turned away.

"Wanna dance?" Cam slipped his arm around Kate's waist, clearly relieved that Jackie left through the front door.

"Sure." She followed him out to the dancefloor.

He caught her hand. Pulling her close, he said, "I'm sorry. Momma spotted her after we dropped them at the door."

"Lady, I'm your knight..." The lead singer crooned.

"I like this song." Kate leaned into Cam's chest.

"Me, too." He kissed her forehead.

"Does she live nearby?" Kate asked.

"Houston, last I heard. I haven't seen her in seven or eight years. She said Jane told her we were here. I'll have a talk with my brother's wife about my business.

"It's okay."

"No, it isn't." He held her close, inhaled the fragrance of her hair. "You smell good."

"Thank you."

"Other than that, are you havin' a good time?" He grimaced.

"Absolutely, I'm with you." She laid her hand on the side of his face.

He turned to kiss her palm; eyes closed. He sighed. "Kate, will you stay with me tonight?" He bit his lower lip.

"What's going on? Like I'd say 'no'?"

He shook his head.

A tall man, in a black cowboy hat stopped behind him, to clasp Cam's shoulder with a large rough hand.

"Excuse me. I wanna dance with your woman." A wide, dentured grin split his weathered face. He was a bona fide cowboy, from his Stetson hat to his highly polished pointed-toe boots.

Kate responded mentally. *Guess I better get used to it.*

Cam turned, keeping a grip on her waist. "Hey, Randy. This is Katrina. Honey, this is Randy Sutherland, our ranch manager."

Randy removed his hat and folded his lanky frame into a sweeping bow. "Katrina, the pleasure's all mine."

Cam glanced back, at the older man and winked. "Tell you what, if I get tired of dancing with her, I'll give you a holler. Will that do?"

Randy slapped Cam's back and laughed. "It'll have to, I reckon." He settled the handsome Stetson on his bald noggin and left them.

"I thought it was polite to concede a dance." Kate responded, as Randy walked away.

"I can't bear for anybody to be this close to you, who isn't me." He smiled to soften the set of his jaw. "Besides, we were having a discussion."

Chapter Thirteen

Kate sat on the side of the bed studying the clock. *Eleven-thirty. Somebody's going to a lot of trouble to be quiet.* She tip-toed to the door, yanked it open, and stepped into Cam.

He caught her in his arms.

"Ah!" She gasped, recoiling in shock.

He held onto her. "Kate, it's me! Shh, honey, it's okay," his voice sounded hoarse, his hands felt cold through her silky sleep shirt, as he held her.

She relaxed a little, finger-brushing her hair out of her face. "Why're you out here walking the hall in the middle of the night?" She shivered at his touch and rough manner.

"Couldn't sleep." He eased his grip. "Sorry I woke you up."

"Cam, what's wrong?" She rubbed his arms, still surrounding her.

He peered down and sighed.

"Camden?" Her tone sharpened.

"I'm tied in knots. I just need to hold you."

"Okay, I wondered why you left."

"Didn't wanna wake you up."

He steered her back inside. Ancient rhino horn lamps with raw silk shades, soft browns, greens, and ecru adorned the room. A large mahogany four-poster bed stood in the middle, flanked by matching chests on either side. A dozen framed charcoal sketches, of horses, hung in the space above the headboard.

Kate turned back the covers and slid to the opposite side of the bed. "Now tell me what's going on."

"I just need to hold you." He turned away and removed his robe, tossing it onto a side chair.

"Okay, *I need* something too." She tossed her sleep shirt to join his robe.

He turned to find her watching him. "What's that, honey?" Her thick dark nipples beckoned, even in filtered moonlight.

Kate smiled. "I need more than a cuddle." She flipped the cover back.

Camden caught his breath. "Yes, ma'am."

He lay beside her, his touch as gentle as a breeze. His hands and lips explored her body, her sighs and whispers stoking his fire.

Kate melted into his arms. Their lips met, mouths open and passions soared. She whispered, "You have no idea how much I missed you, while I waited for you to find me."

When she couldn't wait any longer, she led him inside. Her throbbing pleasure sent him into orgasm. They lay tangled, between legs and sheet, relishing the moment of intimacy.

Cam whispered, "Welcome home, my heart."

***

Kate woke on her side, facing the wall, snug in the comfortable bed. She rolled to her back, peering through sleepy eyes. *It wasn't a dream.* She checked the vacant hollow in the pillow beside her. She buried her face in the recess and savored Cam's scent.

After a shower, she crept down the back staircase, eavesdropping on Cam's phone conversation.

He was in the office at the rear of the house with the door open. "…what on earth made you tell her about Kate and me? Jane, it's not her business." He listened for a tick. "She said that. I'm goin' to the courthouse tomorrow to tag Momma's Jeep. I'll check the records. She's looking for my copy now." He went quiet, then growled, "Don't ever mention me to her again. I haven't been her business, or yours, for a hell of a long time."

Kate eased down the hall to the office.

"I'm resolved to get shut of her once and for all. I know she's your friend but…okay then, mm, bye." He hung the office phone back in its cradle, "any progress, Momma?"

"Devious little tart!" Elaine swore. "How dare she show up now to ruin your life. She did her best eighteen years ago." She sighed heavily. "Why can't I find that…?"

Kate knocked on the door jamb. "Good morning."

94

Cam smiled. "Good morning, sunshine." His weary eyes raked over her jeans and his tee shirt, the gaze searing her.

I know that look already. She bit the inside of her mouth, grinned and crossed her arms, then dropped them again when she realized his survey rested on her cleavage, where he'd fallen asleep a few hours earlier.

Elaine's glower had melted. "Hello, dear. I'm sorry. You caught us in a tizzy this morning. We have to find Cam's divorce papers. I had power of attorney while he was in the Navy, so it has to be in these file cabinets somewhere." She pulled a few more files to the front of the drawer. "If we don't locate them and it went through, there'll be copies at the courthouse."

"If they aren't, she's not lying." His voice sparked with sarcasm. "I'll go see Rafe Edwards, if that's the case."

"I just know Jane told me, a few years back, that Jackie *married* Skeet Keller." Elaine's hands rested on her hips.

"Maybe just lived with him. Don't fuss over it. Coop and I were both overseas. Jane lived here, with Jimmy, after her parents ran off to take Jesus to the Philippines. Then Grandma got really sick. Top that off with the drama of a teenage girl in the house and you teaching full-time. You were a tad occupied."

Elaine bent to the task once more. She snatched a file out, thumbed through, and produced an envelope. "There it is!" She handed the yellowed package to Cam.

He opened the seal and scanned the papers inside. "Dated March 2000. Not a decree. It's a letter that says they couldn't contact Jackie's attorney, he didn't return Rafe's calls."

"And I didn't open it." Elaine's head dropped.

Cam tossed the mess on the desk, stood and put his arm around her. "Hey, don't take this on! It's not yours. It's my mess. I'll deal with it."

"She'll do her best to take the ranch." Elaine groaned.

"She can't touch it, in the trust. We'll be fine." He squeezed her arm. "Momma, I need a few minutes with Kate."

"Oh! Of course. I'll see to Harry." Elaine stepped around the small, glowing space heater and swept by into the hallway.

Cam maneuvered Kate into the tiny space and closed the door. "We need to talk."

"Okay." She stood before him.

He sighed. "After you rode the poker run with me, I came to Texas. Grandma passed. I needed to be here for the funeral *and* the reading of the will. She appointed me executor of the estate. I've been helping Momma run the ranch, but it's too much for her, so I took over. Randy's a decent manager. She still signs checks, but I like to have a little more control over the place."

"That's it?" Kate asked.

"Pretty much." He waited expectantly; a scowl settled on his brow. "I want you with me when I have to come down."

"We'll muddle through." She smiled.

"About last night...." Cam's face reddened.

"Yes?" She asked.

"Thank you."

"Well...don't feel obliged to thank me every time we make love. It's a mutually wonderful thing. You've taught me how my body's supposed to feel." She glanced down at his chest.

Cam slipped his arms around her. "That's good to know." He searched her eyes. "I'll never hurt you intentionally. Promise you'll tell me if you feel that way."

"Okay. You haven't told me where you'd been or what was bothering you."

Cam sighed, then began, "I went to the barn, saddled a horse, and rode. Stopped for a while, at the cemetery. Came back, put up the horse, and walked around. Took a cold shower and fought the fire inside." His face flamed. "When I realized you were just a few feet away." He shrugged.

Kate smiled at his obvious embarrassment.

"Nothing *improper* happened, Kate." His intense gaze burned into her. "This time, you're wearing my ring *and* my tee shirt."

She placed her hand over his heart. "The idea that premarital sex is taboo is a fairly recent rule created by angry white men who want to control women's bodies, which they do not understand. Through the ages, if a woman was pregnant before marriage, the family *celebrated* her fertility. Just sayin'."

He nodded. "I like the way you view it, but I don't want to embarrass you."

"You don't." She stretched on tip toes to kiss his mouth.

***

Harry sat at the round table. He said, "You can fly into Las Vegas and get it done in a day, son. Married, too, as far as that goes." He took a sip of coffee; both hands encircling the heavy mug.

"That's an idea, Pop." He checked Kate, manning the stove with their breakfast. "How 'bout it?"

She flipped pancakes. "I'm game."

Harry spoke toward the stove. "Kate, those pancakes smell wonderful!"

"Thanks, they're gingerbread." She sautéed apples from the ranch orchard, in a skillet by the griddle. "I grabbed a bag of my special mix to bring to you."

Cam poured coffee around and replaced the pot. He stopped beside her, resting one hand on the back of her thigh, the other on her abdomen, and leaned in to whisper in her ear. His hot breath on her neck sent shock waves through her limbs.

He reached past her to turn the sliced ham, sizzling in an iron skillet. His hard chest pressed against her shoulder. "Think about it, okay?"

Kate's knees felt like warm honey. Her husky voice replied, "I will."

Elaine came in from the dining room. "Are we close to eating, y'all?"

"Yes, ma'am." Cam answered for both of them as he turned away from Kate.

***

After brunch and cleaning the kitchen, the couple excused themselves.

"Come on, we'll go to the music room." Cam caught her hand, tucked it into his arm, and led her through the house. "Brunch was great, honey."

"Thank you." She smiled.

Cam led her to the Victorian sofa. "Let's sit here."

She sat. He snuggled against her, propping his arm behind her.

"What do you think about Pop's idea?"

97

"I want you to meet my sons." She stuffed her hands under her thighs.

"You cold, baby? I'll build a fire."

She cleared her throat. "*No,* I hope to be through with this before the room could warm."

"Let's get married."

"Cam, we can take a breather… We needn't be in such a rush."

He glanced down to her upturned face. "That was eloquently put, darlin'. He hugged her close and rested his face in her hair. "We aren't children. Our time is limited, on the downhill side these days. Mmm, the remainder of last night was amazing…Waking up and seeing you there, beside me, was comforting, but also…very tempting."

Kate smiled and said, "You should have awakened me. I was a little disappointed you weren't available when I woke up." Her tongue moistened her lower lip as Cam dipped to her mouth for a long kiss.

He shifted. She sat up straight.

Cam inhaled and said, "Enough of that!"

"We have to buy rings and make a plan." She smiled.

"It's done." He grinned.

"Pretty cocky, aren't you?" She asked.

"No ma'am. Hopeful." He slipped a kiss on her neck. "I'm taking Pop out for a ride. You wanna go?"

"I need to spend a little more time with your mother."

"I'll be back in a couple of hours." He stood, pulled her up, and kissed the top of her head.

Chapter Fourteen

Elaine said, "Harry and Zelda were on the prowl, when Cam came in from the cemetery. He usually goes there when he's home. Harry's up several times a night. Always has been. Pilot training. Very little escapes his notice. And you need to know, my boys tell me way more than I need to hear. Camden may break your heart, at times, but you'll always know the truth."

After a sip of water, Elaine continued, "Shortly after Harry and I were engaged, we'd planned a family evening. There was a Boy Scout campout the following weekend. My boys were both Eagle Scouts, by the way. Proud Momma." She placed her hand over her heart.

"A hurricane in the Gulf headed toward the Texas coast and you never know which way they'll blow, but best guess was our way. So, the Scout Master called the boys to camp a week early. Harry showed up, thinking they were home." The tea kettle whistled.

Elaine hopped up to pour water. "We went out dancing. When we got back to my house, Harry came in, like he'd done dozens of times, but that time the atmosphere was different." She set Kate's cup in front of her and sat with her own. "We were totally alone. We slipped. We eloped a few days later. It was a good thing too. I'm convinced Lindy was conceived that night. She arrived forty weeks later, to the day." She shrugged.

Kate sighed. "You have a gift for putting me at ease, sweet lady." She dipped her tea bag a few times and laid it on her spoon, wrapped the string around, and squeezed the richness out. "Will you tell me about Cam and Jackie, please? I know a little, that they had a rough time and lost a baby. But I want to understand why she'd show up now to lay claim to him again."

Elaine replied, "I wasn't going to bring her up. You don't have to know what a witch she's been but…she put my son through the ringer. They married. Cam bought her a house next door to her parents outside Houston." She leaned back. "His Naval career took him all over the world. She'd go with him, stay a few weeks, leave. That went on for almost two years." Elaine sipped her cooling tea. "Then *her* baby was stillborn. She walked out of the hospital and Cam's life for more than a year. He'd buried the little boy by himself. He dug the grave, up in the family cemetery. The baby's death was God's intervention, Kate." She frowned, tapping the edge of the saucer with her fingertip.

"Then what?" Kate asked.

"She tried to mend their relationship, but something inside Cam died with that child." Her eyes filled with tears. "It sounds melodramatic, but life's that way with Jackie, like a damn soap opera. She's bounced from man to man through the years, leaving a trail of husks behind her."

"What does she do—for a living, I mean?" Kate drained her cup.

"Cam put her through nursing school. After they were divorced, he paid for her to finish college. He never returned to her, but he didn't desert her either." Elaine floated an herbal tea bag in her China cup.

She continued, "He's like that, I'm afraid. He feels responsible for people, even when they're finished with him." She shook her head with a sad smile, brushed her hand over her broad, lined forehead. "If she'd walked up to the table last night and asked him for anything, he would've given it to her. But she's in serious error to think she can threaten him like she did."

"How'd she *threaten* him?" Kate dreaded the answer.

"He didn't tell you?" Elaine asked.

"I wish he had, but no." Kate shook her head.

Elaine held up fingers in air quotes. "She told him he'd have to make it worth her while to keep her from telling 'her story.'"

"Mmm, I see." Kate stared into her cup as though there were answers hidden in the bottom. "Do you know what she's talking about?"

"He'll have to tell you the particulars, that's one thing he's never shared."

Harry settled at the kitchen table when he and Cam returned from their ride. "Man, I'll feel that ride in a little while. I don't get many rounds in the saddle these days."

"It felt good to get out. I don't ride a horse nearly often enough." Cam turned on the coffeemaker.

"Do me a favor. Somethin' bothers me." Harry scratched his whiskered chin.

"Sure, Pop, what?"

"You brought down the pink file cabinet full of photos ,from the third floor when you were home last. Elaine's been working on puttin' pictures in albums in the library."

Cam answered, "Yes, sir."

"So many things happened here, at the same time, but I think I remember that we received an envelope from Rafe for you. Go check the summer of '99 folder. Pictures came in the mail, Lindy's prom…and graduation. We go through it all here on the table. I just want to be sure something important didn't wind up in that file. It's happened to us before. Two weeks ago, Elaine found a letter from Cooper, when he was flying cargo into Kuwait, stuck inside a picture sleeve."

"Sure, I'll go look." Cam's long stride carried him toward the library in haste. "Please let the divorce decree be in there," he muttered along the way. He heard Kate laughing, as he opened the door.

He found the ladies sorting through photos. They glanced up at the same time, both looking sheepish.

"Hey, son, what's up?" Elaine deftly slid the stack of snapshots in her hand together, like a deck of cards.

"What're you hiding, Momma?" Cam grinned and checked Kate's less than innocent look. "What're you two doing?"

"Lookin' through old pictures. Is there somethin' you need?" Elaine dropped the photos in an aged envelope and slid it between her thigh and the chair.

"Now I have to know. You're going to too much trouble to keep it from me." Cam chuckled.

"Your naked baby pictures." Kate admitted, tucking a slipped curl behind her ear. She failed to make eye contact. "You do have sweet dimples." *And to think I can see them for a wink!*

"As long as I enjoy your favor." He shook his head and laughed. "You two are a pair. I can't imagine the mischief you'll be up to when Ruth makes it a trio."

"You didn't say why you're in here. I thought you and Harry were out riding." Elaine reminded him.

"We're back. Coffee's on. Pop sent me to look in a file, summer of '99, for missing mail."

Elaine studied her eldest son for a moment before she realized what Harry referred to. "Oh, I know!"

She twirled her chair to the cabinet behind her and produced a brown accordion folder and slid the contents onto the desk blotter. Her well-worn hand sorted through large photos of Lindy posed in cap and gown, formal dresses, and a cowgirl outfit, propped on a bale of hay. "I have to get busy and put these in albums. She may want to take them next time she's home."

An envelope appeared among the photographs. She liberated it, to hand to Cam.

"It's from Rafe." He opened the envelope and unfolded the paperwork inside. "This is it. The divorce was final May 18th, 2000. Thanks, Momma." He laughed.

"Thank God! That's driven me nuts since Jackie showed up at our table last night. I didn't sleep a wink." Elaine blushed fury. "I could wring her neck!"

Kate and Cam's gazes locked. He raised his brows, "Well, Miss Kate?"

"What?" She looked away.

"Tomorrow at the courthouse or tonight in Las Vegas?" Her attempt to avoid his eyes amused him.

She shrugged, shook her head. "I think we can wait until tomorrow."

"Blast it, woman!" He turned on his heel and walked out of the room chuckling.

Elaine eyed Kate sympathetically. "What'd I tell you?"

Chapter Fifteen

Kate's packed bag sat by the open bedroom door of the pink room. Cam reached inside for it, hefting his own.

"Ready, honey?" He put the bags in the hall and approached her.

"I am. I've enjoyed dressing in here. Your mother's dolls are adorable. Their faces are exquisite, details so perfect; you could brush away a tear." She smiled up at him.

He smiled back, reaching for her. "They creep me out."

"Not for everyone then." She rested her head on the niche in his shoulder.

"Our itinerary is to fly into the county airport, let them go over the plane and gas it up. We can run to the courthouse and take care of the Jeep and us, then we'll dash down to Austin for the evening." He held her back at arm's length. "And you're mine—legally!"

***

Cam's cell phone rang. He swung his legs over the side of the bed to answer. "Fletcher."

"Prepare yourself for annoying phone calls, son." Harry's voice rasped through the line. "The sheriff just left here. They found Jackie yesterday, in a local hotel room, badly beaten. She's in ICU, hanging on. They think it happened Saturday night. They want to talk to you."

Cam glanced back at Kate's bare shoulders. "I expect they do."

"They asked where you were, after we left Pappy's. I told them you were on the ranch. Is that right?"

"Yes, sir. I didn't leave until Kate and I flew out." Cam ran his fingers through his hair.

"You returned to the house after 10, but before 10:15? It was between clocks chiming."

"Yes, sir."

"Then what?"

103

Cam hesitated, then admitted, "I was with Kate, in my room, until I came downstairs" He stretched.

"No judgment, Camden. You go to the cemetery?"

"Yes, sir. Pulled weeds awhile, by my phone's flashlight."

"We're good. I'll call Rafe; put him on standby, in case we need him." Harry assured his son.

"Thank you. We're going home today."

"You get married?"

"Yes, sir." He smiled. "Pretty incredible feeling—belonging to someone else."

"I understand." A hoarse chuckle clamored across the phone line. "I love ya, son."

"I love you too, Pop." Cam laid the phone on the bedside table and turned to his wife.

Kate lay watching him, curled on her side. She pulled the blanket up to her chin.

"Cold? I think I can fix that." He joined her.

"No doubt." She giggled.

***

They sat at a diner's corner table after breakfast, holding hands by the condiment tray. Kate watched the overhead light reflect off the coffee in her cup.

"Pop said she was in ICU, hanging on. I'll go into the Sheriff's Department to make a statement, before we leave." Cam turned her hand to catch the light's gleam off the gold wedding band under her engagement ring. He'd bought it the day after their second "first" meeting.

"Do they have a time frame yet?" Kate asked.

"Pop said Saturday night."

"Are you worried about what can happen?" She frowned.

"No, I wasn't anywhere near her. He said she was in a local hotel room. He didn't say where. I was at—riding, then the family cemetery, then back—with you. I have about an hour and a half to account for without a witness." Cam bit his lower lip and frowned. "You don't think I...?"

She responded, "Absolutely not! I wasn't implying that you did. I just don't want a storm cloud hanging over us."

104

"You mean like this muddy coffee?" Cam cracked a smile.

Kate surveyed the mid-morning crowd of diner patrons. "Can we start for home?"

"Yes ma'am." He glanced around for their waitress, spotted her, and signaled for a check.

She bustled toward their table with a slip of paper and a smile.

***

"Tell me what Jackie threatened you with, please." Kate said.

They sat in the plane, on the runway, waiting for clearance to take off.

Cam took in a bushel of air, then sighed. "The 'don't ask don't tell' policy was a landmine for the military." Cam's wide hand brushed down his whiskers. Weariness etched his face. "I'd been assigned a new co-pilot. A bunch of us were going to meet at the Officer's Club at Pensacola NAS for dinner. Charlie needed a ride, came with me. He'd been in the unit for about a month. I stopped for gas. A surge in the flow spewed gas on my pants and shoes. I ran home to change."

His voice shifted into monotone. "I said 'gettin' a shower, be right back.' Beat it to the bathroom, was gone maybe twenty minutes. Jackie returned from a month-long sabbatical, unannounced, as usual. I walked out to a screaming cat fight. The MPs rang the bell at the same time I stepped into the room. There was an incident report. From there, an inquiry." He checked the control panel, fiddled with a switch.

"He was gay, had ideas. I was clueless. Looking back, I could see the signs, but working with him every day...I didn't know, couldn't ask. He couldn't say. We were both in a pickle. It cost him rank. They slapped my wrist and I was embarrassed. Jackie said he started in on her about leaving me. She picked up on him right away. She never let me forget it, always made catty remarks. There you go." He leaned toward her, waiting for some kind of feedback.

Kate listened in silence, then said, "I waited tables, in college, at a five-star restaurant. I was on the schedule to close one night and the head waitress stayed late, waiting for one of

105

her tables to leave. She was married with two small children. I was drying silverware when she physically accosted me. I thought it was an accident until she made it clear that she wasn't playing. I was shocked. I'd led a sheltered existence. It took days to get over it."

"Did you quit?" Cam asked.

"No, the tips were way too good." Kate grinned. "I asked, politely, for her to remove her clitoris from my knee. Said that I wasn't inclined to her ways, got up and left. The thing is, we aren't always sensitive to our surroundings, especially when we're tired, and we can't read minds. I can see how that story might have hurt your career and public perception, if it became common knowledge. But, it's nothing to be ashamed of. Why people can't just accept other people, who don't share their ideas or lifestyles, is beyond me. We're all just human, doing the best we can do with what we are."

"Yeah, but honey, *we* don't rule the world." He squeezed her thigh, as the tower called up their number and runway.

Once airborne, Kate brought up another subject she was curious about, "Tell me about your aunt and uncle. Elaine told me how they came to be part of her family, but tell me their particulars, please."

"Okay, Uncle Han was an engineer. He designed and built bridges. He's done really exceptional work, but you have to hear about it from somebody else. After he closed out a job, it was archived in a file and his mind. Never married. He's always been a loner.

"I went to Israel once, when I was a junior in high school. Summer break, for six weeks with him, working on a bridge. He showed me the methods, the materials, the framework. His assistant told me Han had designed every inch of that bridge.

"Mossad approached him early in his career, so he has an inside to all sorts of intelligence.

"The only time I've seen him lose his cool was after the Preacher died. Han walked into our house, which the church gave us a week to get out of, to find a church deacon tearing into Momma about her lack of care for her marriage. Said if her husband had been getting sex at home, he wouldn't have had to go elsewhere. Han walked straight to that man and grabbed a handful of his jacket and shirt at the nape of his neck. The deacon outweighed Han by about 80 pounds. Didn't make any difference. He literally dragged him out the front door and dropped him on the ground in the yard. Told him his attorney was filing a lawsuit, on Momma's behalf against the church. Seems they had a $100,000 life insurance policy on the Preacher. Momma wound up with half of it, after the settlement. Then he had the attorney file a defamation suit against the board members. She won that a year later. "We had nowhere to go, until Han showed up.

"He'd rented an apartment in San Antonio. Coop and I had to change schools and Momma had to find a new job, but Han had all that covered, too. We stayed there three months while he bought and renovated a house, in the same area, for his sister. She got to pick the paint colors and everything. She'd never had the pleasure of that experience. We lived there until we moved onto the Kendal Ranch.

"I never knew Elias, Momma's oldest brother. He was gone when I was growing up. I met him in Amsterdam, when I took a few days off from the Iraq war. He'd been in the US Air Force, stationed in Germany. He stayed, after he retired. Married, had no kids and his wife had passed from cancer. We had a little time to get to know each other." Cam checked his panel and reset a dial.

"Aunt Greta's a pediatrician. She married late in life, but has two daughters, through IVF. She's married to a preacher, but she's still Jewish, still worships her own way. She goes to the church and helps with a lot of the superfluous doings, like Momma used to, but she's not so into the congregants. That's a weird situation." He chuckled. "When you and I met in San Antonio, my cousin Sicily, one of her daughters, was supposed to come down, with her husband. She had to cancel because Aunt Greta's best friend had been in a bad wreck. Worked out great for me though."

"Me too. Do you see them very often?" Kate asked.

"Not like you do Aunt Evie and Uncle Leroy, for sure, but we have family gatherings a few times a year, at the ranch. Sometimes, my sister even makes it across the pond. Elias has come twice. I would love to know him, but he's—dark. Was in Hitler Youth, before they left Germany. So, maybe the darkness comes with his heritage."

"I look forward to the family reunions." Kate smiled and looked down at the patchwork quilted fields below. "This is so lovely."

Cam grinned. "Glad you like the scenery." *Me too*, he thought.

Chapter Sixteen
One month later
The Boys

Asher Klein watched for his younger brother among passengers disembarking the plane at gate three. At 6'2 he could stretch to see over most of the mob before him, but Isaac was 5'8 and hard to spot. He turned to find the object of his quest behind him.

Asher asked, "How'd you do that, runt? I've been watching for you." He raked a lank of dark hair from his brown eyes.

"Until you turned to ogle the cute redhead who sashayed past." Isaac pushed his black rimmed glasses up his pale aquiline nose.

"Come on. Mom has a rental waiting for us. We're off to Gram's. It's at least a 4 hour drive." Asher propped his elbow on Isaac's dark, curly mop.

Isaac ducked. "Do you wonder what this *guy*'s like?"

"No, Mom told me a few things about him. She's crazy about him, so he's okay in my book, as long as he's good to her." He hoisted his bag on his shoulder.

"Dad was good to her. What would he think about all this?" Isaac trotted to keep up with Asher's long stride.

Asher stopped abruptly and grabbed Isaac's thin arm. "Really? How many times did you see *The Lion King?* Circle of life and all that?"

"I know Dad's no longer alive. I mean, what if he was?" Isaac rolled his hazel eyes and pushed his glasses up again, with his knuckle.

"Then maybe this wouldn't have happened. He's not! Move on." Asher slapped the back of his brother's head and stepped past him.

"What did she tell you about her *boyfriend*?" Isaac nearly tripped over his own feet, trotting to keep up with his brother's long stride.

"He owns part of a roofing company, has a plane, was a Navy pilot, and won't talk about it much." Asher made a sharp turn at the corner and nearly lost Isaac until he felt the tug on the strap on his backpack.

"Oh, she didn't tell me much." Isaac scurried to catch up.

"She probably did. You don't listen. You're captivated with yourself and *your* feelings." He squeezed Isaac's head in his large hand, like he handled a basketball. "There's no room for anyone but you in there." Asher shook off his irritation. "Be nice, polite and act happy for her. If you argue with her, I'll smack you."

"Yeah, yeah, yeah." Isaac wrinkled his nose as his glasses slid down again.

***

Kate met the boys at the back door with hugs. "Both of you are still growing." She pulled back to survey her offspring. "At least a foot, since I saw you a few months ago."

"I think you only remember us smaller, Mom." Asher tossed his bag on the backstairs. "Where's Gram?"

"Right here, handsome." Ruth wrapped him in her arms and squeezed.

"You're cracking ribs." Asher groaned.

She released him to embrace Isaac. Her younger grandson patted her back gently. "How are you, Gram?"

"Splendid, Isaac, and you?" She held him back for inspection. "You need some sunlight, boy."

He sighed. "I'm fine. What's for dinner?"

"Lasagna, salad, and focaccia bread are prepared, beyond expectations, by your mother. I made strawberry ice cream for desert."

"I'll nap until it's time to eat, if it'll be a while." Isaac's thin shoulders sagged.

"Well, I think we'll be ready to eat as soon as *all* our guests have arrived." Ruth snapped.

The noise of Cam's motorcycle electrified the air. Kate peeked out the window in the breakfast room. *He wore his*

leathers! I've never seen him so decked out. Whew! He's hot.
She couldn't hide her delight.

Asher glanced out the window. "Whoa! You didn't tell me he had a Harley, Mom. Very cool!" He crossed his arms and glared at Isaac who pushed up his glasses, trying to appear bored, and shrugged.

Kate met Cam at the back door for a quick kiss and a chance to stow his gear. Then she ushered him into the dining room to meet her sons. "Asher, Isaac, this is Camden Fletcher."

Asher reached to shake hands. Isaac turned away until Asher grabbed his shoulder.

"Remember my promise, runt." Asher mumbled.

"Y'all have a good flight?" Cam asked as he tucked his gloves into his jacket pockets.

"Yes, sir." Asher responded.

"Are you from *Texas*?" Isaac asked with a grimace as he pushed his glasses up again.

"I am. A little burg north of Austin. Ever been there?" Cam smiled.

"No, it's hot. I don't care for hot." Isaac glanced out the window. "One of my many hobbies is regional accents and dialects. That's how I got the read on you."

"Ah, I see. Well Texas isn't for everybody. It leaves a lot of wide-open space for the rest of us." Cam leaned on the back of a chair.

Asher softly inquired, "Will you show me your bike before it gets dark?"

"Sure, come on." Cam led the way to the door.

"Dinner's in about fifteen minutes." Kate announced.

Isaac watched Asher and Cam leave the house before he approached Kate. "Mom, what do you see in that man? He's *nothing* like Dad."

Kate counted to ten, before she replied. "That's one of his finest points. He's kind, he cherishes me, and he's a lot of fun." She ripped salad greens with fervor.

"Dad was a lot of fun." Isaac scowled.

"I'm glad you remember him like that, honey." She whisked dressing with zeal and dispensed it into a cruet, with a dash of fury.

Isaac whined, "Couldn't you just be satisfied with what you had?"

"Can you?" Kate stopped to return his glare and dropped her hands to the counter.

"What do you mean?" Isaac pushed his glasses up and studied her, his head tilted back.

"If I said 'Isaac, you're a smart kid. I think you've wasted enough time at school, read enough books to last a lifetime.' Would you be satisfied to never learn or experience anything new or different?" Kate propped her hand on her hip.

"We're always growing, evolving into more complex beings until we come into what Elohim created us to be. We *must* reach our full potential." Isaac pushed his glasses up.

"Please let that statement make the trip from your head to your heart. That does not negate anyone over 40. Where are your contacts?" Her frustration began to shine, with her youngest son.

He grinned. "I packed them."

"Put them on. If you push those glasses around one more time, they're in the trash—after I use a hammer on them." She shooed him out of the kitchen, up the backstairs. "Little jerk." She mumbled under her breath.

Ruth chuckled. "He's always punched your buttons, just like his father."

"Please save me! My memory failed for a moment." She shook her arms away from her body and readjusted her apron.

Ruth considered her only child. "You can't shake that off, sweetie."

Cam handed the keys to Asher. "Climb on. You ever ride?"

"My mother would have a cow if I rode around the yard." He squinted back at the kitchen window with concern. "I have a friend at school with a Vespa, that I borrow to run to the store sometimes. Mom doesn't know." He straddled the big machine.

"Your Mom rides." Cam choked back a chuckle at the incredulous look on Asher's face.

His chin dropped. "Mom rides this?"

Cam laughed. "Not alone. She doesn't think she can hold it up. It's not bad. Try it. It's kinda like a Vespa, but it has a lot

112

of power and it's heavy. Take it slowly." He stepped back to give the young man space.

Asher donned Cam's helmet, inserted the key and cranked the big bike. He started out too fast and stalled. His face paled as he made another attempt. He bounced along the grass for a moment until he hit the trail to the barn. He rode all the way down the track and back.

"Wooo!" He shouted when he returned to the yard. "This is great. I love it."

Cam applauded, then said, "Ride out to the road. I'm goin' in to help the chef." Cam turned his back to Asher who sat there a moment, before accelerating down the gravel driveway.

Cam glanced back from the porch and smiled. *You're like your mother. Your happy trigger's easy to find. But your brother's a different bird altogether.*

***

After dinner, Kate walked out with Cam, who said, "Thank you for the evening."

He pulled her into a hug. "It'll take a little while to adjust to each other, but we'll be fine. If we have nothing else in common, we all love you." He sat down on the bike and looked up at her. "We'll figure out what Isaac's target is." He kissed her hands.

"Thank you." She leaned into him.

"It bothers me that Reggie and your dad couldn't get along. We'll have to find where we exist, without conflict, and stay in the boundaries." He kissed her cheek. "I'm gonna miss you tonight. Our bed will be stone cold, my heart." He pressed his face into her chest and sighed.

"Me too."

"Tell me goodnight, my love."

"Goodnight, my love." She smiled as he pulled his helmet on and cranked the bike. She went to the porch, turning to watch him leave. He'd want her inside, but she wasn't ready to go yet.

The night was cool and damp. *Fog shrouds the morning as mist rises from the creek, where beloved lodges.* She threw a kiss to him, as he rode away.

Ruth poured coffee in Kate's cup. "How'd Cam take it?"

Kate answered, "Like he does, with a grain of salt. He isn't easily offended." Kate sipped coffee as Ruth sat in her chair.

"Asher's up, out for a run with Dixie. Do we wake Isaac and take him to breakfast with us or leave him here?"

"I'd have more fun without him, but it isn't fair to Cam to leave him. I'll go up and wake him." Kate said.

"Let me, dear. He's never as problematic for me." Ruth headed for the stairs for her daily climb.

"He's afraid of you." Kate smiled as she said it.

Ruth turned and nodded her wavy silver-crowned head. "Exactly!"

***

Ruth drove her family to Cam's home in her Cadillac. She pulled into the driveway amid exclamations from Asher.

"Whoa, cool! Look at this place, Isaac. It's beautiful." Ash bailed, as soon as the car stopped and bounded up the stairs to meet Buddy, who allowed him the privilege of rubbing his ears.

"Come on in." Cam called out from the kitchen.

Asher walked into the front room, past the Baby Grand piano in the middle of the floor. A few chairs were scattered around the room. Turning he saw each one situated to the view.

"Good morning!" Ruth cried as she entered the room, amused that her grandson was aghast with delight.

"Y'all come on in for coffee." Cam indicated the service on the bar where he poured and prepared the ladies' coffee.

Cam smiled at her approach. Kate beamed when their eyes met. He took her hand in his discreetly and kept it. "Good morning, beautiful lady." His voice was low.

"Good morning, my love." She answered quietly.

"Boys, come on in, make yourselves at home." Cam spoke to them without taking his eyes off their mother.

Isaac stopped at the piano, ran his hand over the lacquered mirror finish. "Do you play this?"

Cam grinned. "Yep."

"What kind of music do you play?" Isaac asked, his face scrunched in confusion.

"Anything I want to." Cam replied.

"Country? Bluegrass?" Isaac probed.

"Yes, though you can't do justice to Bluegrass without a dulcimer and fiddle. My stepdad plays the fiddle and I play the hammered dulcimer. Have one down in the cabinet, below the bookcase. Belonged to Pop's mother's family. They were Irish, settled in the Appalachians, like Ruth's ancestors."

"I see." The thin, pale lad moved past the others to the dining room. Buddy bounded ahead of him. "Where does that go?" Isaac pointed out behind the house.

"About a quarter mile back," Cam answered. "There's a creek and a party spot. We like bonfires and horseshoes."

"I see." Isaac returned to the kitchen. "Do you cook a lot?"

"No, sir, that's your mother's specialty. All I do is breakfast, well mostly." Cam grinned.

"But he does it well *and large*." Ruth commented.

"Comes with the territory, ma'am." Camden nodded.

"What's on the menu this morning?" Kate asked.

"Venison sausage and gravy, the gluten free biscuits you made, grits, and wild mushroom omelets. Did you remember the jam?" Cam watched his bride's every move.

Kate produced two jars from her bag. "As ordered."

"Did you shoot the deer you cooked?" Isaac asked.

"I did. I hunt with a crossbow. Don't have a lot of use for fellows who run deer to the ground with dogs and blow 'em up with high powered weapons on the other side. No sport in that."

"I've never eaten a deer. I think they're just nice to look at." Isaac searched for an argument in everything Cam said.

"I do too. A herd grazes within view of our deck most evenings. Maybe we'll see 'em while you're here. We're ready then. Let's eat, crew."

***

Cam held Kate's hand as they walked to the creek, her face hidden under her sunhat. She watched Isaac growing anxious for something to complain or debate over. *Speaking quiet to that boy's spirit and mind. Used to work when he was younger, might still.*

"Hey, Mom!" Asher rolled up the legs of his jeans and waded in the creek.

"Yes?" She knew what would follow.

She mouthed the words.

"Come here. I want to show you something." He motioned to her.

She and Cam strolled toward the water.

"There's a dam over there. Cam, is it a beaver?"

"Probably, I haven't seen it before. Buddy and I'll have to keep our eyes open. I don't want to flood out my horseshoe pits."

Asher grinned. "That's cool!"

Ruth called to Asher. "It's too cold to be in the water. You'll catch your death…." She headed to the creek, grumbling.

"It's not bad, Gram. Just takes a minute to get used to it." He laughed and stooped to find a rock to skip.

Isaac hung back and studied the party site. He dug around in the fire pit with a long stick and worked at looking bored.

"Does Isaac play music?" Cam asked Kate.

"Yes, he's fluent on the keyboard. He played percussion in high school and a mean tuba in marching band."

"There you go. We'll play when we get back to the house. See if we can scare up a concert."

She laughed and gazed up into his face. "I'm dying to kiss you, but there're too many watchers and where it leads is private. What do you say we steal away later and make out?"

"I'm game, Mrs. Fletcher. Anytime." He muttered.

***

Isaac had disappeared. Ruth glanced around the campsite and surrounding woods but couldn't spot him. "Isaac?" She shouted.

No answer.

Kate turned to scan the area. "Mom, he's almost nineteen."

"With very little common sense. Has he ever been near woods or a creek before, Katrina?"

116

"I'm sure he has, though Asher was the Boy Scout. Okay, maybe not. He's never been one to be outdoors. He's probably at the house waiting."

"Well, we aren't hurrying back to him." Ruth declared with her hand propped on her hip and headed toward an Adirondack chair.

Cam shook his head and grinned. "I'll go." He took off up the trail at a trot.

When he neared the house, he heard the piano. *That's what I thought, couldn't wait to get your hands on the ivory.*

He took the steps softly and eased into the kitchen's open door, to listen. A peek past the bar revealed Isaac, lost in the tune he played. Cam listened for a quarter hour before he stole to the front room. He rescued the hammered dulcimer and its stand from the bookcase and dropped into his favorite chair.

He picked out the tune and key Isaac played and joined in. At the end, Isaac moved into a jaunty Irish jig that gave the dulcimer center stage. A sweeping ballad followed which highlighted Isaac's prowess on the keyboard.

Applause broke out. Kate, Ruth, and Asher eavesdropped from the kitchen, unnoticed by either musician.

Isaac stood for a bow. "That was great, Cam. I've never tried a dulcimer. May I?"

"Sure, why don't we take it to Ruth's and play around with it. It's not difficult once you figure out the keys. You'll master it in an hour." Cam stood and stretched, checked the clock. "Ladies?"

"We can get out of your way. I'm sure you have things to do." Kate offered, standing beside him.

"Actually, I'd planned to be with you, if you'll let me." He took her hand and leaned to her ear. "You promised me we'd steal away."

"Oh, yes I did." She shrugged. "We can go back to the house and the boys can do what they do and we'll go for a walk."

Ruth spoke up. "A walk would be lovely, dear. We can pick up pinecones and check for holly berries on the hill, bittersweet by the creek. Perhaps pick chestnuts for roasting. I can put them on to boil and they'll be ready to pop into the fire this evening. We can decorate for Thanksgiving as well."

"Splendid, Mom! Let's, by all means." Kate stole a glance toward her husband.

He winked.

Chapter Sixteen

"What about Christmas?" Cam asked.

"What about it? We're working on Thanksgiving and you want to talk Christmas?" Kate whisked gravy, with a smile.

"No, where are we having Christmas or do we split it between here and Texas?"

"I don't see any reason to do that. We can go there. Asher and Isaac will be at Reggie's folks for Hanukkah. Aunt Evie and Uncle Leroy are headed to Florida. Mom and I are flexible. What works for you?"

"I need to go down there for a few days. I have some business to tend to." He crossed his arms and leaned against the counter. "There's something else."

Kate turned the stove off and stood in front of him. "Okay, talk."

"Jackie woke up. The investigator wants me to see her. She isn't talking to them. Coop tried to draw her out, but nothin' doin'. I need you to go with me. Is that an issue?"

"Maybe. When do we leave?" Katrina asked.

"We fly down in the morning, come back Saturday or Sunday." His voice dropped. "At least we can sleep together."

She grinned, kissed his mouth greedily. "Yes!"

"Why not just tell Ruth? Better yet, I'll tell her. I bet she'll be fine with our situation."

Kate winced. "I don't want to disappoint her."

"Honey, I'll handle Ruth." Cam pleaded.

His mother-in-law rounded the corner, from the butler's pantry. "Oh, you will? And who are you, to think you can, buster?"

"How long have you been eavesdropping, woman?" He pretended to be gruff with her.

"Long enough to know you're keeping something vital from me. I love surprises, but I hate secrets. Now, cough it up, both of you. What are you hiding?" She folded her hands in front of her and waited.

Cam shook his head, looking sadly at his bride, "We're found out. Let's just get it over with." He turned back to Ruth. "We eloped while we were gone. We're married and we've been sneaking around to be together for the past few days."

"Oh, I knew that, dear, your mother told me. I thought we were keeping it quiet because of the boys. They'll be away in a few days and you can live freely again. But, now, I could tell them…."

"No, Mom, please." Kate waved one hand in the air. "Let's let sleeping dogs sleep. There's no need for them to know right now."

Cam's head tilted; his eyes narrowed. "I'll tend to that. I think I need to have a man-to-man chat with your lads, Mrs. Fletcher."

Kate blanched; gulped, feeling dread grip her stomach. "Could we leave this until after dinner?"

"Yes, ma'am. Want me to put a salad together?" Cam turned to the sink to wash his hands.

"Please." Her sons would know they had a stepfather before bedtime. She knew better than to think he'd forget.

The mudroom door opened to Evangeline and Leroy bearing cake and cranberry relish. Evangeline called out, "Happy Thanksgiving, family!"

Leroy looked on, with a smile, as his wife bussed cheeks and loved on everyone.

Jackets were deposited in the mudroom. Asher and Isaac appeared, smiling. Asher always got the first hug, Isaac hung back until Aunt Evie came to him.

"Law! These boys are no longer boys. Kate, look at this." She turned her back to Asher, who propped his head on top of hers. He reached around her and gave her a big squeeze.

She gathered Isaac into her arms. "And you, professor, you're looking mighty handsome. How do you keep the girls off?"

Isaac grinned and blushed. "It hasn't really been much of a problem, Aunt Evie."

"Well, their loss, sweetheart." She pulled him into a side hug.

Cam walked by with the cake, asking, "What sort of cake is this?"

Evangeline answered, "It's our momma's recipe for Lane Cake. Baby girl asked for it. You'll love it, Camden. Good Appalachian food." She reached out to make room, on the sideboard, to display the cake.

Asher asked, "Where's Rickey?"

Leroy replied, "He and Marion are with his parents today. We get 'em at Christmas, along with our new twin *granddaughters*. I have pictures!" The grin he wore said the rest. Leroy held up the photos his son had mailed to him. Kate glanced through them, passing them around with oohs and aahs, admiring the new additions to the family.

***

After dinner, Ruth nodded at Cam, as they began to clear the table.

He glanced at the boys. "Asher, Isaac, let's adjourn to the music room, shall we?" He made a sweeping gesture toward the opposite side of the house. He looked back at his wife when the boys started that way. "We'll be back in a little while. No need to come help, understand?"

Kate cut her eyes Cam's direction, with a wry smile. "Yes, sir." She traded a glance with Evangeline, who winked and slung her hand in a gesture that said 'that's hot'.

Cam followed the boys to the music room.

Isaac sprawled on the velvet settee. Both Dachshunds joined him, vying for a cuddle. Asher sat properly in a tapestry covered Queen Anne chair. He addressed Cam, before he reached the piano bench. "What's up?"

"Your mother and I are married. We eloped." Cam wore his serious look.

Asher nodded and shrugged. "Okay, cool! Anything else?"

"We'll go ahead with a formal wedding and reception, in March at my family's church. Block the dates off your calendars. I'll send you plane tickets."

"We still have to wear penguin suits?" Asher frowned.

"Yeah, but there's beer and girls at the reception," Cam responded.

"I'm in." Asher turned to his brother.

"You're not going to have *babies,* are you?" Isaac asked, with a grimace.

"No, we discussed that. Any other questions?" Cam checked each of the boys, studying their body language.

"Will you teach me to ride a motorcycle?" Asher grinned.

His smile is so like Kate's, a little crooked, one eye almost closed. It'd be impossible not to love this kid.

"Absolutely, when you get good at it, I'll buy you a Vespa, if you prefer." Cam wasn't fooled by Isaac's lack of immediate response. Nor was he worried.

"And talk Mom into letting me take it to school?" Asher sat on the edge of his seat.

"You drive a tough bargain, but I can probably handle her. Isaac, questions?" Cam trained his stare on the problem child.

Thin fingers tapping his forehead, his eyes half closed in meditation, Isaac reveled in a moment of undivided attention.

Asher raised his voice. "Squirt?"

"I want to learn to fly your plane." Isaac blurted out.

"We can get you signed up for lessons." Cam continued calmly.

"For real?" Isaac shot up off the settee. The Dachshunds rolled to the back of the cushions, scrambling to their hairy feet.

That's the most action I've seen from that boy. "I said it." Cam paused. "We leave in the morning for Texas, staying one night, maybe two. I had an emergency arise. If you wanna go, be packed and ready no later than eight o'clock."

Both boys nodded and answered at the same time. "Yes, sir."

"I'm goin' to help the chef." Cam rose to leave the room. Asher scooped up his laptop from the floor. Isaac snagged his iPhone from the ebony coffee table, resettling his thin frame between the dogs.

Cam found Kate racking plates. She watched the door, concern etching her brow. He walked straight to her and kissed her hard on the mouth. "So, you want to go home with me tonight?"

"How'd they take it?" Kate asked, looking doubtful.

"They're cool." He nodded.

She shifted to disbelief. "Isaac too?"

"Yes, ma'am. He's going to take flying lessons. I'll check the internet and see who I can find in Iowa City."

"You bought 'em off?" Kate's frown deepened.

Cam grinned and said, "We're male. We have to see the advantage of compliance, before we relent. They were actually pretty easy." He absently scratched his forearm.

"Asher wants a motorcycle and you said…"

"When he gets good at riding, I'll get him one and talk his mother into letting him have it at school."

"You're incredible." She grinned.

He nodded with a smirk. "Yep! Pretty darn."

***

Cam and the boys hauled bags out to Ruth's Cadillac. "Are we taking dogs?" Cam asked.

Ruth answered him. "Asher already took mine down to Evangeline, so just Dixie. Since you've dropped Buddy with Mark, we're ready." She climbed in the back seat with Isaac and Kate.

Cam drove to the county airport and parked in front of the hangar. Everyone piled out, as his cell phone rang. "Fletcher."

Harry's voice sounded tired. "I'm sorry, son. Jackie didn't make it."

"What?" Sensors keen, alarm rushed through him.

"Jackie died this morning at the hospital, in ICU."

Cam sighed deeply. "We're loading at the airport now. See you in a few hours, Pop." He turned to find Kate lowering the trunk lid on the car.

"Who called?"

"Pop." He wrapped her in his arms. "Jackie died this morning."

She stretched on tiptoes and kissed his cheek. "I'm sorry." She kept Dixie's leash tight in her hand as the Border collie stood guard across the back of her legs.

123

"Something's not right, Kate." He stared beyond her, for a moment. "Her folks need to ask for an autopsy." He frowned; his lips compressed. "This situation runs deep. No telling who all's involved. Let's get to the plane, honey." They started that way, his hand at her elbow.

Everyone carried or pulled their bags across the tarmac.

Isaac scurried to Cam's side. "May I ride up front with you?"

Cam donned his headset and handed the co-pilot's set to Isaac. "Excellent idea. We need to look into flight training in Iowa City. I'll put out feelers, maybe run into somebody I know. Remind me when we get a minute on the ground, okay?"

"Yes, sir. Hey, Ash, I get to co-pilot. Cool, huh?" Isaac bragged.

Asher laughed. "Very cool, runt." Dixie had climbed into Asher's lap, shaking. "It's okay, old girl. You're safe with me." He hugged her to his chest and buried his face in her fur. She licked his ear and settled.

***

On the ground, Cam and the boys loaded the yellow Jeep with bags. "Momma, we'll walk down. Kate and I need a few minutes. The boys can help me unload in a little while."

"Are you alright?" Elaine walked toward him, zipping her fleece jacket against a cool breeze.

"Yes, ma'am, but troubled about circumstances." Cam hugged her close.

She pulled back and pecked his cheek. "We'll see you at the house. I'll tell you about my phone conversation with Jackie's mother." Elaine climbed into the driver's seat and strapped on her belt, studying her son with concern through the windshield, as he turned to his wife.

Kate shrugged deeper into her red plaid fleece coat, flipped her hood on, and buttoned it. "What're you going to do?"

"Suggest an autopsy. There's more going on than a lovers' spat. She was beaten almost to death. They could've been high. Maybe she owed money. I don't know. It doesn't sit well with me." He stopped their progress, turned Kate to face him. "I can't see you around that hood." He stepped into her body pulling her neatly into his. "Now, if you have objections, say so."

"How could I?" She frowned up into his handsome face. The sky was clear, as blue as a spring day, but the air was crisp, with an icy edge.

"You're my priority. If looking further into what happened to Jackie bothers you, I won't do it. We have a nice visit with my folks and go home tomorrow. What do you say?" He watched her eyes closely.

"Well, I don't object to the suggestion of an autopsy. Can we see, after that? I mean, what else would you want to do?"

"Hire an investigator? We're in it together or it's a no go." Cam answered.

"Justice has to be served. But you must love her an awful lot to go to so damn much trouble." Kate turned away.

Cam reached to draw her back and shook his head, frowning. "No, never did. *That's* the issue. The guilt I carry for what I did to her… I never loved her, Kate. She was a convenience. I liked her well enough, for about a month after we were married." He glanced up at a hawk circling the tree line, searching for lunch. "Then I just never wanted to be near her again. Half of me feels like she wouldn't have made the bad choices she did, if I'd been more patient—kind. I wasn't."

Kate turned away, back into the wind and wondered how she really felt about justice in Jackie's circumstances *It shouldn't matter who it is, I should feel glad my husband has a strong sense of fairness. Am I jealous? No, that's not it. Maybe I'm jaded by the frequency of her name and circumstances interjected into our lives. Do I have to wait for her ghost to vanish to feel like Camden Fletcher is all mine?*

She glanced back at Cam's determined demeanor. *Yeah, I'm jealous.*

Chapter Seventeen

Elaine and Cam stood in the back office with the door closed. Elaine spoke quietly to her eldest son, "Her folks had been to see her and told she was on the mend. I don't believe there'll be any trouble convincing them to ask for an autopsy. The doctor said it happens sometimes; a patient appears to be recovering and takes a turn for the worst. Occasionally, he said, it results in death. I don't think her dad's buying it."

"I'd rather not be the one to suggest an autopsy. You and Coop talk about it and see if he can bring it up without a fuss." Cam brushed his hand over his mustache and beard. "I want to stay as far as possible from the whole thing. There's no need for them to know I'm even here."

"Did you discuss it with Kate?" Elaine's arms crossed against the chill of the tiny room.

"Absolutely, she says go for it. We'll take it a step at a time. The person Jackie met at the motel was more business than pleasure. Coop said the manager overheard the conversation when the man inside opened the door to her. No telling what she got herself mixed up in. Coop said he couldn't get any more information." He propped his fist on his hip.

"Tread cautiously, Camden. *Don't* risk what you have with Kate over Jackie's mess. *Please*, walk away from this and let the authorities handle it."

He nodded. "I'm not rushing headlong into anything, Momma. Just don't feel right about what happened. She needed money or she wouldn't have pulled the stunt at Pappy's. If she hadn't been in a pinch, she'd have called. To put on that show, in public, cost her. She took a risk and lost." Cam reached for the doorknob. "Come on, let's join the family. You're gonna love Asher. Isaac's way different, but a likeable young man. Very musical."

The family met in the music room, at Cam's insistence. Everyone chose an instrument. Kate returned, from upstairs, with her flute case. Cam nodded approval and grinned. He leaned to her ear. "I should've guessed, with those lips, you'd play a woodwind."

Isaac settled on an African Djembe. He parked on a hard back chair, balancing the drum between his boney knees and ankles to pat out a beat. Elaine sat at the piano. Harry tuned his violin. Ruth chose a penny whistle and rain stick and Asher, the harmonica. He blew a brisk intro tune as the discord of various instruments struck the room.

Cam adjusted the harpsichord, plucking the strings with a guitar pick. "Momma, what'll we start with?"

"Something light, how about *Greensleeves*?" She ran through chords to set the tone and key then checked the room. Everybody nodded, as they were ready. She began.

As a first song with unfamiliar musicians, it turned out well. Elaine laughed when they wrapped up. "That was great, y'all, let's do another. Boys?"

"How about the *Tennessee Waltz*?" Isaac suggested. "Mom plays the melody really well." When Kate glanced over at him, he winked.

She felt her face flush and smiled. *He's never winked at me before.*

"Anybody need music and are we good in C?" Elaine asked.

"We know it." The boys chimed together.

"No ma'am, C's good." Cam responded.

"Give me a minute." Harry adjusted his violin. "Gotta string trying to go out."

"I'll change it for you, Pop." Cam offered.

"It'll do for now." He plucked and tightened it again. "I'm ready."

"Lead us out, Harry."

Harry drew the bow across the strings to begin the waltz, everyone joined in by the third chord. Kate began the melody at the end of the first stanza. At the beginning of the second stanza, Asher picked up the melody on the harmonica.

Kate and Cam snuggled in his bed. She said, "The jam session was fun. The boys and I haven't done that together since Daddy died."

"You didn't play at home?" Cam asked.

"Not too often, as they got older. We were on the road with tutoring and soccer, football and basketball, Scouts. Asher was always on his way *to* something. Until Isaac was well enough, he wasn't involved. He's more of a specialist. Ash is good at a lot of activities. Isaac excels at a few. If he can get his mind around a subject, he'll try it, but if he can't be its master, he's indifferent. Mediocre isn't for him."

Cam whispered, "I saw him wink at you."

"Wasn't it funny? I don't recall that he's ever done that before. He's becoming cheeky!" She smiled.

Cam said, "Kate, you're the kindest person I've ever known. If I had to deal with an ex showing up…I'm not sure I'd be nearly so gracious."

"I'm feeling less gracious every time her name interrupts our lives." Kate stayed snugged, against her husband, to soften her reprimand.

He smirked. "Been wondering how long you'd put up with it. I'd have shut it down already, had the shoe been on the other foot."

She pinched his arm on tender flesh. "Are you trying me? Cause, I've gotta tell you, between Jackie and Isaac, I'm near boiling point, so don't push your luck."

He chuckled, trying to look sheepish. "Yes, ma'am. Not another word."

"Or thought," She finished.

He nodded.

The following morning…

"Are you going to the funeral?" Harry asked as he hefted his coffee mug.

Cam answered after a moment. "No, sir, don't see any reason to."

"You shared a child, Camden. A dead child, but there's still a connection."

Cam glanced around the brightly lit kitchen, to be sure they were alone. "He had my name. That was all, Pop." His voice dropped. "Nobody else knows, but Kate, so I'd appreciate it if we keep it between us."

Harry nodded. "I wondered. Elaine did too. She always doubted because you'd had the mumps…anyhow, I don't think we'll go." He paused. "Do you know who…?"

"Got an idea." Cam replied.

"Skeet?" Harry asked.

"Most likely."

"I need to tell you something, Camden. It may be the source of some of your difficulty." Harry sipped his coffee. "Before I met Elaine, I kept company with Shelley Keller. I already knew her. We'd dated some in high school. After, I left for Annapolis and she married Keller. He deserted her shortly before Skeet was born."

Cam listened intently. "Yes, sir?"

"Well, it was just one of those things you do, when you go back home. She was a decent dancer. Every time I was around Skeet acted up. She failed sorely with discipline, doted on him when he needed stern guidance.

"I met your mother a few months later, and fell head first for her. I'm not saying I left Shelley for Elaine. We went out occasionally, nothing serious. I wondered, when I heard Skeet was tangled up with Jackie, if maybe he was takin' another shot at you."

Harry picked up his mug before continuing, "In high school there were plenty of times, on the football field, I felt he took advantage of cover and slammed into you or Cooper. It may not mean a thing, but I always thought…he was jealous of you both."

Cam rubbed his chin in the quiet moments that followed. "Makes sense, Pop." He inhaled deeply. "Baby Jacob had auburn hair. I thought since Jackie was adopted there's no telling what her biological parents looked like. She took one look at him and decided to get outta that hospital, as fast as her legs and my checking account carried her."

"Well…let that go. Skeet had his way. Give him to God to handle." He drank his coffee. "Why don't we take your crew

129

for a ride? Saddle up the horses and spend a little time in the fresh air?"

"Sounds good. Let me check with Kate. We'll stay tonight, but we need to have the boys back to the airport by early afternoon tomorrow."

"You gettin' along alright?"

"Yes, sir. They're fine young men. She and Reggie did a good job with them."

***

Isaac found Kate in the parlor lounging in an overstuffed chair, Dixie curled up at her feet. The light from a sunny window illuminated her magazine. He pulled a Victorian stool, with foot long fringe, over beside her.

"What're you up to?" She asked, as she dogeared the page of the article she read and set it aside.

"I need you." His eyes filled with tears as he seated himself, squirming. "Mom, I miss Dad." He leaned across the chair arm and laid his head on her shoulder.

Kate placed her hand on his cheek and pressed her face against his head. "I wondered if that's what's going on with you. Tell me, Isaac."

"Just…I don't know, hanging out with him, going for walks. We used to read and play Scrabble for hours. Do you remember?"

"I do. Ash and I hated to play Scrabble with you because, you always beat us. You were accustomed to your dad's vocabulary and we couldn't compete." She smiled. "Do you remember all the hours he spent rocking you? I'd have to go to work early on Tuesday and Thursday afternoons. He'd make a light schedule for classes, so he could be home with you before I left. He always wanted one of us to be with you, never a stranger. We had enough of that every time you were in the PICU." She stroked his smooth skin. "Gram would come up to help when your Dad had finals."

"I remember that. He'd read test papers to me in his story-telling voice. I thought he was really reading stories, until I was four." Isaac laughed again and let silence fall. "Mom, do you ever miss him?"

"I can't as long as you and Asher are around." She nuzzled his curly dark hair.

Isaac took her hand and held it.

Cam watched from the parlor door as they sat in murky sunlight, almost ethereal. A twinge of grief swept through him. *How on earth am I going to fill Reggie's shoes?*

He glanced back at the two of them. *Would I have been so concerned for my son that I'd give up work or anything else so he never had to be comforted by strangers?*

He studied his boots, for a moment, and turned to leave quietly. He'd give them a few more minutes alone. He set out to find Asher.

Chapter Eighteen
Back home

"Fletcher." Cam answered his cell on the first ring.

"Camden, it's your mother."

He grinned. "Yes ma'am, I recognize your voice."

"We've been to Coop's. Jackie's folks asked for an autopsy. The results are in." Elaine drew a shaky breath. "Their daughter was suffocated. The coroner says by a pillow or thick towel. It's become a murder investigation. I wanted you to know." She sounded exhausted.

"Okay, keep me up to date on how they're doing. Pop still has friends in the sheriff's department, doesn't he?" A scowl replaced his good humor.

"He does. They'll release her body, for burial, in a day or two. The coroner's waiting for toxicology reports." Elaine sighed. "Another thing, they found one clear fingerprint in the hotel room. We assume it was local law enforcement. The state's come in to take over the investigation."

"Sloppy cop or something else?" Cam asked.

"Something else. Sheriff's department tried to keep it internal, but some wise soul went to the state anonymously."

The connection went mute for a heartbeat.

"Let me know when you hear something, Momma. I love you. And, hey—no need to bother Kate with any of this, okay?"

"I would not dream of darkening one moment of her day with all this B.S. I love you too, son." She disconnected.

He stood in the middle of his kitchen and pondered how the revelation affected his life. *Not so much anymore. But, I tread a delicate line with Kate sometimes.*

Kate ambled into the kitchen, fresh from her shower, to find him studying the pattern of the parquet floor. "Are you okay?"

He nodded, brushed his hand over his beard. "Momma called. Everybody's doing fine. She misses us already."

The Bailiwick

Kate climbed the six-foot ladder and held up the drapery panel. "Like this?"

Ruth stepped back to view her handiwork. "I think it works, dear. We'll put the panels on each end and a thick layer of sheers in the middle. The scarf across the top ties it all together. This is the only economical way to cover a fifteen-foot row of windows. It'll soften the noise in the room as well. Cam and Mark did an excellent job pulling the carpet. The floors look fine. And the walls are looking good. I'm glad it didn't take a lot of patching. Means the foundation's mostly still solid."

"We can put down an area rug. I found an outlet on-line who'll give us a deal on multiple purchases. Cam can fly to Dalton, Georgia to pick them up." Kate climbed back down after handing the panel to Ruth.

"We haven't discussed how you're handling the news of his ex-wife's murder." Ruth studied her daughter.

Kate shrugged. She chose a bit and a driver for her drill and dropped a handful of screws into her shirt pocket. She climbed the ladder and laid out her tools and drapery hardware on the tray. "Not my business, Mom."

"It's like that is it?" Ruth threaded panels on the rod and laid them out across the bed.

"Yes, ma'am. So far, she put a kibosh on our engagement celebration and our first day of wedded bliss. If I never hear her name again, I'll be satisfied. Cam feels like he needs to be in Texas to keep an eye on everything. I don't have to go just because he does."

"Do you really want him running back and forth without you?" Ruth watched her only child carefully.

"I don't get his obsession with someone who used and abused him." Kate marked the pilot holes with a pencil. She stuck it back in her ponytail. "He's not had a kind word to say about her, but bent to her will, at every turn."

"I don't think it's all guilt, darling." Ruth's voice softened. "She came from foster care into an adopted home. Her new dad asked Cam to take care of her. He made a pledge to do

133

that. Even though she never kept up her side of their bargain, didn't mean he could release himself from his."

Kate climbed down the ladder and sat on the end of the bed. "I never thought of it like that. He didn't do all he'd done for her, because of who she was, but because it's part of his character."

Ruth smiled sadly and nodded. "Exactly."

Kate met her mother's gaze. "I need to apologize to him."

"There's something else I want to discuss with you, Katrina; this monstrous house and the upkeep of it. I don't think I can do the bed and breakfast. Even a hostel feels overwhelming. Have your feelings changed since you married our roofer?" Ruth slid the ironing board closer to a plug and situated the scarf across the bed.

Kate smiled, as she eyed her mother. "To tell the truth, yes, ma'am. It would be nice to relax for a while and be a wife. As it is, I'm wiped out at the end of the day and I'm not seeing this place finished for at least another year."

"Bishop's Bailiwick is *your* inheritance. What you do with it, is your decision. If you want to wrap up loose ends and sell, I'm with you."

Kate studied Ruth. "Really? You'd do that?"

"Sweetie, I'm dog tired of wading through snow and ice in the winter. Just because we get the place up to snuff, doesn't mean it won't be a money pit when we're done. We still have to maintain it. Leroy's talking about retiring and moving closer to the boys and grandgirls. Speak to Camden, and let me know what you think." She shifted the scarf forward on the ironing board. "Elaine and I've been talking…."

"About what, Mom?"

"…about me moving to Texas, with her, to help with Harry and the house. She'd appreciate the companionship and, honestly, I would too. I'll die a nurse, so it isn't like I don't know what I'm doing. She needs surgery on her knees, but has too much else going on to be off her feet, any length of time."

Kate grinned. "Okay, I see we have a lot to resolve. What about Aunt Evie and Uncle Leroy leaving? Any idea when?"

"Leroy is way past retirement age and Evangeline wants to go. I expect we can sit down together and work out a schedule."

Katrina responded, "Cam's managing the ranch affairs from here and wants to be there and so do you. We'll discuss it at dinner and see if he has ideas." She stretched. "I think I'll walk down for mail and get some exercise." She flew down two flights of stairs and out the front door with Dixie on her heels.

Kate jogged the quarter mile to the mailbox. It was stuffed. She took a moment to sort Leroy and Evangeline's mail out, and started back at a decent pace to drop it off. No one was in, at the Turner's cottage, which had once been a guesthouse on the property. She tucked envelopes and a magazine inside the screen door.

She and Dixie loped back to the house. Out of breath, but revived, she rounded the corner, to the back, to find Cam's truck in the driveway. She took the steps quickly.

He saw her coming and opened the door. "Happy lunchtime, wife." He caught her in a hug and kissed her chilly mouth. "Mmm, you taste good, slightly on the cold side, but yummy."

"Give me a minute and I'll get us set up for lunch." She tossed the mail on the counter in the mudroom.

"I'll help. I just got here. How're curtains comin'?" He washed his hands in the kitchen sink.

"Well, thank you. We're almost finished with the last room on the third floor. Tomorrow, we start on the second-floor bedrooms." She set out sliced roast turkey, lettuce, homemade sweet pickles and peppers from the fridge. "Mom's talking about selling out and leaving the area—for Texas. What do you think, want to move home?"

"Home's where you are. What brought this on?" He turned to face his bride, as he dried his hands on a tea towel.

"She's been talking to your mother." She laid a loaf of fresh sourdough bread, on a cutting board, by the turkey.

"You bake this morning?" He pulled a bread knife out of the butcher block.

"As soon as I arrived. There's hillbilly cobbler too, peach with gingerbread."

"I like meeting you for lunch, but I need to be more diligent about running. I generally worked out in the evenings but…." He glanced up from slicing bread and winked. "There's a room I need to show you when we get home tonight."

Her head cocked to one side. "A room? I thought we'd made the tour." She cleared her throat, her eyes widened.

He grinned. "Yeah, mostly have. Tonight, we'll explore underground."

"What's that?"

"Panic room, tornado protection and a secret passageway."

"I'm intrigued."

"Entertaining you keeps me on my toes." He grinned.

Home

Cam and Kate stood in the upper hallway of their home. He opened a door that appeared to be a closet. "This is the elevator." They stepped inside the aluminum structure. He pointed to the top of the open box.

"It's set up with a simple cable pulley system. Crank this handle and we glide down." He turned the handle and they slowly descended past the first floor and garage. "Now we're about ten feet underground." Dim light came from the skylight in the roof forty-eight feet above, piped into the lowest level.

Kate gazed up and around. "We're lower than the garage?"

"The elevator's built in between the walls of the house and garage. We could've stopped there or on the first floor. But I want to show you this, in case you ever need to know how to get out of here, undetected, or shelter from a tornado." He slid the back panel up. "There's a key to this door attached to the chain, by the panel in the elevator. There're three more hidden. I'll show you where they are, later." He took the key and opened a steel plated door. It swung into a brightly lit room. "Watch the drop." He stepped down inside and caught her arm.

Kate turned around, inspecting the concrete room full of exercise equipment. "*You* work out down here?"

"Helps the claustrophobia. Bright lights are a boon. Solar powered by the roof panels on the pool house, which power the battery." He gave her a minute to get her bearings. "Down this way is the back of the house." He walked toward a narrow tunnel. Halfway down he stopped and pointed out a niche in the wall. "The safe's here. I have duplicate credit cards, driver's license, and my passport's down here. We'll have to get you set up for that too. There's always a thousand dollars in small bills." He spun the combination lock and turned the handle, as she watched closely. "Got it?"

She nodded.

"There's a Glock 17 and a .38 in here." Both guns were holstered. "They're loaded, but not registered. Know how to use these?" Cam asked.

Kate looked up without raising her head. "I am my mother's daughter. Of course, I know."

Cam nodded, then continued, "There are boxes of extra ammo." He pulled each item out of the safe, as he spoke. "There's a light jacket, a poncho, a knife, and matches. There's also a key to get out."

Kate's arms crossed. "Okay."

"Proceed down the tunnel." He replaced everything except the key in the safe and spun the knob. He took her hand, feeling her hesitation. "It's all right, honey, come on." They walked twenty more feet, to concrete steps at the end. "If there's a weakness in this place, it's right here." He patted the wall beside them. "Twenty-five thousand gallons of water rest on the other side. It's reinforced with steel, but you never know. Worst case scenario it'd be ankle, maybe shin deep by the time it filled the panic room and tunnel. There's only one drain in here to expedite it, until the water reaches the shower."

Kate nodded and glanced up at the steel plate at the top of the steps. "This comes out in the pool house?"

"Yes ma'am. Buckets of chemicals ordinarily sit on top of that plate. I moved them, so you can open it." He handed her a key. "Go ahead. The lights would have to be low at this point. You'll get used to the routine."

She scampered to the top, bent low and turned the key. The cover slid away quietly. "Now we go out?"

"We wait, listen. You can't be seen in the pool house from outside, but you may make noise. It's best to take your time, even if the pool's cracked and leaking water. The point to a panic room is to *not panic*. You're safe down here, if you can handle it. I need for you to handle it, Kate." He studied his bride.

She sat on the top step, her head a foot above the opening. Her eyes closed as she identified every sound, drifting to her, through the cool night air. *Distant thunder, wind whipping through treetops, a coyote howling, the restless current of the creek…*

Danger lurks as curtains of darkness slowly settle in the dale,

Beloved insists I learn to be furtive.
No matter how scary, I must prevail.
This place of peace and sanctuary….

"What're you doing, honey?" Cam asked.

"Listening." Kate peeked below.

"You can come down now. Lesson one's over." He caught her hand as she descended, after locking the steel plate back in place. "We'll start spending a few evenings a week down here. I need the exercise."

"I saw the recumbent bike. Mine's in storage."

"It's good for warmups. Nobody, but Pop and Mark know this place exists. It was Pop's idea. He put one in at the ranch. My folks use the elevator when they're here. The panic room is our secret."

"Okay. I hope we never need it, but if it helps you with the claustrophobia, it's worth the trouble." She took his hand and shivered, as they passed into the middle of the room again.

"A chemical toilet and shower are behind that door." He pointed to the left side of the tunnel. "There's storage in the closet, beside it, with cots, water, and MREs; enough to survive down here for about a month. Anything more than a day you'll have to shoot me." He sat on the upholstered weight bench, pulling her down with him.

"Can you tell me what caused the claustrophobia?" She met his uncertain gaze. "Please."

Cam looked away. "The Preacher was serving at a church two doors down from the house we lived in. Momma sent me there with a message that someone had called the house needing pastoral care. I was nine and a half." He studied the floor. "He was *engaged.* The woman left, after she dressed. The Preacher was furious that I'd walked in on them. The door had been closed, but not locked. I'd knocked, then barged in. After screaming at me, for a little while, he dragged me into the supply closet in the hallway and locked the door. Told Momma I'd gone to spend the night with a friend. She was suspicious, called my friend and then swiped the keys to the church from his desk at home. She found me late that night. I'd been in there for about seven hours." He looked up. "I never felt comfortable in a tight place again, that wasn't an airplane. Always sit in the window seat on a commercial liner."

She watched him digest the restrictions of four gray walls. "That's a good explanation." She glanced around. "Are we going to try out one of the cots? Make sure they're comfortable?" She posed her question with a hint of amusement.

He grinned. "Weight bench is padded."

"Mmm, I see, well then…."

He unbuttoned her denim shirt to find her braless and smiled.

***

Shirt left open and shoes in hand, Cam guided Kate into the elevator and closed the door, locked it and pulled down the side panel. He turned the crank that raised them to the first floor and slid the panel up.

"We're beside the coat closet. It takes the key to open the door, only from the inside." He unlocked and opened the door into the living room.

"Okay, cool."

"But we always take the elevator to the top. It may be our only way down."

"Ominous, but good to know." She nodded.

Cam remained subdued throughout the evening.

Chapter Nineteen
Bishop's Bailiwick

The garden had died back enough that Cam spotted Kate picking kale and chard at dusk. He parked in the driveway.

She lifted the frost blanket from her Brussel sprouts and cabbages then resecured the edges. Dixie stayed close by her mistress, her nose in the air, ears perked, sensitive to every sound.

Cam rested for a moment and admired the view. The sunset was beautiful from their back deck, but something compelled him to see about Kate and the Bailiwick.

His wife stood, turned, stretching her back, and spotted him. He waved to her as he left the truck. Tension electrified the air. He scanned the area, but saw nothing out of the ordinary. *Feels like a storm is imminent. What's happening that I can't see?*

"Hello, beautiful lady." He met his wife halfway and kissed her. "Mmm, you taste good."

"Thank you. I thought you had a ton of paperwork to wade through. What're you doing out here?" She brushed her fingers over her hair.

"Don't know. I finished early, so Buddy and I sat on the deck waitin' for you. Always been satisfied watching the sunset, until now. Had to come. Can I carry the basket?" He grabbed it.

Dixie scurried to Kate, taking a stand behind her and growled toward the gloaming, beyond the reach of mercury vapor lights on the outbuildings.

"What's the matter, Dix?" Kate reached down to pet her, found her hackles raised, she crouched, ready to attack what she could only feel.

Cam surveyed the area, but saw nothing amiss.

They walked on for a tense moment, listening. In the quiet distance they heard a man yell. Dixie pushed herself broadside across Kate's legs. She barked, four short, sharp warnings. They froze. Cam turned to the pasture beyond the fence, pulling Kate behind him. A shot echoed through the hills.

"Rifle by the sound of it! Did you see a muzzle flash?" He grabbed her arm and steered her toward the house. They moved at a trot. Dixie guarded their rear flank.

Kate shook her head as she ran. "No, I'm not sure where it came from. Uncle Leroy goes to the upper pasture to bring in calves who lag behind, sometimes." She made the porch and reached for Dixie.

Cam commanded, "Stay in the house. Lock the doors."

He loped to his truck, jumped in, and tore down the path toward the fence line. At the gate, he pulled on a watchcap and scrambled out with a rifle from the rack over his arm. He secured a flashlight from the pocket on the door. He eased through the gate.

The cows crowded each other, trying to reach the barnyard. One Hereford blocked progress, bawling. She struggled to return to the field, pressing against the spooked animals spinning her like a sailboat, in an eddy.

Cam sprinted toward the hill between him and the pasture beyond.

At the crest, he dropped low and shifted to a clump of brush. A survey of the lower pasture revealed dark silence. *Nothing's moving.* He checked his watch. *Four minutes since the shot. Time enough for nature to recover unless men are still around.*

He headed to the creek, on the east side of the pasture, bent low. A thick leaf mold carpet silenced his steps. At the nearest ash tree, he straightened to survey the paddock. In the distance he heard a low moan. He trod lightly toward it, bent double.

Leroy Turner lay in a heap at the edge of the pasture. He groaned, rolled, and tried to stand. Cam crept near him.

"Leroy, Cam Fletcher, can you hear me?" His deep voice fell flat in the night.

The older man groaned and tried to speak. "Hit hard. Think they gone." Again, he attempted to sit up.

Cam fell to his belly, beside him, and whispered. "Lay still until we're sure. Tell me what happened." He checked

Leroy's coarse, kinky hair for wounds, and felt the stickiness of fresh blood.

Leroy lay back and took a shallow breath. "There's at least two of 'em. After calves. Got away with one, maybe two. Light's low. I couldn't see clear. One man's big, the other skinny, tall."

"Drive in here or walk?"

"I reckon they drove in the backway, through the woods." Leroy's voice became stronger. "Man, my head hurts."

"I'll go for the truck and get you back to the house, in a few minutes." He laid his rifle under Leroy's arm. "Put your hand on the stock, feel it? Safety's off, so go easy. I'm leaving the flashlight with you too." He pushed it into Leroy's left hand. "I came in from the house, so I have to get the truck through the gate and the cows. When you hear me, extend your arm; shine the torch straight up to mark your location. If anybody else walks up, shoot to kill. We'll sort out details later."

Cam's step was as light as fresh snowfall through the carpet of leaves. Attuned to the sounds of the woods, he followed the creek up to a treeline that dumped him near the gate.

When he climbed into the truck, he called Kate. She answered before the first ring ended.

"Hello."

"Me, I found Leroy hurt. Going back after him in the truck. Could've carried him out, but he wouldn't've liked it. He says calves were stolen, Kate. Call the sheriff and report it. We won't be able to see until morning and there's no sound of rustlers in the area now, that I can make out."

"Please be careful." She begged.

He smiled to himself. "Yes ma'am. I'll take Leroy to the house for Evangeline to tend and come back to you. Phone her, please ma'am?'

"I will. I'll be waiting."

Cam helped Leroy out of the truck. Evangeline stood on the front porch of the cottage. She wore a rose printed housecoat. A silk scarf held her dark curls away from her creamy mocha skin. Her shaky hands covered her mouth to keep from crying out.

When the men mounted the porch, she muttered. "Leroy, honey, what happened? I've been sick with worry, since I heard that gunshot."

Cam answered her. "He's been hit on the head a pretty stiff blow and kicked in the ribs. I wouldn't be surprised if he doesn't feel like a truck hit him in the morning."

"Feels like that now." Leroy replied weakly.

They entered the front door and Cam got his first good look at Leroy in the light.

The older black man had two open gashes at his hairline on either side of his craggy face.

Cam's voice assured Leroy, "Head wounds bleed like crazy, but these don't look deep enough for stitches. If you want, we can run to the hospital for stitches and x-rays."

"I'll check him out, Camden. I can take him in, if needs be." Evangeline set about wiping Leroy's wounds with a soft rag dipped in warm water she had ready. She fussed over him for a moment.

Cam looked on, hands on his hips. "Leroy, I'll be here in the morning to tend the cattle and talk to the sheriff. You may as well sleep in. Get some rest tomorrow. I'll swing by to check on you and let you know what we find, okay?"

"That'll be fine. Thank you for helping me home. Man, my head hurts!" Leroy tried not to move his head when he talked.

"Shh…hush now, you gonna be alright." His wife cooed, "We'll get you bandaged up and a few ibuprofen down. You'll be right as rain in the morning."

Cam turned to the door. "Evangeline, you have my number. I'll be up at the house." He let himself out the front door and stopped to listen to the quiet. He could still hear two cows bawling. They would need milking in the morning.

Kate waited at the kitchen door for Cam's truck to appear. She sighed in relief as he bounded up the steps.

"I was getting worried about you. How's Uncle Leroy?" She asked.

"I'd rather have taken him for x-rays, but Evangeline didn't think he'd need it. She's the nurse, so I bow to her wishes. How are you?" He braced his hands on her waist.

"Concerned, but okay. There'll be somebody from the sheriff's department out first thing in the morning." She held onto his arms.

"We'll stay here. I'll run to the house and pick up Buddy and some clothes. Be right back. Will you be okay?"

"Everything's locked down. I have Daddy's four-ten out, cleaned, and loaded. We have an arsenal of barking dogs to sound an alarm. We'll be fine for an hour or so. Mom's sewing curtains and she's never far away from a loaded gun."

Cam smiled. "We may have to rethink our strategy of living at our house. It's too dangerous to leave Ruth in this big place alone."

"Mom met a girl from church who wants to rent a room."

He held his wife tenderly, buried his face in the curve of her neck. "Mmm…."

"I know what you're thinking. She needs a young man out here."

"That wasn't what was going through my mind, but it's true. If I don't go now, I won't leave. We'll tell Ruth about this when I get back, thirty minutes tops." He released and kissed her. "Kate, I love you. Call me if you even *think* you hear a boogey man, promise?"

"Promise. I love you, too." She released him.

Cam had been away for more than an hour. Kate let Dixie and the Dachshunds out to potty. As she stepped outside, she heard a noise at the barn. Dixie returned to the porch at a skid, growling, Cinnamon and Shuga barked and started toward the racket. Dixie pressed Kate's legs to herd her back inside.

"I heard it too, baby, but we have to get those little terrors to come in." She pushed her way around the Border collie to the yard, her voice low. "Cinnamon! Shuga! Get here now!" Dixie took off to cut them off the path to the barn. She roughly pushed each of the small dogs back, with her nose. They turned and merrily made their way back to the house.

They rushed toward Kate; their ears flapping as they ran. She jumped up the steps and opened the screen door as they passed by in a blur. Dixie growled at more movement and noise down at the barn. Once the inner door closed, she stood guard, with her nose pressed to the jam.

Kate dialed Cam's cell number. No answer.

"Where are you, Cam Fletcher?" She sighed.

She went to the sewing room. "Mom, we're staying here tonight. Cam ran home for Buddy and clothes, but he's been gone a long time. I can't get him on the phone. I'm worried."

"Well, let's ride over there." She began to put away her sewing.

"I'll go. You stay here. I'll probably pass him on the way back, but it's been more than an hour. He always answers his phone."

"Call me as soon as you get there, Katrina." Ruth picked up the drape she'd worked on and pulled pins from the hem. "I'll come if you need me."

"I will." She slipped into a light jacket at the backdoor and eased through.

There was no more noise at the barn. *Maybe it's just wind.* She got into her Camry and backed out without headlights. She pulled out the gate of Bishop's Bailiwick toward Cam's house, switching her lights on as she passed the apple orchard.

Ten minutes later, she drove down his driveway. Lights blazed at the garage. His truck sat in front, driver's door open, pinging indicated keys in the ignition. She parked on the passenger's side of the truck and studied the area. Seeing no one, she got out and walked around the front.

Cam sprawled face down on the flagstone bleeding through his watch cap. Buddy lay beside him whining.

First, she thought he was dead. She checked his pulse— strong. She called the ambulance and sheriff's department on her cell phone.

She dashed up the stairs to the house and found kitchen towels to soak in water to clean the blood. Her eyes dropped from the horrible words spray-painted on the handsome knotty-pine cabinets. She shivered and hurried back out to kneel at

Cam's side and gently clean the blood away from his face. She left the wound alone, as it had almost stopped bleeding.

Kate reached for the Boxer to rub his ears. "It's okay, Buddy, he'll be alright."

She brushed her fingertips across Cam's hand. She tried to avoid anything that may interest the deputies.

Kate called her mom.

Ruth answered the phone at the first ring. "Where are you, Kate?"

"I'm at Cam's house. He's been badly hurt. Mom, Uncle Leroy was attacked earlier by rustlers. They got 2 calves. Cam brought him home and Aunt Evie's seeing to him. We didn't want to worry you. Deputies will be out in the morning around daylight to see what they can. I'm waiting here for an ambulance and the sheriff's department." She wiped her face clear of tears with her sleeve.

"Kate, I love you. I'll tend to this end. Be careful." The connection dropped.

She knelt beside Cam to check his pulse again, laid her hand over his and prayed softly. "I speak life into you, Camden Fletcher."

Footsteps on the gravel held her spellbound. *No weapon was handy.* Buddy left her side and barked. His nubby tail wagged, at someone he knew.

Cracker leaned over Buddy and rubbed his ears. "Hey, how you doing now, Buddy?" He rounded the truck and saw Cam on the ground, Kate by his side. "Is he dade?" he growled; his face devoid of expression. He stank of whisky and swayed on his feet.

She shook her head and refused to lower her gaze from his.

"Have you called for hep?" He took a step closer.

"Yes, they should be here by now." As she spoke, she heard a car pull into the driveway.

Cracker turned and left hastily, cutting across the front of the house toward the shop.

Two deputies climbed out of their car. They approached carefully, taking in the scene as they came. "Ma'am, are you the one to report this?"

Kate stood, nodded, and wiped her face again, with her sleeve.

The other deputy dropped beside Cam to check his pulse. "He's alive, let's get an ambulance."

"I've called already. I'm Kate Fletcher. Cam was on his way to my mother's, Bishop's Bailiwick. He'd run home to get clothes and Buddy, so we could spend the night there. We had trouble earlier. I made a report about six-thirty."

She stopped and gathered her wits, glanced again at the man she loved, lying on the concrete unconscious.

"Who was leaving when we pulled up?" The deputy asked.

"His name is George Fleming. They call him Cracker. He works for Cam. He's a foreman. I don't know what he's doing here so late, but he's stinking drunk." Kate answered.

"Did you talk to him?" The other deputy asked.

"He wanted to know if Cam was dead." She reported flatly.

"Here's the ambulance. We'll have to ask you to step back and get that dog, please. Let's give these fellows room to work."

Kate tugged on Buddy's collar. "C'mon, boy, come outta the way." To the deputies, "You might also be interested to see inside the house. I only went to the kitchen. It's been vandalized." Her face flamed at the memory of the words she'd seen. "Please, I saw his cell phone just under the bumper of the truck. I need a number from it. Mark Miller."

The younger deputy dropped to his knees to look, used an evidence bag to pick it up. He scrolled the numbers and read Mark's out to Kate.

"Thank you." She dialed her phone and turned away from the two men.

"Hello?" Mark answered.

She squeaked, "It's Kate. Mark, Cam's hurt. I'm at his house—come quickly!"

"I'll be there in a few minutes." He rang off.

Kate crossed her arms and tried to stop shaking. She walked Buddy away from the truck and leaned against her car.

147

Emergency lights whirled red waves against the foggy darkness. The ambulance driver maneuvered in as close as possible.

Mark Miller's long stride brought him to Kate's side in a flash. "Kate, what's goin' on? I'm close behind the ambulance." He studied the scene with a dark frown.

"Cam's hurt, been hit, um, a gash on his head." She couldn't stop shaking.

Mark reached for her, squeezing her shoulder. "How'd it happen?"

"Uncle Leroy was attacked in the upper pasture at the Bailiwick. Cam, maybe an hour later."

The paramedics had Cam on a stretcher, his head wrapped. He was still unconscious. She glanced back at Mark. "I have to go with him."

Mark nodded. "I'll be there directly. Let me get Buddy up to my house." He snapped on a lead.

The deputies were inside, the door stood open to the world. Kate watched the medics load Cam in the ambulance.

Mark ambled past, getting a good look at Cam. "What hospital are you going to?" Kate didn't hear the answer. "Much obliged."

She went back to her car, opened the door.

"Excuse me, Mrs. Fletcher!" A deputy called her from the top of the stairs. "We need you to hang around. We may need to ask more questions."

She shook her head. "No! I'm going with my husband to the hospital. You have my phone number on the report." She made a mime of a phone at her ear. "Call me." She climbed in, reversed the Camry, and inched past the patrol car. In moments she was behind the ambulance.

Chapter Twenty

Kate sat in a recliner in Cam's hospital room. She ran her hand over her hair and realized it hadn't seen a comb in eighteen hours. She dug in her purse, found one, and went to the mirror.

"Kate?" Cam's bass voice rasped.

She returned to him. "Hey, how're you feeling?"

He reached for her, saw the i.v. attached. He growled, "Where in sam hill are we?"

"At the hospital." She tried to smile.

"What am I doing in this bed?"

"Healing, hopefully." She touched his face gently.

He blinked, trying to focus. "I didn't get back to you, did I?"

"No, I found you in a pool of blood about an hour and a half after you left."

"I remember pulling the truck in. There was a log across the driveway. I got out to move it…that's all. My head hurts."

She patted his hand. "Relax. You have eighteen stitches and a major concussion. You were out for a long time. When we arrived, they sedated you."

"Buddy…?"

"Went home with Mark." She began to braid her hair.

"They could've killed him."

"Do you remember seeing anyone?" She wrapped the end of her braid with a band.

"I don't think so. Felt like a boulder dropped on me. I don't recall even hearing a noise."

Kate said, "Cracker showed up, right after I got there. He asked if you were dead *and* he was drunk. Cam, he's creepy. What is it about that man?"

"When Leroy told me one of the guys in the pasture was big, Cracker was my first thought. He's a good foreman, brings in a job on time and on budget. It's not a personality contest. I've never liked him, just can't put my finger on why."

A nurse interrupted them. "Excuse me, is Mr. Fletcher awake?"

"Yes, ma'am, I am. Can I get something to drink, please?" He grimaced and blinked. "I'm dry as a bone."

"I'll call the doctor, after I check your vital signs. Mrs. Fletcher..." She nodded toward the door.

"I'll step out to call Mom. I'll be back." She left for the waiting room.

Kate rang off after assuring Ruth that Cam appeared to be on the mend.

A man stepped out of the elevator and glanced around the expansive ICU waiting room. His eyes landed on Kate. He approached her with assurance.

"Would you be Kate Fletcher?" His gray eyes matched his hair and suit.

"Yes, and you are?" She felt the hair on her arms and neck rise.

"Leo Burnham, with the Sherriff's department," he handed her a card. "I'm investigating the incident at your house." He hitched a pant leg and sat in the chair beside her.

"Well, I found Cam, but I can't tell you much about what happened before I arrived. He said he was pulling the truck into the driveway..."

"He's awake?" Detective Burnham made notes on an electronic pad.

"He was a few minutes ago. Nurse sent me out so she could evaluate him."

"I'll get in to talk to him. You were saying?" He returned to the pad.

"When he pulled in the driveway, there was a log across it, in front of the truck. He went to move the log. Something hit him."

"The report says there was another person there, who left the scene?" The investigator asked.

"George 'Cracker' Fleming is a foreman. I have no idea why he was there so late." She shrugged.

"I saw what the vandals wrote on the kitchen cabinets. Can you shed light on that?" He continued to make notes.

"I'm the Jewish *person* the writing referred to." She felt the silence strain as it fell between them.

Finally, he nodded. "Any idea who would do that?"

"No clue." She rubbed her hands over her arms as a chill swept over her.

"Do you think there's a connection with what happened at your mother's place?"

Kate tried to smile. "It would be odd if there wasn't, Mr. Burnham. This harkens back to the days when civil rights first had a fighting chance. The KKK burned a cross in front of our house. It's set a quarter mile off the road. Daddy didn't see it, until it became a raging brush fire." She paused, studying his reaction.

He nodded without making eye contact. "We're seeing a resurgence. The world goes through these cycles and the scape goat's always the same. Anti-Semitism is on the rise in these quiet little burgs."

"Well, I've had my eyes opened to something I haven't had to face too often. I've never had a personal attack like the writing on Camden's kitchen cabinets."

The policeman glanced up and spoke, "Be prepared for this to escalate, if we don't catch them. Even if we nail down the individual there's a gang mentality involved with these groups."

Kate nodded. "I'll keep that in mind. The doctor said the cuff of Cam's wool watch cap probably kept the wound from being fatal. "

"Take precautions. Stay alert to your surroundings. I'll check in with the nurses and see when I can get an interview with Cam. I have your number. May I call, if something comes up?" His smile failed to warm Kate's chill.

"Certainly. Do you know my husband?" Kate's narrowed eyes studied the lawman.

"Like a lot of folks around here, he put a roof on my house after bad weather." Leo Burnham turned away to Camden's room. Kate studied his stride.

3 days later

Kate parked her car in the driveway. Cam opened the passenger's door and climbed out slowly. They stood, for a moment, studying the surroundings, before they started up the steps to the house.

He said, "Honey, Leo told me what's been done to the kitchen and bathroom. I don't want you in either one. Let me get a few things and we'll go fetch Buddy. Stay at The Bailiwick." He climbed the steps stiffly.

"I'm a big girl. I don't think I'll faint at the sight of vulgarity." She followed.

"I have a call in to a fellow, whose business it is to clean that up. He's due out in the morning."

"We'll soldier through." She unlocked and opened the door.

He stepped inside, removed his sunglasses, and looked around. "You ever get a feeling about a place; know you'll never be completely comfortable again, no matter what?"

"Yes. I felt that way, after Reggie was killed while jogging in our neighborhood. It wasn't safe anymore. I called a realtor after the funeral and sold the house." She rubbed his back.

"That's what I'm feeling now. As soon as the guy gets the crap off the cabinets and walls, we're selling out." He sat down on the piano bench, and patted the seat beside him.

"Give yourself a few days; you may grow out of it." She sat on the bench facing the back wall.

He shook his head. "Don't think so. I'm not afraid. I'm *pissed.*" He played the scale to limber his fingers before he began a tune.

Kate watched his hands glide around the keyboard like a pro ice skater in the rink. She smiled when she recognized the melody; *Piano Man.*

Ruth topped the front steps, followed by Buddy. Kate saw her mom lean on the doorway to listen. When the song was over Cam kissed his wife.

"Mom's watching us." Kate whispered in his ear, as Buddy jumped in his lap, to lick his face.

"Hey, Buddy. I missed you too." Cam rubbed the Boxer's ears.

Ruth proceeded in, while her two favorite people interacted. She put her hand on Cam's shoulder. "How do you feel?"

"Head's still achy. It'll be okay. I'm glad to be out of the hospital. Once I was conscious, all I could think about was escape. I've never been overnight in one of those prisons. I don't see how people do it."

"Not everyone's as claustrophobic as you are. Most folks are content to sit inside occasionally." She bent to kiss Kate's forehead.

"Did Amanda get settled in, Mom?" Kate asked.

"She brought most of her things out this morning. She'll stay tonight and get the rest after work tomorrow." Ruth held Kate for a moment. "I missed you, darling."

"Hello!" Mark called out from the steps.

"Come on in." Cam called back, as Buddy launched himself to meet Mark.

The lanky black man scrubbed his shoes, on the mat at the door, while Buddy jumped up on him. "You ran off and left me." Mark rubbed the Boxer's ears. He turned to Cam. "How you feeling?" He grabbed Cam's hand in his.

"I'm alive to someone's dismay, my friend." Cam replied.

"Yeah, talked to Leo Burnham yesterday." Mark sat in a nearby chair and crossed his legs. "Cam, lay low for a while. Let the cops do what they do."

"How many years have we known each other?" Cam's eyes narrowed.

Mark shook his head, smiling. "Long enough to know you'd say that. More than a quarter of a century, give or take. The folks doing this are in it for blood, man. We have no authority over them."

"I'm not sittin' here waitin' to see what else they have up their sleeves." Cam scowled.

"Why don't you take some time off, maybe go on a real honeymoon? I can tend to this end." Mark laced his fingers together, stretching to pop his knuckles, studying his partner.

"It's not in me to run. You know that. I'm choking an urge to take the fight to them. If I knew where to look, they'd have it. Any talk around the shop?"

"Nah, it's quiet as a tomb. Nobody's gonna say anything around me." Mark shook his head.

"That speaks volumes. They should be chattering like magpies." Uneasy silence settled around them for a minute, before Cam added, "They spray-painted filth in the house. That tells me they walked past Buddy. This was done by somebody he let inside."

Ruth spoke up. "Years ago, when Leroy and Evangeline were married, we had trouble. Evangeline's father, my step-father, came for the wedding. Kate, do you recall the burning cross out by the highway?"

"I remember that. It was scary." Kate nodded.

"Richard had an illegitimate half-brother, John Bishop Maynard. He was tied in with the local group of the Klan. We put it down to him, at the time. He and Richard had an altercation in Bass Pro Shop earlier the same day." She mused for a moment. "Bigots are cowards, they terrorize anonymously." Ruth continued. "They hide themselves in sheets, masks, and darkness because there's no bravery in their actions. They never confront directly, but skulk around in shadows."

Mark glanced at the ladies and took off his ball cap to rub his hand over curly gray hair. "Guess I never thought of it that way, Miss Ruth. They feel emboldened to catch a man alone, like Leroy down in the pasture gathering calves or Cam rushing off to Kate. They don't have guts enough to face off, man to man."

"That's why they run in packs, like wild dogs." Ruth turned to Cam. "You're looking for a charlatan. There's someone you may even consider a friend, who is not."

"Mom, what did Daddy do to stop the harassment?" Kate rose from the piano bench.

Ruth smiled at the memory. "He and Leroy visited every bar around here, with an ax handle in hand, and announced that the next time the cowards trespassed they'd meet with armed resistance, by men who knew how to fight. He began with, what's now, Homer's Saloon when Homer's daddy, George ran it."

Cam listened in silence but his mind raced. "Sounds like a good start, anybody up for a steak?"

"I'm with you." Mark smiled. "Janiece is still in Texas with our new grandbaby."

"Me too." Ruth and Kate answered at the same time.

Cam rose from the piano bench and held his hand out to Kate. "Come on, beloved. Let's go see what crap we can stir up."

He snagged a driving cap from the antique halltree by the door, slipping it on backwards, carefully over the stitches.

***

The foursome walked into Homer's Saloon before the dinner rush. Cam held Kate's hand and led the way to a booth. Kate and Ruth sat on the inside against the wall.

Lucy sauntered over with menus and flopped them on the table. "Hey, Cam." She struggled to make her voice sound normal.

Cam glanced, at the bar, to find half a dozen patrons watching them. "Hey, Lucy. Bring me a glass of tea, please. What do y'all want to drink?"

Mark, Ruth, and Kate ordered and scanned the crowd. Kate felt chills run up her spine. Tension thickened as seconds dragged past.

Lucy popped her gum and ambled away. A huddle, at the bar, sent glances their direction.

Mark mumbled, "I don't believe we're imagining the intimidation factors at work. When was the last time you were in here?"

Cam thought for a moment. "Cracker and I came in about three weeks ago and had lunch and a long talk about his attitude. Before that, Kate and I ate here on our first date. Didn't we, sugar?"

She nodded when he kissed her hand and said, "You're provoking.…"

"Yes ma'am. We might as well dance." He slid out of the booth. "If it gets that far, y'all order a rare steak for me. If it doesn't, Ruth, we'll meet ya at the car. What do you want, Kate?"

"Baked potato and salad, please." She replied.

"Cam, you've just been released from the hospital, is it a good idea to start a fight?" Ruth scolded.

He glanced down and nodded after a moment. The Texan's drawl deepened, "Right now's as good as any, I reckon."

Cam dropped quarters into the jukebox and made two selections. He led Kate to the dance floor, held her, then whispered in her ear. "When this goes bad, you get outta here by the front door, if it's not blocked. Ruth will slip out the emergency exit, by the booth. Okay?"

She nodded, shivered, and felt her throat tighten. "Okay. Please be careful."

Cam smiled, "I've got a lot to look forward to once this is done, sweetheart." He furtively scanned the crowd.

She nodded. "Me, too."

He threw back his head and laughed. "That'll do. Here comes Ruby. You can't say I didn't warn you."

Ruby's ragged fingernails dug into Kate's shoulder. "Get outta here, you filthy Jew." She struggled to drag Kate from Cam's embrace.

Cam encircled Ruby's wrist and applied enough pressure to make her fingers go numb. "Ruby, be nice." He smiled, checking movement from the bar, peripherally.

Homer, short and stocky, flew out from the back bar. "Ruby! Ruby, this ain't the time. You stop that nonsense." He wrapped one arm around his sister's waist, pushing his round black-rimmed glasses up his stubby nose, and hauled her away. "Sorry, Cam." He called back over his shoulder.

The place fell silent. Mark stood beside the jukebox with his feet spread, and tossed the plug to the floor. Two couples followed Ruth out the emergency exit. Cam escorted Kate to the entrance twenty feet ahead of them. As soon as she cleared the door he whirled and met every eye in the place.

"My home and property have been violated. I've been assaulted by a thug. My mother-in-law's livestock has been stolen and Leroy Turner badly beaten. If any of you are involved and you're man enough, we can settle this outside in the parking lot." No one acknowledged him. "Well, then, you're on notice. There won't be a successful next time—either."

Ruby spouted filth until Homer covered her mouth with his hand. "Shut up I say!" He growled in her face, before he responded to Cam's taunt. "Don't know what you're talking about, Cam. Nobody here means you and yours any harm, I'm sure."

Cam chuckled. "At least Ruby's got the guts to face me. Homer, it's a shame…" He threw a ten dollar bill on the bar. "Remember who drew first blood." He looked at every man at the bar who would meet his eyes.

Mark joined Cam as they left. The crunch of gravel underfoot was the only sound heard until they climbed into Ruth's Cadillac. Mark sat in front with her. Cam climbed in behind her to sit with Kate.

He kissed his wife and said, "Let's just sit here a minute, Ruth, and see what manifests. I believe we stirred a hornet's nest."

A few minutes later, six men piled out the door, sweating and swearing. When they realized they auditioned as suspects, their steps slowed. One man even threw up a hand to wave and tried to smile.

"That's about what we figured, Cam." Mark chuckled. "Word will spread fast. I'm glad they didn't decide to jump us, but I've got a question."

"What's that, my friend?" Cam asked.

"We didn't get to eat. What're we doing about supper?"

Kate responded, trying to keep her voice from wavering. "I used to cook for a living, Mark. I imagine I can feed us."

Cam gazed at Kate. "Honey, do you have grass fed beef?"

She shook her head. "No, but I have veggies and…."

"That's what I figured. Ruth, remember the new steak house we went to, last Spring, in Ozark?"

"I do."

"Let's see if we can get a table." Cam turned to Kate. "We need to come to an understanding about red meat, beloved." He took her hand, kissing her fingertips.

"Mmm." Kate replied.

"I'm a carnivore. Vegetables, at best, are side dishes. Now," he looked down at her legs, "if you aren't using the top side of your lap, may I?"

"Sure, come on. Does your head hurt?" She lifted the cap to check the glued stitches.

"A little, mmm." He lay his head down, squirmed to find a niche in the leather seat for his shoulder, caught her scent, sighed, and closed his eyes.

Chapter Twenty-one
Ten days later

Buddy whined at the bedroom door. Cam dragged himself from sleep. Pain medication and the constant headache still slowed his reflexes. He sat up and watched Buddy scratch at the floor.

"You gotta go out, Buddy?"

"Huh?" Kate rolled over.

"He needs to go out." He pulled on jeans and grabbed a shirt. When he opened the bedroom door the smell hit him.

Smoke!

Alarms failed to sound.

"Kate, come on, honey. We've gotta hurry. There's a fire."

Kate sprang up, grabbed jeans, off a hook in the closet, and pulled on a sweatshirt. Her clogs were handy to slide on her feet.

Cam's head cleared as he slipped on his shoes.

They crossed the hall to the elevator.

Smoke from below rolled up to the ceiling. A thick cloud gathered at the roof's peak. Flames ate away at the oak floor like it was sugar.

The cable slid smoothly through the pulley as Cam manually lowered the metal box.

When he reached the panic room, he turned the key in the lock. The door swung inward at his touch.

They passed through. He closed the door and locked it.

Buddy whined. "Shh, Buddy, it's okay. We've practiced this enough to do it in our sleep. You all right, Kate?"

"I think so. Buddy has more experience at this than I do." She clasped her arms to herself.

Cam navigated the maze of exercise equipment in the fifteen by twenty-foot concrete room. Lights glowed brightly.

"A drawback to those pool shed roof panels is that they'll melt if fire gets close. We have light for a little while, as long as the battery holds the charge. I'm gonna head outside and see what I can."

They hurried down the narrow tunnel to the wall safe. He spun the dial. The door opened.

He pocketed his stash and pulled on a black watch cap gingerly over his bandaged wound. He buckled on the holster and adjusted the Glock. He placed the .38 in Kate's hand. "You know what to do."

She nodded mutely. Ruth had not failed to teach her daughter about guns.

SSShrew…. boiling sap whistled and exploded. *Whrump!* The house, above them, shook.

"That was the balcony or part of the roof. Better scoot in case the vibration cracks the pool." He handed Kate the poncho, slipped into the black lightweight jacket, and grabbed a leash and muzzle from the safe. He hefted a chunk of charcoal.

They continued a few feet farther down the tunnel. Cam dimmed the lights.

"I need you to stand here and turn the lights off, as soon as I get the trap door unlocked. I hate to leave you in pitch dark."

"Go, it's okay." Kate took up post, nervously. She reached under her shirt and clipped the holstered pistol to the waistband of her jeans.

Cam stopped to leash and muzzle Buddy. He handed Kate the leash.

Cam smeared charcoal over his face, neck and the back of his hands. "Wait here. I'll be right back." He whispered. "Crap! I smell chlorine." He felt along the concrete wall. "Wet!" He glanced back at Kate. "Just give me a few minutes and move Buddy up with you."

Cam ran up the steps, two at a time and unlocked the trap doo,r into the pool shed. He looked back and nodded.

Kate hit the switch. Light filtered in through smoke in the small opening around Cam's body. He slowly eased into the shed. He sat inside listening for a moment, before he stood.

He set two buckets of chemicals out of the way and studied his surroundings through lattice. No one was in sight. The fire lit the night like midday.

A loud crack from below caught his attention.

He dropped back through the portal and down the stairs. The boxer whined against the muzzle and pranced, attempting to escape the water. The gouge in the pool wall widened.

Cam's voice softened, "Shh…okay, pal. This is the real thing. You gotta be quiet."

The three of them climbed the stairs. When they neared the top Cam hesitated, his voice dropped.

"Hang here. I'm going out and scout a path to the trailer by the creek. Don't be afraid. I'll be right back."

"Yeah, you said that the last time I let you outta my sight." Kate whispered.

He grinned. "I did, but I mean it, this time." He held up his hand, pointed to his ear.

Kate nodded.

He halted at the top step, straining to hear. Voices were too far away, to make out the conversation. He exhaled as manmade noise grew fainter.

He eased up and through the shed. Flames licked the sky from forty feet above. Eerie shadows danced through the lattice enclosure. Knots in the structure of the house, he'd built by hand, popped like firecrackers, as resin overheated.

He studied the landscape for a minute, holding his breath against acrid smoke that swirled through the air.

He unholstered the Glock, slipping off the safety. He eased through the outer door, took two steps, and dropped below the patio behind shrubbery. The air was almost free of smoke. He waited, scouring the area for movement.

If somebody's out there, he's better, at this, than I am. He stooped, keeping close to the low wall, and headed to the opposite side of the house for concealment.

He dropped low and crept through broom straw and buffalo grass, his way well-lit, by the inferno behind him. He heard racket from the shop. *Must be where they parked.*

He crawled toward the back of the shop, crouching in shadows. Cam stole along the path with calculated steps. He checked two work trucks parked in front of the bay, a third he knew, and a fourth he didn't recognize. He memorized the Florida license plate number. Voices rose, from the front of the house. Cam eased to the corner away from the security light. He dropped flat on the ground.

C'mon, boys, let's see who you are. Creep on up here.

Four men rounded the driveway. Laughter erupted at one man's remark. "…where the hell is he?"

"Burnt up I expect." Cracker's deep voice rang clear.

"That'll teach 'em," replied Larry Martin.

"Larry, that's dumb. A dead feller ain't learned nothing useful." Cracker replied.

"You know what I mean. It'll make other folks take notice and stop inbreeding with Jews and blacks. That's what's wrong with this country, boys."

The third man, a local, had been at Homer's, and rolled out with the group that followed Cam and Mark. He grunted agreement with Larry.

The fourth man was a stranger. He wore sunglasses, a gray fedora, and carried a walking stick. He stopped, pulled a pack of Big Red gum from his shirt pocket, opened it, and methodically folded it into fourths, before popping it in his mouth. The wrapper was crumpled and stuffed into his pants pocket.

Six feet tall, one seventy or eighty with the jacket on, gray hair around the edge of the hat, and a limp in his left side, not leg, hip.

The stranger spoke, his deep voice raspy. "Larry, that's a lot of hate you're toting around."

"Well, it's like this. That woman's husband got my brother *unjustly* accused of whipping some Jew boys at college. He was kicked out, no questions asked. And him there on scholarship, the smartest one in the family. Naw, I had enough of bein' pushed around. It's like Jews, queers and blacks got more rights that we got. I'm drawing the line, by god; the buck stops here, fellers. Tell you this, though; Billy's out of Federal prison tomorrow. Let's talk about retribution!" Larry chuckled after the diatribe.

"Cracker, what's your stake in all this?" The stranger turned his shaded gaze to the foreman as the inferno reflected off his mirrored lenses.

The big man chuckled. "Hell, I got mine the other night, meant to kill him and that Nigro that works at Miss Ruth's place. Those damn Texans come up here and start a business, they don't know nothin' about. Sittin' on their duffs, they're making the big bucks, living high while the rest of us struggle paycheck to paycheck."

Cracker's blank stare swung in Cam's direction.

Cam held his breath and narrowed his eyes almost closed to avoid light reflection. *If you're thinking of comin' this way, you're a dead man.*

Cracker removed his cap, scratched his head, and turned back to his peers. "Anyhow, we better pick up the other boys and git outta here. Fire depot'll be here directly."

The four men clambered to their trucks and left swiftly, gravel flying against the side of the shop.

Cam sneaked away.

He made the trailer site, dropped on his belly, and stopped to watch for movement.

He caught a shadow peripherally and froze.

Life fluttered, beyond the trailer.

He didn't dare blink for missing the culprit.

Wind began to howl out of the north. Fiery embers swirled into a vortex and spun into the broom straw.

Glad, we had rain earlier. I'd be in a pickle.

The shadow leapt, startling Cam with its sudden burst of speed. A young stag glided from the gloom, behind the trailer, and into the woods across the creek.

He inhaled deeply and exhaled slowly. *Okay, time to move Kate and Buddy.*

He backtracked covertly, stopping every few feet to listen for voices and movement.

He rolled up, over the edge of the concrete patio and crept into the pool shed.

"Kate, let's go." He whispered. He took Buddy's leash in hand. His wife's body quivered under his touch.

Cam checked his watch. *Two-thirty.*

They exercised caution getting to the trailer. Once inside, he sighed with relief.

Kate's teeth chattered. She wrapped her arms tightly around herself. Cam enclosed her in his. She began to cry softly into his chest.

"Come on." He led her to the back of the trailer, removed his jacket and shoes and her poncho. "I'm sorry, honey. I had no idea it would turn into this. I'm glad we were here and not your house." He pulled her down on the bed and held her tightly, wrapping his leg over hers.

"Shh, baby, it's over, for now." He rocked her gently.

She shook her head against him. Her body vibrated in shock.

"I'll call Mark. He can pick us up, in a little while and call the fire department." He rested his face on her hair. "We've got a long way to go til daylight." He kissed the top of Kate's head and held her.

Mark's phone rang three times before he answered. "Yeah?"

"House is burning, call the fire department, please. It's best if they think we didn't make it out, right now."

"Got it." Mark disconnected.

Cam returned his free arm to hold his wife. They dozed in the quiet of predawn. Kate stirred against her husband; his grip loosened. He looked down to find her fingers plucking the buttons on his shirt.

"You sure?" He stretched.

She met his eyes and nodded.

***

Cam rang the doorbell on Ruth's kitchen door. At the noise, her kenneled Dachshunds raged. Dixie made the back door, barked, then whined when she picked up Kate's scent.

Cam dialed the house phone. "Hello?" Ruth's sleepy voice answered on the second ring.

"It's Cam. Will you be so kind as to let us in the kitchen door, please?"

"What are you doing here? You have a key. What time is it?"

He responded, "Six o'clock, my key no longer exists and it's a chilly, damp morning."

"I'm on my way."

The door opened. Ruth tied her robe. Kate and Cam tromped in. Mark watched for Cam's wave before he pulled out the driveway.

"What's going on?" Ruth asked. "I smell smoke." She was immediately awake.

"They burned the house down." Cam loosened Buddy from the leash. Then he removed the poncho from Kate and slipped out of his light jacket to reveal the shoulder holster and pistol.

Ruth took a step back. "Oh, no. Come on in. We don't want to wake Amanda."

"On the bright side, I know who they are." Cam rumbled as they stepped into the kitchen.

Ruth turned on the coffee pot. "Who?" She closed the door to the backstairs.

"Cracker and Larry are part of the group. There's a third man, local, whose name I know and a fourth I've never seen. I'll call Leo as soon as the sun comes up. No need to wake him; these guys aren't goin' anywhere." Cam opened a cabinet door and found a bottle of peach brandy.

Ruth shook her head. "I'm so sorry, Cam. To think men who've worked for you, would do such a thing. It's ghastly."

"Yes ma'am, it is. I'm ready for this to be over. They were discussing my demise on the way back to their trucks, two of which I own." He poured two ounces of peach brandy in a juice glass and added a shot of water. "This is an eye-opener for me. I wouldn't've suspected people working for us involved in this kind of mess." He placed the glass in front of Kate. "Sip it, honey," his voice gentle. He rubbed her shoulders, for a moment, while she obeyed. He bent to kiss the top of her head, unbuckled the shoulder holster, and hung it with his jacket in the mudroom.

"It makes sense, though. Who else would've noted Leroy's schedule, bringing in cows and going back for calves?" Ruth puzzled over the quandary.

"I considered that the night he was beaten. Taunting me out in the open can only be explained as somebody who knew me." Cam sat beside Kate and held her hand.

"How did you get out of the house?" Ruth poured coffee around.

"The panic room Pop insisted I build. Thank goodness I never got around to running electricity to the elevator I put in for him. Since it was a manual pulley, we rode down undetected. Nobody else, but Mark, knew about the elevator, until Kate and I made a practice run the other night."

Kate hadn't said anything in a while. Her mind was a jumble, her heart torn. She listened as Cam and Ruth talked over the problem with no clear idea of what to do.

Cam addressed Ruth, "I'll need you to run into Springfield for clothes for me, if you don't mind. It's probably better if they think I'm dead, at least for now."

"We can do that, can't we Kate?" Ruth took note of her daughter's silence.

Kate nodded. "You have two clean sets in my room upstairs. I brought them a few days ago…just in case."

***

Ruth stopped the Cadillac at the entrance to Bishop's Bailiwick. Kate got out for mail from the box. She sorted through, separating Leroy and Evangeline's out. She found a business envelope hand addressed to Kate Bishop in a sloppy script. She stuffed it in her jacket pocket.

When Ruth stopped the car in the driveway at home, Kate got out. "I'm going to run mail down to Aunt Evie's. Be back in a few minutes." She gave the rest to Ruth and took off at a brisk pace for the Turner's house.

Kate tore open the envelope, addressed to her, on the way back. Crudely cut and pasted words from magazine pages warned '3rd X's a charm.' She wadded the paper up and crammed it back in her pocket. She'd decided what to do. She needed to have a few hours alone, to carry out her plan.

Kate sat on the window seat, in the music room, and watched the raindrops gently roll down the panes. Internal conflicts battled for her attention. She could leave and see if the violence stopped or stay in the protective shield of her family and ride it out. After hours of ruminating, she left the window seat and climbed the stairs to her bedroom. She brushed her hands over the new jeans Ruth had bought in Springfield, for Camden.

She sat down to write a note to her mom and her husband. **I have to get away for a while. I'm going to Jaimie's to ride out the torrent of terror that continues. Hopefully my absence will make it stop. If not, the two of you need to seek protective custody, which I'm sure Jaimie can arrange. I love you both and feel this is the best thing for us all. Mom, you have the phone number for Jaimie's house in your directory or call my phone, should you need me. I'm not coming back until the villains are caught and behind bars. Camden, I love you with all my heart and cannot bear for you to lose everything, on account of me. Mom, you'll never be safe as long as I live here. I know you understand. Thinking back to the day that Maynard burned the cross in front of the house, it terrifies me what can happen next. I love you, Katrina**

She whispered, "Hope I'm choosing what's best for all of us." She opened her jewelry box and picked up the note Cam left on the nightstand in San Antonio. She opened it to read the words she could recite by heart:

Sweetheart, I didn't want to wake you when I leave at 3:30, so I'm saying goodbye, for now. My lady, you need time to heal from your loss. Take it with leisure and confidence that we'll find love in the future. I hold you and feel home.

My entire life, my mailing address has been my parent's. (I bought a house once, but never set foot in it. Another story, I'll tell you later.)

After this mission, which may take up to a year, I'm free to make a home for myself and hopefully you; if you'll have me, or haven't been swept off your feet already. I look forward to coming home to you every day. I want only the best for you and keep you close to my heart.

I put my phone numbers in your phone. Call me if you need me or just want to talk. I'll always come for you."

She returned the note to her jewelry box.

Kate called Jaime Manville. It went to voicemail and she left a message, "Hey, it's Kate. I'll be needing a place to hide out for a few weeks. I'm leaving Springfield, within the hour, going to your house. Will explain everything when I see you." She ended the call and wiped the tears from her cheeks.

She removed her wedding band and engagement ring, kissing each one and placed them, in her jewelry box, laying the letter on top of them. She felt the tether of Camden's love snap away, freeing her to try to save them all.

She snagged her phone from the charger and found the number. It rang four times before he answered. "Leo Burnham, Kate Fletcher." Her voice dropped.

"I'm sorry about the house fire, Kate. Hope you're alright What can I do for you?" The detective offered.

"I've received threatening notes. Not mailed, but in the mailbox. They'll try to kill Cam again. I have to do something to make this roller coaster stop. What're my options?"

"I think protective custody might be the answer. Why don't you pack a few things and meet me here at the office." He paused for a moment. "It'd be handy to get Camden and Ruth outta the way too. I can take care of them, as soon as we get you tucked away."

"Okay, I'll be in later today. Thank you for your help." She felt nauseous. A chill ran down her spine.

"It's my job." Leo Burnham responded.

Chapter Twenty-two
Taken

"Ruth, you don't have a *clue* where she is?" Cam's deep voice boomed in the kitchen.

"Kansas City's all I know. She didn't leave us anything, but this note and Dixie. She said to call her cell."

"I've done that. She doesn't answer." Camden raked his hand over his hair and brushed the recently stitched wound on the back of his head. "Ouch!'

"Give her time. She needs a chance to work through all this. The fire at the house put her over the top. She blames herself for what's happened."

"It's not her fault, it's mine for being so damned provocative. The wedding's in a few weeks. What do we do about that?" He exhaled loudly.

"I think the best idea is to cancel. You send emails. I'll make phone calls."

Cam huffed. "I can't believe she'd walk out on me."

"She didn't, dear. She ran. It has nothing to do with you, it's about the circumstances. Living in a large city, Kate rarely confronted anti-Semitism. She and Reggie worked and played with people, who were above it all or in a similar situation. She had no delusions about coming back here. She knew she'd hit rough spots."

"Was Reggie's death investigated as a hate crime?" Cam scratched his forearm and frowned.

"There was talk about it, but the police thought it could be accidental, the vehicle jumped the curb. It took out the stop sign, before hitting Reggie." Ruth pondered the memory for a moment. "Has Kate told you what Reggie involved himself with, at the University?" Ruth asked.

"She never talks much about him— to me anyway." Cam answered.

"There was an incident on campus, at UMKC." Ruth leaned forward, warming to the tale. "Two Ultra-Orthodox Jewish boys were attacked, beaten, and spray painted with swastikas. Reggie taught both of them and put himself in the middle of the fray. When the administration tried to keep the lid on the attack, Reggie went public. He brought a lot of trouble on himself, but it forced the school to acknowledge the problem and find the ring leader." She paused, in deep thought, before mumbling, "Hmm…I hadn't thought of that in years."

"What?" Cam's tension mounted.

Ruth's finger wagged his direction. "Larry Martin, the young man who works for you?"

"What about him?" Cam frowned.

"It was his brother who was behind the attack. Billy was kicked out of school. He was sent up for the attack on the Jewish boys. If I remember correctly, he should be through his prison term soon."

Cam leaned back in his chair. "It's starting to make sense. Larry mentioned it, the night of the fire. Said he was being released from prison. That he would seek revenge."

Ruth continued, "Reggie couldn't find a local reporter willing to take on the University, so he made a few calls. He found the sister of a school chum in the editor's office of the *Chicago Tribune* who was more than thrilled for the opportunity."

"So, it could've been neo-Nazis taking Reggie out." He slowly rubbed his knuckle across his chin. "Unless somebody in admin was hooked in with them… Nah, that doesn't add up."

"The only item I recall from the accident report was that he was killed by an older model white truck. I forget the make. They said they could tell by the tire imprints what type of vehicle…drove over him. Then, of course, there was paint left behind on the sign and…flecks on Reggie's body." Tears slid down Ruth's cheeks. She dabbed her face with a hankie and tucked it into her sleeve. "Camden, the world's such a cruel place."

Her voice brought him out of his reverie. He replied, "Yeah, but the tide's about to turn."

Ruth unfolded a piece of paper and smoothed it flat on the table. "Sometimes we come in with mail and toss it on the counter, in the mudroom, before sorting. Katrina must have missed this one, but I'm guessing it wasn't the only warning sent."

Cam reached across the table and picked up the smudged page. Patchwork from magazines formed the words; *You leave, Jew, we won't kill him.*

"Well, they've tried." He wadded the paper and stuffed it in his pocket. "Hasn't work out for 'em, so far."

***

Kate stopped at a traffic light, on Glenstone Avenue. An older model white pick-up truck had followed her since she'd entered Springfield city limits. She looked back again and said, "A girl could get paranoid followed so close, boys."

The light changed. She hung back, to be the last car to go through. The truck ran through the red light, as it passed her. She peeked at the driver, who wore a straw cowboy hat. No one in the truck looked her way. She slowed down, cruised behind, allowing distance to build between them. She exhaled with relief when they were out of sight. *Finally, I've lost them.*

She reached for her quart stainless steel water bottle, for a drink, her fingers feeling for the handle on top, while she watched the street ahead.

Traffic surrounded her, waiting at the longest traffic light in town. Just a few blocks from Leo Burham's office.

Suddenly the truck pulled up beside her. She caught a glance of a passenger, from the truck, his face hidden beneath a straw cowboy hat, pulled low, sidled between vehicles.

The light turned green, with six cars ahead of her.

She put the car in park. Unlatched her seat belt.

Dashboard monitors pinged. She opened her door.

He slammed her door shut, as the back window shattered from the impact of the hammer he carried. He was inside her Camry before she could see hime. He grabbed her braid, snatching her head back.

Cold metal pressed against the warm softness of her neck.

His icy voice demanded, "Drive! Follow the truck. Try anything, I'll kill you now."

She steered into position, behind the truck, and wondered if anyone around her saw what happened and called the police.

My God! What have I done?

Two Days Later

"Hey, Coop." Cam answered on the second ring.

"Bro, we need to talk. Sit down." Cooper was out of breath.

"What?" Cam sat.

"The clear fingerprint the cops found in the motel room belonged to Deputy Skeet Keller."

Camden growled, "What're they doin' about it?"

Cooper sighed. "They've known for a while, but looked for DNA to strengthen their case. Anyhow, they went to arrest him, but somebody must have tipped him off. He scarpered."

"What else? I know you." Cam rose, starting upstairs.

Cooper proceeded, "Pop went out, with Zelda, for a walk this morning. He didn't come back. Momma called me. Randy and I found Zelda tied to a tree up in the pasture. No sign of Pop."

Cam demanded, "You think Keller has him?"

"Yep." Cooper responded, dragging his hand through his longish blond hair.

"Pop shared something with me not long ago, about Skeet. I think you're right. I'll be on my way as soon as I can. Is there a team searching for him?" Cam's brain fog cleared. He snatched a backpack and started packing.

"Yep, forty-two men showed up, a bunch of folks are taking off work to come help, before it gets dark."

"I'll be there shortly. Coop, put the best trackers out front. Don't let the ground get churned up with footprints."

"I have. Momma's a hot mess." There was a catch in Cooper's voice. He rubbed his forehead and hoped the migraine headache would ease.

"Figures. Be there in a couple of hours." Cam pondered his brother's call, for a moment, before dialing Kate's cell. It rolled over to voicemail. He kept moving.

"Katrina, this is your husband. Please, call me. Have to go to Texas. Don't know how long I'll be but…" He sighed. "I love you more than life, woman." He listened to the silence. "Please, honey, I need you with me. We can whip this devil together."

His hands shook, as he pocketed his phone, and went downstairs.

He found Ruth in the sewing room. "I'll be back. I have to see about Harry. Coop called; Pop's disappeared."

"What?" She left her chair. Fabric tumbled from her lap to the floor.

"Ruth, whatever happens…please tell Kate I love her." He felt a sob rise in his chest, but choked it back.

Ruth shrieked, "Camden, what's going on?"

"More of the same, different day. Somebody's snatched Harry. Found Zelda tied to a tree. Coop's got a crew tracking him. He needs me. I have to go, Ruth. Call Leroy and Evangeline to stay, until I get back, or I can call and ask for a deputy." He turned to the door.

"Amanda's here, don't worry about me. You get to your mother. I can try to get a flight into Austin."

"Ruth, stay put…in case Kate calls or comes home." Cam demanded.

"Of course! As you wish. Let me know when you find Harry." Ruth lowered herself into her sewing chair.

"Yes, ma'am." He left the house, climbed into his new black Dodge Ram truck and pulled away, thinking, *I wonder if I'll ever see this place again.*

He felt bereft of hope.

As the plane taxied to a stop, Cam found Cooper waiting with the Jeep. He bailed out, snatching his duffle bag off the co-pilot's seat. He regarded the cheerful bright yellow Wrangler among the fallow grays of late winter. *Like a canary in the midst of sparrows.* A pang of grief struck him for his wife.

Coop met him with a hug and slapped his back.

"We'll go to the house first. You need to see Momma. Miz Preston, the neighbor's, with her. Then we'll come back for the plane. I want to get an aerial prospective before dark."

Cam opened the back door of the Jeep and demanded, "Let's do it now. Momma can wait, Coop— night won't." He tossed his duffle in the back and returned to the plane.

Cooper climbed in the Jeep, backed out of the way, and parked in a grove of scrub oak. He trotted to the plane and climbed into the co-pilot's seat.

Cooper updated Cam, "State's got their choppers out, but I want a quick look to see what's amiss." He pulled on his sunglasses. "Fifty thousand acres is a lot to cover and the spotters aren't familiar with much of it."

"Have you been up with 'em?" Cam steadily increased power to the engine and taxied out the pasture runway.

"I did for a little while. Then I decided I was more use on the ground checking the line shacks. I think I covered everything I could with the Jeep. What's left we'll need the horses to get to. If I had to guess, I'd say that's where he's holed up, but who knows?" Cooper rubbed his face with both hands. "Where's Kate?"

"Away, at the moment. Had some things to take care of in Kansas City." Cam's heart was near bursting.

"Well…is she on her way down?" Cooper needled his brother, while unrolling the sleeves of his flannel shirt.

Cam turned his scowl on his brother. "Don't reckon so."

Coop glanced away, nodding.

The men rode in silence for ten minutes. Cam banked the small craft and headed over rugged terrain toward outlying shacks. Cooper scanned the area, looking for any signs of recent activity. After twenty minutes of studying trenches, ditches, and berms, he yelled, "Let's make another pass! I think I saw tracks back there. Could just be kids four-wheeling, but let's be sure."

Cam banked the plane and circled again, gliding over treetops.

"There," Cooper pointed off to the east.

"I see it." Cam circled a third time. "Not torn up, so it's not kids. Definitely two sets of tracks. Get on the horn and let them know we're up here. He came in and left by the same route. We'll follow as long as we can."

Cooper called in to the base operation, set up at the ranch, in the parlor. "Yeah, this is Coop. My brother and I are down in the southeastern quadrant. We found four-wheel tracks, two sets. We'll follow, in the air. If you can get somebody to meet us on the highway mile marker 27, they can take it from there." He waited. "That's correct. Yes, sir. I will." He disconnected.

"What?" Cam asked.

"May take forty-five minutes for them to get around here by vehicle. We have enough gas to wait on 'em?"

"Topped off in Waco. We're good for a while." Cam replied.

"When they get here, let's go back for the Jeep. I want to be ready to follow them." Cooper continued studying the ground.

"Any ideas where Skeet would hole up?" Cam asked.

"A few, let's see where these tracks lead." Coop said.

Cam circled back and picked up the tire marks, flying as low as he dared. "There's a cliff about a quarter mile ahead." Cam stole a look at his brother.

"Don't even think that, bro." Cooper strained to see toward the cliff.

The tracks ended at the edge. A dark green Jeep Grand Cherokee had driven straight off the cliff, landing in a ravine at least 30 feet deep.

Cooper slammed himself back in the seat, grabbed his head. "Please, God, no!"

Cam circled and dropped lower for a look. "Can't get close enough to see inside. Call the boys at the ranch and tell them we found the vehicle. That *is* Skeet's, isn't it?"

"It is. Damn!" Cooper waited for someone to pick up the call. The sergeant answered. "Coop again. We found Skeet's SUV at the bottom of a cliff. Can't see if anyone's inside." He listened for a moment. "Your fellows can probably backtrack from the road."

"I'm gonna set the plane down in the highway. You fly back for the Jeep. I think I know where he is, if he got outta that." Cam headed toward the blacktop. "I'll hike in the backway."

The small plane touched down, on the two laned road, smoothly.

"What're you thinking?" Cooper asked.

"Remember the line shack on the far southeastern corner? The one we camped in on our deer hunting forays when we first moved out here."

"Yeah!" Cooper raised his fist. "That's less than a mile from the cliff. Makes sense. He wouldn't be able to walk Pop any great distance without his dog."

They coasted to a stop.

"If they aren't there, I'll call you to pick me up. There're two other spots, nearby, we can check." Camden loosened his seat belt. "I'm gonna try to work a swap. There's no reason for him to push Pop off that cliff. He needs leverage, so we'll play. If I can get in, give me a little time."

"What's the password?" Coop asked the same question for forty years whenever they'd part.

"*You're the man.* If Pop doesn't come out the door, stay outta sight. I'll call you as soon as I can."

Camden turned away and walked the hundred yards, through thicket. Once clear, he worked up to a decent jog. He heard the plane fly overhead.

Within a mile, he crossed two sets of footprints on the way to the line shack. He picked up the pace. He stopped short of the clearing and took a deep breath, before he ambled toward the door.

"Stop right there, Fletcher!" Skeet Keller yelled from inside.

Cam held up both hands, palms out. "Alright, it's your show. No weapons. Swap us out. I'm the one you want."

Laughter spilled through cracks, in the decaying tarpaper shack. Skeet's annoying tone demanded, "What makes you think that, buddy?"

Cam's skin crawled at the sound of Skeet's voice. "You got a broken-down old man in there. Harry's no help to you now. He'll slow you down. I can give you what you want *and* get you outta here."

"A'ight, come on in and we'll talk." Skeet shouted.

Cam kept his arms high as he carefully mounted the rotted steps, to a shallow porch of weak and broken boards.

He slowly turned the rusty door knob and pushed the warped oak door inward. The entry opened to a single rough room. Harry sat at Cam's right, a gash in his forehead. Cam stepped in, closing the door.

Skeet propped in a rocking chair, on the left, near the brick fireplace, his back to the corner of the room. A thirty-thirty rifle lay across the chair arms. "Welcome, Camden. Grab a seat and set a spell."

Cam glanced around the room and went for a straight back chair behind Harry. He moved the chair within a few feet of the door.

"Before you sit, how 'bout emptying your pockets? You can drop it over here in front of me." Skeet indicated the spot with the barrel of the rifle, his finger resting on the trigger.

Cam obeyed. His cell phone, keys, and wallet lay in a pile. He returned to the chair.

Harry spoke. "Camden, did they find Zelda?"

"Yes, sir. Coop and Randy did. She's back at the house. She's fine." Cam answered.

Harry nodded and sighed with relief. "Thank you, Skeet, for not killing her."

"No need to waste a good dog." Skeet scratched his head. "Me and Harry been sittin' here talking about the good ol' days. You know how it is, when you reminisce." He scrubbed his nose with his fist and drawled, "Life seemed simpler when we were kids. Took a downhill slide for me, when Harry married your momma—after he threw mine over." He yawned and scratched his head again. "I decided there and then *you'd* pay for that sin."

Cam nodded and leaned forward, elbows on his knees. "Cut to the chase, Skeet. What do you want? This place will be swarming with Texas' finest in a few minutes."

Skeet's face screwed up in a scowl. "Camden, you're always in a hurry. Take time to enjoy a moment, will ya?"

"Okay." Cam shot a side glance at Harry.

"I'm gonna need money." Skeet grinned and wiped his sleeve across this mouth.

"Figured. How much?" Camden studied Skeet. *He's sweating, it's maybe 45 degrees in here. What's up?*

"A million dollars seems like a nice round number." Skeet answered.

Cam grinned; his drawl deepened. "I hope you brought supplies. I can't get that kind of cash in less than eight, maybe ten days. Have to liquidate stock, sell some land."

"It ain't funny. Wipe that smile off your face. Make me an offer. But, if I don't like it, I'll shoot Harry." Skeet's face twisted in anger, making him more repulsive.

"I can't help that. The most we can put together in a crunch is maybe twenty thousand. I'd have to call the bank and see how long it'll take to get it...unless you'll take a check." Cam soberly met Skeet's gaze.

"Coop's got money too." Skeet leaned forward in the chair.

"Not his accountant, Skeet. I can't speak for my brother. I can get what I have and fly you outta here. That's my best offer."

"Call him. If you're in here, he's out there. See what it's worth to him."

"He's nowhere nearby. I walked in the backway. I don't want him caught in the crossfire, when the state police show up."

"You're awful brave, Camden. Come sashaying in here like your leavin' in less than a body-bag. My boys gave you a scare when that fine place you built, burned down around your ears!"

"Wondered if you were behind that." Cam answered.

"I'm the *mastermind* of the whole operation. Had Jackie working for me, running drugs, after you put her through nursing school. Miss her. She was a decent piece, if I may say so. That little boy you thought was yours? *He was mine!* You laid a Keller to rest in the hallowed ground of the Kendal family cemetery." He threw back his head and laughed.

"Did you get me all the way down here to review the failures of *my* life or do you wanna barter?" Cam mentally shook off the creepiness of the atmosphere.

"I *want* you to know who caused those failures. I'm your nemesis. It'd take all the fun out of it, if I just got the money and flew to Guatemala, without rubbing your face in the dirt. I've dreamed of this moment, having you and Harry together so you could both know exactly who did it to you. You can comfort each other in hell."

Cam nodded. "Mmm. Well, let me know when you're ready to barter." He leaned back in the chair and crossed his arms. His right hand touched the hilt of a thin-bladed filet knife sewn into its scabbard on the chest of his jacket. He closed his eyes.

A cell phone rang.

Skeet leaned over the pile on the floor and snagged the phone. He read the screen and giggled. "It's the current Mrs. Fletcher. Shall I tell her you're unavailable?" He wiped his hand across his mouth again. "Too bad she's a Jew, she's a pretty woman. Had to talk my men outta takin' her for a little sport."

Cam felt his face burn.

Harry mumbled under his breath. "It's just a dig, son."

Cam swallowed his anger, rolled his shoulders back and straightened.

Skeet's tone changed to a whine, "May need her later. Although...you could tell her to get to that plane of yours and she could ride down south with us. Would she like that? A little south-of-the-border vacation to ease the stress of nearly bein' roasted alive?" He laughed again, noise bubbling out of his throat. Skeet had a coughing fit, spitting the results on the floor.

"Don't know if you could handle her, she's a tad difficult." Cam yawned, covering his mouth with his hand.

"Hate to bore you, Camden." Skeet's head dropped, as he studied Cam from underneath bushy red eyebrows, with the look of a mad dog.

Cam answered, "Then get on with your demands and I'll call the banker." He glanced at his watch. "They close in thirty minutes."

Skeet looked confused for a moment, then burst into laughter again. "You can get the president of the bank outta bed, if that's what I want you to do. If he won't get up, I'll shoot you both. Got nothing to lose at this point."

The whisper of clandestine movement in the woods, surrounding the shack, blew in through the cracks. Cam squinted toward the door and back at Skeet.

"I think we got company." Skeet stood, draped the rifle over his arm. He stayed to the side of one of the shack's two windows and peeked out. "Yep, there's lawmen here now. Think they're hot stuff, those state fellas do. I could've kept Jackie under wraps, but some yellow-bellied coward called the *big* law in." He inched toward the rocker, to pull it closer to the window.

Harry sighed and stretched his back. "Skeet, don't play this wrong. They'll kill you. Let Camden talk to them and take us outta here."

"Do I look crazy, old man?" Skeet's voice became manic. "You're my ticket out that door. With Camden at my back, they ain't gonna take the chance of hittin' either one of you."

A bullhorn sounded. "Hullo the house! We have you surrounded!" Echoes reverberated through the valley below them.

Skeet found it amusing. He yelled, "Big deal! Shoot the place up for all I care!" He snickered and muttered, "hot stuff."

"You're not ready to die, Skeet." Harry's voice coaxed the madman.

"How do you know that?" Skeet frowned.

"Too much life left, son. Dying's for old men. Let Camden take us outta here. We'll get you south of the border safely. They'll let *us* go."

Silence settled in the shack. A limb cracked at the edge of the woods, when a trooper stepped on it.

Skeet flinched, then shook his head to clear the fog.

They sat in silence, as darkness fell.

A full moon rose. Soft light oozed through the dirt-clouded windows of the cabin.

Occasional stirrings in the woods came to their ears.

A barn owl hooted nearby; his wings flapping violently when spooked from his perch.

Cam checked his watch again. "'Bout time for your medicine, Pop. Skeet, what d'ya say we call Coop for Pop's meds and some sandwiches?"

His lopsided grin spilled drool down one side of his face. "Damn practical of you, Cam." He tossed Cam's cell phone to him.

Cam scrolled to Cooper's number. His brother answered on the first ring. "Yeah?"

"How about you bring us supplies? Looks like we'll be here for a while. We need sandwiches, water, and Pop's medicine. Pull up by the porch and toot the horn twice. I'll come out to fetch it from you. Got that?"

"Sure, anything else?"

"You're the man." Cam ended the connection.

Cooper pulled onto the highway, cell phone at his ear. "Momma, get Pop's medicine, water and sandwiches together, please ma'am. Cam's inside, with Pop and Skeet. He's got a plan. I'll be there in a few minutes."

Elaine scurried around the kitchen, shaken. Mary Peston helped her make sandwiches and pack the picnic hamper.

Jane, who'd brought the boys to Cooper, said, "I'll put in a small jar of hot pickled peppers. Maybe Cam can figure a way to use that fiery juice. What about flatware?" Jane brushed back her stylishly cut blond hair, with her manicured fingertips.

"Pack just like you would for us, nothin' outta the ordinary. You don't want Skeet alarmed or suspicious, dear." Elaine dabbed her fingers on the tea towel draped over her shoulder. "You might put a flashlight in, at the side, though."

"Good idea." Jane straightened and stretched her back. Three hours sitting in the hardback kitchen chairs made her thin frame ache. "I feel like a lot of this falls on me. If I hadn't told Jackie about Kate ,maybe none of this would've landed in your lap."

"It didn't make a difference to Jackie. They'd have killed her just as dead, for stealing from them. If Cam had given her the money she demanded, it may have kept the wolf from the door for a little while. But you can't get mixed up with a nest of vipers and not expect to be bitten." Elaine traded a glance with Mary.

Jane affected her little girl whine, "I was no part of what she was involved in. I need to say that to you, not because I think you're holding anything against me. I just need to be sure you know. I'd never put my *family* at risk, by getting mixed up with illegal activity." Her blue eyes brimmed with tears.

Elaine paused in her chore and met Jane's eyes. "I never, for a moment, thought you would be. We can't determine the path our friends, even our children, will take. We try to love them through their worst times. That's all I've ever considered your connection with Jackie. You've done your best by her. You have to let it go." *Why does this have to be about you?*

Jane nodded and wiped her cheeks free of tears. "Yes, ma'am, thank you for understanding. I don't know how I'll explain this to Kate."

"You won't have to. Kate doesn't blame you for Jackie's decisions." Elaine shook her head.

"You don't think?" Jane asked, sniffing and blinking away the waterworks.

"I'm pretty sure I know that her heart's merciful." Elaine added.

The backdoor flew open, as Cooper tromped in. A blast of cold air rounded the corner with him. He spoke to Jane, "Boys here?"

She nodded.

"You don't have to hang around." He looked at the hamper, "Is it ready?"

Mary Preston closed the lid to the hamper. "Right here. Please, let one of the Rangers get this to the door, Coop."

"Don't worry about a thing. It's under control. My brother has a plan." Cooper grinned.

***

An hour ticked by slowly, in the chilled cabin. Darkness deepened, as the grim silence of their captivity deepened. Cam fidgeted, in the hard chair, stood and stretched; his ears attuned for the Jeep's engine.

Outside lawmen shifted positions. A vehicle left for supplies.

Cam envisioned the snipers, hours on end, eyes pressed to their scopes, awaiting an opportune moment to take out the target. Numb to the cold ground and dormancy, barely blinking, they'd stay steady, until the end of the standoff. *Could never have that job.*

"Coop should be here in a few minutes. How we doing this, Skeet? He can't come in here." Cam sat after a moment.

"He can if I say he can!" Skeet snapped. He cringed when a noise from outside startled him.

"What are you going to do with another one of us in here? Sure, you may get one shot off, but most likely not." Cam taunted.

"Oh, yeah, I forget I'm dealing with elite Navy pilots! What was I thinkin'?" He slapped himself on the forehead. "You boys are *bad,* aren't cha? Lady, you ain't seen *bad* til you deal with the cartels. Those fellas are flat-out wicked."

"Mmm, well, what's the plan?" Cam was unimpressed.

"I'm thinkin', okay? I'll know by the time he gets here." He sat straight in the chair and tried not to doze. After a few minutes, his head dropped to his chest.

Minutes crept past. Cam whistled a low tune between his teeth.

Harry turned toward him, searching his memory for the movie theme song from *The Magnificent Seven.*

Branches crushing beneath the weight of the Jeep, brought Skeet bolting upright.

Cooper blew the horn.

Skeet gave orders, "Alright, Camden, holler to them we're comin' out."

Cam rose, stepped to the door, feeling the rifle leveled at his back. He opened the door a crack and yelled. "We're coming out." He pushed the door closed.

"Hold your fire!" The bullhorn blared, echoing down the valley.

"Here's how we'll do it," Skeet leaned forward. "Harry's in front of me. You walk behind. Keep your hands on my shoulders. Stay close enough they won't be tempted to shoot. If you peel off, I'll kill Harry." He produced a .45 automatic from under his jacket and laid the rifle across the chair arms.

"We can do that." Cam glanced at Harry. "You up to it, Pop?"

Harry stood. "Let's go." He waited for Skeet to grab the arm of his jacket and turn him to the door. In the darkness, Harry failed to make out their forms. Skeet pressed the pistol to Harry's temple.

Cam opened the door wide. He stepped behind Skeet. They moved through, one slow, shuffling step at a time.

Cooper waited with the hamper just ahead of them, ten feet away.

Harry cleared the door frame.

Skeet turned slightly, to get through the narrow doorway, with his arm bent, holding the pistol.

Harry's body blocked the Ranger's fire.

Cam turned with Skeet. Quick as lightning, his right hand slid the blade from the sheath sewn into the jacket. His left hand shifted, from Skeet's shoulder to his chin, as Harry pitched his weight forward. The razor-sharp edge of the filet knife slid effortlessly across Skeet's throat, as a rifle's report blasted nearby. Cam drew back with all his strength, spinning Skeet toward the interior, of the shack, aided by the power of the sniper's bullet.

Skeet's reflex snapped the trigger of the .45.

The pistol shot exploded into the doorjamb.

Wood chips dispersed like shrapnel.

Cam hauled Skeet all the way down with him, back into the cabin.

The surrounding thicket roared, with the racket of thirty-eight policemen dashing toward them. Harry lay still ,until grasped by strong hands.

"You all right, Mr. Kendal?" A Texas Ranger dropped beside Harry's prostrate form.

"Think so, felt the impact of a few splinters. Where's my son?" Harry pushed himself up.

"Inside. Let's get you up and I'll check on him." The Ranger gently lifted Harry to his knees, then helped him to stand.

Cooper grasped Harry's arm. "C'mon, Pop. Two steps down. Let's get you outta here."

"Where's Camden?" Harry demanded.

Cooper glanced up. "Behind you. He just got off the floor. He's alright. It's over. Let me get you home."

"See to your brother first." Harry barked, taking hold of his walking stick, that someone placed in his hand.

Cooper held onto Harry's arm. "Mama'll want to get you to the hospital. Make sure you're okay...."

"Cooper! See to Camden." Harry snapped, planting his feet.

"Yes, sir." Coop opened the passenger door. "Get in the Jeep and I'll see about him." He glanced back toward the entry, packed with officers, as he held Harry's door open.

Cam stood, exhaled, bent forward, then straightened. He looked for a clean spot on his jacket to wipe his face. There wasn't one. He shrugged out of it and wiped Skeet's blood off his face onto the sleeve of his chambray shirt.

"You Camden Fletcher?" A ranger asked.

"Yes, sir." He picked up the filet knife and dropped it in an evidence bag the trooper held open.

"That was a piece of work. We could've gotten a better shot once you cleared the door."

Cam said, "Or not. I couldn't take the chance. He was on somethin', shaky hands, giggling like a schoolgirl. His reaction time was unpredictable." He inhaled. "If it had been your dad, with a gun to his head, what would you do?"

Cam's eyes fell on the bloody mess that had been Skeet Keller, most of his face blown off. He turned away.

The ranger dropped his gaze. "Same thing, I reckon. I'm gonna need a statement from you."

"Have I got time to clean up?" He checked his clothes, covered in blood.

"Want to get it fresh. How about you ride to the house with me?" The ranger offered.

"I can do that. Let me talk to Cooper a minute." Cam stooped to retrieve his keys, phone, and wallet. "Reckon you don't need these. I do."

Cam pushed his way through the crowd, on the porch, to his brother.

185

"Hey, I was comin' to find you. Pop wants to know you're okay." They picked their way through the crowd of law enforcement officers to the Jeep.

Cam rolled his sleeves up and leaned in the open window while Cooper climbed in the driver's seat. "Hey, old man, you did well in there. You feel alright?"

"I haven't had that much excitement for a while. Long for the old days when I could look danger in the eye. We're gonna see about your mother. Come on when you can." Harry's deep voice sent a sense of calm over both of his sons.

"I'm riding up with a ranger. Be there directly." Cam patted the door and stepped away as Cooper cranked the Jeep and rolled out.

The ranger stood beside him and said, "We'll have to interview Harry."

"Momma needs to tend to him first. He's not likely to forget a moment of this debacle." Cam sighed. "He can still quote, verbatim, orders for sorties he flew over Nam." He stretched. "Well, let's follow them and get this over with."

Cam stood in his mother's kitchen freshly showered. His statement was on its way, with the ranger. The parlor was almost free of police equipment and men. He saw Jane, perched on a hardback chair, at the table stirring her coffee.

"You okay?" Cam asked.

She looked up, offered her best church lady smile. "I suppose."

"I'm takin' off. Give Momma a hug when she gets back. Tell her I had to go."

"Want me to drive you up to the airstrip?" Jane offered.

"Nah, I'd rather walk." He watched the shadow pass over her face.

"Jane, it's okay. What I mean is…adrenaline rush…I need physical activity, to get my mind clear. Sitting in the line-shack for four and a half hours wore my nerves thin." He waited for her reply.

Jane nodded, dropping her gaze.

"We alright?" He tilted his head watching her lowered face.

She glanced up. "We're okay, Cam. Give Kate my best, please."

"I'll do it." He took a few steps to the hallway, grabbed his duffle bag off the stairs and left.

He made the plane, winded. He tossed the bag in the co-pilot's seat and climbed in. As the engine warmed, he closed his eyes and remembered that last look at Skeet.

His cell phone rang. "Fletcher."

"Camden Fletcher?" A woman's crisp British accent queried.

"Yes."

"This is Jamie Manville. I'm a friend of Kate's." The voice said.

"You have my undivided attention." He straightened.

"She was supposed to have arrived at my home four days ago. She hasn't, nor has she phoned. Have you any idea where she may be?" The FBI agent asked.

"No ma'am. Have you called her cell?" Cam closed his eyes, fighting tears.

"Repeatedly, there's no answer. I'm deeply concerned. It's taken me a while to locate you. I've only just spoken to Ruth. Kate was coming here in protective custody. We need to find her. I've put in a call to the locals for an APB on her car."

"I'm on my way in from Texas. It'll be a few hours before I'm back at the Bailiwick. Let Ruth know if you hear anything, Miss Manville. I'll check in when I land." Cam disconnected.

He pondered the call for a moment, then dialed Leo Burnham. His call rolled to voicemail. "Leo, Cam Fletcher. My wife's missing. She's supposed to be in Kansas City, but she isn't. It's midnight. I'll be in the air for a while, getting in from Texas. Call Ruth for details." He rang off.

Chapter Twenty-three
Finding Katrina

At 3:35 am Cam killed the headlights before turning into the driveway, at the Bailiwick. He parked near the house and decided to drop his seat back and close his eyes, for a few minutes. The rain made a comforting sound on the hood.

Dogs barked and danced around his truck at 6:40. He climbed out and made his way, through the puddles, to the back porch, where Ruth held the door open. Dogs followed.

His mother-in-law asked, "Did Jamie Manville get hold of you?"

Ruth closed the door and turned to Camden. He studied the floor for a moment, before responding, "Yes, ma'am. She's been out of town and was surprised to not find Katrina where she should have been. She's notified the locals here, and every little burg in between, to put out an APB on Kate's car. No news yet, I talked to her 6 and a half hours ago."

The house phone rang.

"Hello?" Ruth's voice faltered.

Cam caught her movement peripherally, glancing up.

Silence clenched the room.

Ruth paled, her shaking hand moved from the phone to cover her mouth; her face ashen. "Camden," her voice broke. "Leroy found Kate in the ditch—at the end of the driveway."

"Get a blanket and the car! I'll be there." He dashed to the foyer, threw the front door open, and leapt off the porch. He made the quarter mile dash in seconds.

"Hold on, baby girl," Leroy's wailing voice reached Cam, before he stopped running.

Cam found the older man perched on the side of the ditch, holding Kate in his arms, rocking. His face was against Kate's alabaster cheek, her mouth slack.

"Camden, they've left her near dead! My gawd! Sacked her naked body up in a trash bag. Get here and help me get this

188

damn thing off her." Leroy attempted to stand, then sank to his knees.

Cam slid down the bank, landing in front of them. He realized there was enough water in the ditch to drown his wife. "Yes, sir, I've got her. You shuck the bag as I lift her." He gently placed his hands on Kate's ribcage, levering her arms over his and lifted her torso onto his shoulder.

Leroy snatched off the filthy trash bag, plucking off bits that stuck to her skin.

Cam straightened, shifting his wife into his arms, her head on his shoulder.

Ruth jumped out of her parked car, with a quilt in hand, screaming. "No! No! No!" She skidded on the berm, but kept her feet.

Cam looked up, his face pale, eyes tearing, and shouted, "C'mon, Ruth, need the blanket!" He lifted Kate's legs, at her knees and allowed her mother to wrap her, in the quilt she'd grabbed off her bed. Cam moved toward the car, carefully scaling the side of the rain slick ditch, with Leroy behind him, his hands on Cam's lower back, pushing with all his might.

They made the roadbed and Leroy snatched open the back passenger side door. He helped Cam climb onto the seat with his burden.

Leroy reached out to pull Ruth up the embankment and commanded, "Ruth Ann, get in the back seat. I'll drive." He got her door closed and jumped into the driver's seat.

Turf flew, when he put the car in gear and gunned the engine, spinning onto the highway in the opposite direction.

Cam told Ruth, "Call the Sherriff's Department and have them meet us on the intersection to 65. We aren't slowing down. We need an escort." He tucked Kate's blue hands under his armpits in his shirt.

Leroy called out, "Evie's at Cox South this week. It's closest!" He floored the gas pedal and had the Cadillac up to 90 miles per hour, before the first curve slowed the big car slightly.

Ruth made the call. She fussed over Kate's bluish feet, rubbing each one frantically. Once off the phone, she unbuttoned her blouse and leaned over her daughter to warm her near frozen toes, trying to fight off frostbite.

Two deputy's cars waited, with lights and sirens blaring. They covered the Cadillac, front and back until they reached the Emergency Room at Cox South, then parked in an adjacent lot and jogged to the entrance.

Camden was out of the backseat, with Kate in his arms, wrapped securely in the quilt.

A gurney met them. He reluctantly laid his wife on the stretcher. He followed closely, on the heels of the orderly who pushed buttons and dashed through, to the nurses waiting for their arrival.

***

"I'm staying here." Cam declared.

The nurse begged, "Sir, this room is tiny. You make it smaller. Please step out. We'll let you know when you can come back. The doctor needs to examine her."

"You can do that in my presence." His arms crossed; his glare drew tears from the young woman.

"Please, sir, I'll have to call security…" the nurse pleaded through sobs.

The curtain opened and a familiar face appeared. "Camden, what are you doing here?" A delightful Jamaican accent flowed from a dark-skinned beauty.

"Dr. Martin! I refuse to leave my wife." Relief swept over him. "She's been missing for days. We just found her. She's not coherent…"

She held up her hand, as she turned from the sink. "Enough." She slipped into examination gloves, then peeled back the sheet. "Katrina Fletcher?" Her dark fingers gently pinched the dry pale skin of Kate's arm.

"Mmm?" Kate moaned.

"Start an IV, Jan. Katrina, can you tell me what day it is?" She gently probed her upper torso, found a sensitive spot, among obvious burns.

"Nooooo!" Kate cried, teeth clenched; her hands flew up, trying to protect herself. She shivered from cold and fear.

Dr. Martin lifted the other side of the sheet. "The cut over her right eye is nasty and may need stitches. Jan, clean it up and put a butterfly bandage on it for now. There's a lot of bruising, numerous small burns. Let's get x-rays, be sure there're no broken ribs or bones." She listened to Kate's chest and lungs. "We need confirmation on pneumonia. Sounds like there's fluid in her left lung. I need to look in your mouth, sweetie."

Kate opened as wide as she was able. The light revealed a gash inside her left cheek.

Dr. Martin said, "There'll be a few loose teeth, on that side. She's been viciously beaten, Camden. How long was she gone?"

"This is the fifth day." He ran a hand over his beard and fumed. *Why didn't I report her missing earlier?*

"I'll need a rape kit, Jan." Dr. Martin turned to Cam. "Will you trust me, with her, for a few minutes? You can wait outside the curtain. Please?"

He nodded and stepped through, propping on the divided wall. *I thought she'd left me. I didn't call Leo because I thought she'd run away from me.* He listened helplessly as Kate cried. Dr. Martin's gentle voice soothed his wife.

Ruth stepped through the door, paperwork in hand. "Is the doctor with her?"

Cam nodded. "Doing a rape kit right now. She has pneumonia." He swiped the tears away and continued, "Ruth, I don't know what to say. You entrusted your daughter to me..." He sighed. "Did the front desk call the police?"

"They're sending someone out, dear. You can't blame yourself. We didn't know. She left the note. We thought she'd be in Kansas City, with friends."

"If I loved her well, I'd have asked for an APB on her car."

"The police would have refused, because wives leave husbands every day." Ruth firmly remarked. She squeezed her son-in-law's arm.

"I could've tried. Can you talk to them, when they get here? I'm not letting her outta my sight." He scanned the entry behind her.

"Of course. I'll take care of the report. Is she talking yet?" Ruth asked.

"No, ma'am. She moans or cries when they touch her. She has loose teeth, a gash inside her cheek, abdominal pain. I saw a lot of burns, looks like cigarette. I think the rape kit's standard. She's badly dehydrated. That's all so far."

"I'm just thankful they didn't kill her." Ruth swiped a tear. "It could've been so much worse."

"Yes, ma'am, for us." Camden peered down at his mother-in-law.

"Yes, for us." Ruth patted his crossed arms again.

Cam heard whispering beyond the curtain. He listened hard. Dr. Martin said, "Get OR ready immediately for an emergency DNC. Jan, pass me an evidence bag."

The nurse answered, "Yes, ma'am. I've never seen anything like that, what is it?"

Cam stepped around the corner silently and saw Dr. Martin removing something from the pad between Kate's legs to the evidence bag. It was partially disintegrated, about six inches long and had been hairy.

Dr. Martin answered, "It looks like a dead young rat. We need to know what it died from ASAP. If it was poisoned, there may be arsenic, or worse, in her system." She caught sight of Camden peripherally and turned. "Out! I'll be there in a minute. Let me clean her up as best I can." She looked frightened.

Cam stepped back and dropped his head.

Dr. Martin ripped her gloves off. She quietly delivered the verdict, "Camden, the creature you saw was stuffed inside Kate's vagina. Any thoughts?"

He shook his head and answered just as quietly, "Only one, and it isn't what *you* wanna hear." His icy green eyes met the doctor's warm brown ones.

"Okay, the surgeon will take over in a few minutes. We remove to OR now."

A nurse and orderly hurried into the cubicle, raising the safety bars and rolling the bed forward, as Dr. Martin and Cam stepped out of the way.

Dr. Martin watched the bed roll away, attendants rushing. "I'll see you tomorrow, with more news." She left him.

The following four hours became a blur, as Kate's family waited for her to come out of surgery into recovery. Camden wore a path, pacing.

Finally, the surgeon appeared. His green scrubs was blood flecked. He stripped off his mask as he approached, his hand extended.

"Mr. Fletcher? I'm Dr. Winter. Just finished with your wife. Sorry, everything took a backseat to keeping her alive when the tox screen came back. They found heroin in her blood and also another opioid, yet to identify. We had to get her rehydrated and stabilized. I hated to do the DNC with her partially aware, but I didn't dare give her anesthesia. We went ahead with a few more tests, to get those out of the way. Because of the heroin, we searched and found injection sights. She have a problem with opioids, that you know?"

Cam glanced at Ruth then answered, "No, sir. My wife gardens organically, is a chef and shudders at the thought of needing acetaminophen, for a headache."

"Then there's a chance the injection sights can become inflamed, with a dirty needle. But, more importantly, the needle may be reused after an addict, and could pass on HIV, Hep C, numerous other problems. We did a scraping of the sight to see if we can pick up anything, but we'll need to check her bloodwork monthly, after this. At least, for a while." He glanced down at his notes, to avoid Cam's searing gaze. "Oh, yeah, we checked her ears, there was a tiny shard of glass in her left ear. Anus review, anywhere else they may have stuffed something deadly. We did a sonogram on her intestines, to see if there were balloons with drugs or poison, all that was clear. I will tell you this, if she hadn't made it in here when she did, she'd have died. The 'insertion' in her vagina was full of bacteria, viruses and several poisons, including arsenic. The DNC will be followed by antibiotics via i.v. for the next week or more. Then by mouth, if possible for two more weeks." He inhaled, then continued, "Dr. Martin will be back with you in the morning. Are you staying over?"

"Absolutely!" Cam barked.

"Let me get an order for a bed in the room, then. I wouldn't leave my wife either. Can't trust anybody else to mind her like you can." He made another note, stood, extended his hand again and said, "I never tell people I'll see them later. Take care and good luck, hope the cops catch the bastards who did this to her." He turned and left for the double doors, his white coat flying about his legs.

The following morning, Camden waited outside Kate's room, while Ruth and a nurse bathed his wife. He paced and argued with himself, because no one else was available. When the door opened for the CNA, Cam hurried back in to his bride.

"Hey, how you doing?" He smiled and tried to focus on her eyes, ignoring the serious burn beside her right eyelid.

"Better," she mumbled. Her voice was hoarse. Her short hair clung to her skull; the beautiful long tresses crudely chopped away. "Cold."

He tugged the blanket up to her chin and asked, "You gonna be able to eat something?"

Kate shook her head, struggling with a deep cough.

"Can you tell me what happened, honey?" He covered her feet, taking note of cigarette burns on her ankles and toes, but not the soles of her feet. Going barefoot paid off.

Her large dark eyes filled with tears. "Why?" Her voice roughened, her upper lip bruised and bulging, her eyes blackened.

"We made a police report. We need to talk to the cops again. How did they get ahold of you?" Cam asked.

She considered his question, swallowed, then whispered, "Block traffic—broke window—open door—gun…." She pointed to her head.

"Do you know where they took you?" He dreaded the answer to the questions, but he'd have to know sooner or later.

She shook her head, a small jerking motion. "Hood," she pointed to her head again. "Blindfold…." Tears spilled down her cheeks as her body shuddered.

Cam grabbed a tissue, gently dabbing her face, cringing at the bruises, burns and cuts. "Big like a warehouse? Did noises echo?"

"Yes—cold." Kate closed her eyes, wanting nothing but sleep.

"Did you recognize voices? How many were there, could you tell?" Cam continued to prod.

"Three." She mumbled. She coughed again, wincing in pain.

"Who?" Ice flooded his veins. He flexed his hands, rolling his shoulders back.

She slowly shook her head, barely moving, as she watched him through slitted eyes.

"Please, Kate, tell me." He begged.

"No. Don't know." The dam of tears spilled over her wrecked face.

His head dropped. *Get the right words, dumbass, without scaring her.*

He looked up and smiled, got a grip on his body language. "Sweetheart, I'm not leavin' you. No matter what's happened, I'm staying *with you*. The police can handle this. Okay? We'll go home to the Bailiwick when you're released. I—am—*not*— leaving you ever again—understand? You'll be lucky to get a shower without me."

More tears spilled down her face. She struggled against the agony every breath seemed to bring. "Put me—in a box. Closed!"

Stunned, he grabbed the water glass and positioned the straw in her mouth for a sip. "Just a sip, baby." His hands trembled.

She lay back with a sigh. "No more, please."

He replaced the glass on the tray table.

Her eyes closed.

"I'll let Leo know what you remember. He's taking over your case since he's already involved." He tried to smile again and rubbed her arm, beneath the blanket.

She flinched. He looked down at the raw flesh on Kate's left arm, inspecting the number tattooed by the bend of her elbow: A30001 with a triangle underneath.

"Why...what's this?" Cam looked confused.

"Warning." She mumbled, pointing toward her head. "This too."

"They cut off your hair as a warning?" Cam asked.

"Death camp...." Kate replied.

He paled, nodded and leaned over her arm to gently kiss the ugly, obscene blue tattoo.. "Just rest now, honey."

A knock at the door woke Camden, from dozing in the chair beside Kate's bed, the fingertips of her left hand clutched in his palm. He opened his eyes as Leo Burnham stepped in. Cam gently released Kate's hand and met him in the foyer of the room.

Cam kept his voice barely above a whisper. "Hey, Leo. She's sleeping right now. They said she needs to rest as much as possible."

"What's the diagnosis?" Burnham asked.

"She was beaten, has a couple of fractured ribs, pneumonia. They patched her up as well as they could. She's badly bruised, but thank god, no breaks, or internal bleeding. She had no water or food for most of the five days and was left blindfolded in a cold building." Cam took in a bushel of air. "She said there were three men's voices. Sounded like a warehouse."

Leo made notes. "How're you working?"

"Mark's holding down the fort. We have feelers out for a buyer. He's ready to pack it in and go back to Texas."

Leo nodded. "Let me know if she says anything else. We found her car abandoned behind a strip club. Windows are broken out. The lab's going over it now; see if there's any prints we can use."

"They put a tat on her arm, A-3-0-0-0-1. I Googled it. Found out the death camp complex, at Auschwitz, kept track of Jewish women with tattoos that carried a letter in front. The last number issued in the A series was A30000. After that, the Nazi's dropped the A. He glanced back at Kate. "Their hair was cut off, first with a knife or shears, then shaved with a razor. Kate called it a warning."

Leo shook his head. "Man! Where will this end? We're checking on the fourth man from the fire. The ATF expressed interest. That opens up the Fed's data banks to us. We're working that angle now."

"Good, let me know when you find him." Cam studied the lawman.

"Heard you had to go to Texas. Your *dad* was kidnapped?" Leo asked.

"Yeah, worked out okay." Cam's eyes turned to his wife. "I can't stand to see her hurt. Breaks my heart. I don't know how I can ever make this right."

Leo smiled. "We can't always repair what's broken."

"I have to try. It's not in me to quit." Cam replied.

"I'll leave you to it, then." Leo turned and silently slid out the door.

When he was gone, Kate stirred, shifting in the bed.

Straight away Cam was beside her, asking, "You need anything, honey?"

Her swollen eyes opened as far as she could push them; she watched him closely. "Who?" She croaked.

"Leo. I passed on what you told me." He noticed the change in her expression, and sat. "I'm with you, Kate. I won't leave you for a minute. Well, except to take a shower, when Ruth and Mark are both here. The hospital brought in a bed so I can catch a nap occasionally. There's no reason to be afraid."

She shook her head. "Leo?" Her breathing accelerated. She began to quiver.

"Yeah, he said he's made some progress on the fourth man who was at the house when it burned. Feds are interested, so he felt like they'd have better luck finding out who he is." Cam frowned. "What?"

She still shook her head, trying hard to catch her breath. "Went—to—him." She exhaled, inhaled and closed her eyes, tears slipped down her bruised, swollen cheeks. "He knew. Was two blocks away, when it happened."

Cam leaned back in the chair. He studied his bride, beaten and broken.

Later, after Evangeline's shift was over, she dropped in on her niece. Cam dozed in the recliner, instantly alert at the faint knock.

Evie held one finger over her lips, "Shh," she whispered. She quietly pulled up a seat and patted Camden's shoulder. "How's our lovely?" Her deep voice soothing and strong.

Cam's eyes teared. He paused, then answered in a whisper, "Miss Evie, I can't lose her. I can't live without her."

Evie looped her hand in the bend of his elbow and responded, "Don't blame yourself for this. She's the one to take off on her own, refusing the shadow of her beloved. But, she treated you like you were Reggie. Always protected him. The bad guys got him in the end. She's not accustomed to the protection of a real man. Her daddy loved her, but he was never—available. Leroy was the most influential man in her life. He did his best. He's shattered over this, Camden."

Cam said, "As we all are, but he *saved* her. That's definitely an accomplishment. I was sitting in my truck, asleep, when they dumped her. Listen, be careful, keep your eyes open and have security walk you into and out of the hospital."

She nodded and said, "I am. There's a reckoning coming. I've reserved my place in line when that trash is collected. Not gonna burn they lily white asses with cigarettes. I've laid claim to Leroy's brandin' iron. He bought a new battery powered model. We'll be puttin' our brand on they privates too. Never fear, sweetheart, we got your back."

Evie rose, studying her niece's restless sleep. She blew her a kiss and slipped out the door as quietly as she entered.

Cam dozed off again. Later, when he woke, he wondered if he'd dreamed Evie's visit.

***

A tap on the door demanded Cam's attention. He stood as Dr. Martin entered.

"Hey, how's your wife?" Her Jamaican accent lent music to her words. She stopped at the foot of the bed.

"Resting." Cam sighed.

Kate stirred, opened her eyes. "'allo." She coughed, shaking with pain.

"Ah, you're awake, good!" A perfect white smile brightened the doctor's dark complexion. "How are you feeling?"

Kate barely moved her head from side to side. "Hurt, tired."

"You look better than yesterday. Are you in a lot of pain?"

"Yes." Kate answered, haltingly.

"I'll increase medication, now that you're rehydrated." She made a note on the electronic chart. "I need to talk to you about something else." She sobered.

Cam steeled himself for Kate's responses.

Dr. Martin met Kate's eyes before beginning, "Katrina, your body has been through horrendous trauma. We had a DNC performed yesterday. It's a procedure…"

Kate interrupted, "Know it."

Dr. Martin nodded. "The surgeon cleaned up your insides. What the lab has come back with is a list of what all was found. There were a large number of pathogens in your vagina and even into…"

Kate broke in, "Why?"

Dr. Martin responded, "There was a dead, decimated rodent shoved inside your vagina."

Kate's mouth dropped open. Her eyes teared. She looked at Cam for confirmation.

"It's true, baby, I saw it." He said, "Look, it makes some kind of wicked sense. You were in a warehouse sort of place, there's bound to be rodents, traps, poisons…." *What did Skeet say? 'Had to talk my men outta takin' her for a little fun'. Son of a bitch! He really had her all along. The call from her phone to Skeet's was the signal.*

Dr. Martin picked up the thread, "The kidnappers used what was handy, Kate. They didn't count on a rape kit. If we hadn't found it and treated you, you would have died last night. We also discovered heroin and opioids in your system."

Kate cried silently; her throat was too tight to make noise.

Cam held her hand and spoke softly to her, "The point is, it's not over. There will be lingering effects and perhaps worse consequences. Were you awake much at all?"

"No," She squeezed the words out.

Dr. Martin said, "They may have used contaminated needles to inject the opioids. Nothing is back on those tests yet.

"I'm keeping you for two, maybe three more days. When you go home, you'll need round-the-clock care. Your Aunt Evie will tend to you. Camden, will you be able to spell Evangeline?"

Cam answered, "Yes, ma'am. Not leaving her side. Don't want strangers too close."

Kate met his gaze.

Cam turned for tissue and dabbed her face gently. "You need to rest. Know this, nothing has changed between us, except that I will be more vigilant." He glanced up at Dr. Martin. "Any way that we can move her home sooner?"

She shook her head. "Camden, we aren't out of the woods yet. The poisons, viruses, bacteria are all in her bloodstream. An aneurism is a distinct possibility. Exercise patience and caution."

"Yes, ma'am. It's just that…if we're not on hospital property, I can carry a firearm."

"Can you get a law officer to guard the door?" The doctor asked.

He shook his head and answered, "We have no idea how many people are involved and who they are. We're fairly certain that there are officers involved in the hate group, though." Cam glanced back into Kate's deepening silence.

Cam said, "Didn't ask for it. Don't know who's an enemy, who's not. This isn't an isolated incident. We lost our home to fire two weeks ago. I was caught off guard and attacked a few days earlier. Kate's uncle was ambushed, in the field the same evening, and beaten. I think we'll look after ourselves. At this point, I'm not sure I can trust anybody."

Dr. Martin's frown creased her smooth forehead. "Camden, I don't understand! Why?"

"The investigator says it's anti-Semitism, but it's more than that. You might want to ask security to walk you to your car when you leave. It seems our misfortune's contagious." His arms crossed and he glowered. "It'd be good to know what we need to plan for, so as soon as you hear from the lab, call me please."

"I will. Step out with me." She tilted her dark head toward the door.

Cam checked with Kate. Her eyes were closed again, so he joined Dr. Martin in the hallway.

She spent a long moment studying him.

Cam felt prickly. "What?"

"There'll be emotional issues to deal with, because of this." She glanced down at her pad.

"Understood. I don't expect her to skate through it. She doesn't want to talk right now. When she does, I'll be right beside her." Cam swore.

"Sometimes it takes years to recover. You need to be ready for that. A lot of people give up because it's too much trouble." She attempted a weak smile.

"I'm not a lot of people. I gave her my word. I won't run out on her." He stuffed his fingers in his jean's pockets hoping the interview was over.

"Well, I'll give you information on Post-Traumatic Stress Disorder and write a referral for her."

"That'll be fine then. We'll take all the help we can get." Cam declared.

"Both of you need rest, Camden." Dr. Martin nodded, turned, and walked away.

***

Cam sat beside the bed and gazed into Kate's dark eyes. "What are you thinking?"

Her shoulders shrugged a fraction of an inch. She closed her eyes in a long blink and croaked, "Sorry 'bout this."

"Don't be, honey. Our vows are for better or worse. Let's just hope this is the worst."

She looked doubtful, but nodded.

She struggled to swallow, then said, in a raspy tone "They said you went to Texas. Left me."

"No, I went to Texas because Cooper called. Pop was missing. My brother and Randy found Zelda tied to a tree, in the pasture. I'm still workin' through it. Maybe now's a good time to get some things off my chest." He kissed her hand and began the tale of Harry's abduction. His voice broke when he told her he may have been the one to kill Skeet, unless the ranger's shot hit first.

Kate listened, cried with him, held his hand, and silently hoped for solace.

***

Ruth and Mark sat by Kate's bedside while Cam showered.

Ruth chattered, "You look a little better, Katie, but the bruises look worse. I made an herbal salve, for when you come home. I talked to Tere. She's going to come out to the house to cut your hair, when you feel up to it. She said she'd fix it up just fine. Hair grows back."

"Bring cap?" Kate asked. "Cold."

"I did, I'm sorry." Ruth produced a crocheted knit beret from her bag. "I'll just slip it on for you." She left her chair and pulled the cap wide, gently stretching it over Kate's head, as she arched her neck to give Ruth clearance. "There, that's better. You look like you did the first day you left for kindergarten. Remember the little white beret you wore? I'll never forget. You wanted to ride the bus, *on the very first day*." She shook her head, tears coursing down her fine cheeks. "Your daddy thought it was a grand idea. I was terrified. We walked down to the road holding your hands. Richard went because he was concerned that I'd get on the bus with you. At least that's what he said."

Kate smiled at her mother's recollection. She remembered the excitement of riding the bus with other children.

Ruth continued, "I cried a dozen times, throughout the day, before we walked back up to meet you. You were so proud of yourself. All your new friends shouted out 'goodbye, Katie.'" Ruth wiped another tear off her cheek. "You stopped to wave back at them and I knew I'd lost you to the world forever." Ruth's vision blurred as she studied her only child. "I don't know what I'd do if you'd been killed. *This cannot continue.* I love you, darling." She used both hands to look through her purse for a hankie.

Her daughter's hoarse reply was, "Lu-ya too, Mom. Thank you." Kate sniffed.

"Are you eating food yet?" Mark interjected.

"Liquid. Mouth still—hurt." Kate responded.

Mark nodded. "Janiece is back from Texas and wants to visit. Feel up to it?"

She hesitantly bobbed her head.

Tap, tap, tap. The heavy door swung open. A large bouquet of blue mophead hydrangeas interspersed with fragrant white lilies preceded a CNA into the room. The young lady carrying the flowers watched her feet, as she was too short to see past the tall arrangement.

"Mrs. Fletcher?" She asked from the end of Kate's bed.

"Yes?" She covered her mouth as she coughed.

The CNA smiled past the flowers. "These came for you. Where do want me to put them?"

Ruth cleared a space on the credenza, opposite the bed. "How about right here, dear? Can you see them?"

Kate nodded.

The young lady placed the flowers and unclipped the card. "Here's the card. Enjoy." She smiled, revealing a mouth full of braces.

Kate smiled back and mouthed, "Thank you." She opened the envelope and read her husband's handwriting. *I have found the one I love and she is mine...* Tears inched down her battered face again. She sniffed. Ruth handed her a tissue.

The bathroom door opened and Cam stepped out, his wet salt and pepper hair slicked back. He passed a black leather belt through his jeans' loops and spotted the flowers. "Lovely."

"Thank you." Kate mouthed.

"You're welcome. I like your puffy hat, looks like a dollop o' whipped cream. You don't have to be in the hospital to get flowers, in case you need to know that."

Ruth cackled, still swiping at tears.

Mark grinned, shook his head, and rolled his eyes.

Cam stepped over to the bed and placed a gentle kiss on Kate's temple. He glanced at Mark. "Let's step out a minute. I need to talk to you about something."

"Sure." Mark rose.

The two friends walked to the hallway.

"Had a call earlier from a friend of Coop's. He's in Bentonville, Arkansas, owns a construction company. He'd like to take a look at us. Can you handle showing him around and going over the books?"

"Don't see why not. What's he thinking of, buying the company or equipment?" Mark asked.

"He says he's considering expansion to the area. We'll have to see. How're things going?" Cam propped against the wall with a clear view of his wife's door.

"Doing okay, as it's still winterish. It hurt to lose two foremen, but business is good. I hired a Mexican foreman yesterday, fluent Spanish, been on the road with a construction crew. He'd like to be home at night, just got married. Figure we'll be alright, until spring storms hit." Mark passed his hand over his tight gray curls.

"Hopefully we'll be out from under it before then. Are you sure about selling out?" Cam scratched his forearm.

Mark scrutinized the people moving in the hallway. "I'm sure. We came up here to work six, maybe eight months after a bad storm. That was more than five years ago. I wanna get back to my folks. Grandbabies are growing up without me. That won't do."

"You got a figure in mind?" Cam surveyed the variety of medical staff milling around them.

Mark looked down at his boots and chuckled. "You know me too well."

Cam grinned. "I'll let you handle it. When it's time to sign the paperwork, tell me. We'll let Coop know, when he has to make an appearance. You're the best negotiator anyway. I'm just the motivator."

"You mean I have the *patience* for negotiations." Mark glanced up.

"I'm the charming one. You're the brains of the operation." Cam slapped Mark on the back. "It'll be good to go home, my friend. Especially after all this shit."

***

Dr. Martin arrived an hour early on her rounds. "Hello, Fletchers." She strode into the room. "Test results are in."

Cam stood when she arrived. He sat again, waiting anxiously.

Kate stole a peek at him.

Dr. Martin read from the report, "No sign of HIV, Hep C or a dozen more life-threatening problems *yet*. Of course, some of these can come on as much as 10 years later. We'll need to check bloodwork monthly, for at least two years. When you get on your feet, you'll want to see your doctor and go over procedures, but for now, come into the lab at the hospital and have blood drawn. We'll get back to you with results ASAP. No intercourse for 6 weeks, then *always* use a condom." She checked the room chart and made a few notes.

Dr. Martin said, "I think you can go home tomorrow morning. Evangeline will tend your meds and i.v., monitor your bodily functions. You'll need that for a week to 10 days yet. I'll swing by, on the way to the office and sign your release as long as all goes well today."

"Thank you." Kate responded. She looked at her husband.

Cam stood, extended his hand.

The doctor grasped it and said, "I'll see you then." She let herself out.

Chapter Twenty-four
Home to the Bailiwick

Ruth helped get Kate situated at home. "I've moved upstairs, until you can make the climb, dear."

"Didn't have to." Kate protested. She shivered, hovering between exhaustion and excruciating pain.

"It was that or turn the music room into a bedroom. This is easier. You'll recover in a week or two and we'll switch back."

Cam watched the two women interact. "Thanks, Ruth."

Ruth hung the iv bag on a hook above the bed, checking for kinks in the line. "You're welcome. I think we need to schedule a powwow once you've rested, Katie. Amanda's working late tonight, so we have the place to ourselves."

Cam rubbed his hand over his face. "Yeah, there's a lot goin' on and we need to decide what to do with our future."

Ruth teased, "Now, for the bad news; you have to eat my cooking until your bride's on her feet."

"I'll manage, woman. It's not like I'll starve to death." He slapped his firm abs.

Ruth left them to start dinner. Cam watched Kate sit at the side of the bed for a moment.

"Really need sleep." She swallowed the pain, eyes closed.

He nodded his head. "I will do everything I can to make you better, Katrina. We have plenty of time."

"Go run. Get outside. Be okay." Her speech slurred.

He helped her lay down. She eased back on a down pillow. He covered her with a light blanket, turned on the heated mattress pad. "I said I wasn't leavin' you again."

"You're cranky—go. So tired." She closed her eyes so he would leave the room.

"For just a few minutes, then." Cam gave in.

"Mmm." She responded weakly.

Cam checked his watch and set the timer. "I'll be back in twenty minutes." He left, pulling the door closed behind him.

Cam tied on his running shoes in the mud room and hit the ground, leaping from the back porch, Dixie and Buddy at his heels.

Leo Burnham rang the front bell at the Bailiwick. The deputies accompanying him awaited orders. "Cover each door. I need a few minutes alone with Kate. Fletcher's out for a run. When he comes back, keep him occupied."

The young woman, with him, adjusted her cap. "Sir, how're we supposed to do that?"

The detective's cold eyes considered her. "Use your imagination, Deputy."

Cam's legs ate up the distance to the barn, down to the Turner's cottage, around it and back toward the house. His phone alarm sounded as he approached. He stopped beneath an eastern red cedar, leaning, with his hands, on his knees to catch his breath.

His phone rang. "Yo?"

"Me," Mark replied. "You'll never guess who I just spotted. Cracker pulled into his driveway, as I drove past. He saw the truck and tried to duck his head, too late."

A man stepped away from the house into Cam's line of sight. "I'll call you back."

He called the Bailiwick's number. "Ruth, quietly head to the music room and unlock the French doors, please."

"Whatever for, dear? Leo Burnham's here with deputies. He's in with Kate."

"Please! Now!" Cam rang off.

When the man ahead turned away, Cam sprinted for the shadows of the house. He inched around the outside, toward the music room. Hearing footsteps behind him on the wraparound porch hastened his trip. He tried the door handle. Locked. Two seconds later it opened.

"Camden, what's the matter?" Ruth whispered.

He shushed her. Long strides took him through to Ruth's bedroom door. He quietly turned the handle and threw the door open.

From the short hallway he saw Leo in a chair by the bed, making notes on his electronic notebook. "Camden, come on in. Kate and I were just catching up."

One glance at Kate's eyes told Cam her side of the story. She gulped air and was visibly shaken.

Leo Burnham left the chair and stowed his equipment. "Well, thanks, Kate. I'll let you get back to healing." He approached Cam, still parked in the doorway.

Cam stepped aside. "Leo, if you need to talk to her, be sure I'm available. She's still very ill." His icy voice brooked no argument. Dixie stood near his knee and growled, low in her chest.

The detective glanced up, as he passed. "I'm sorry, Cam. That never even occurred to me. I'll call ahead next time."

Cam followed him to the front door and opened it without a word. He stepped onto the deep front porch and watched the investigator and his two deputies pull out of the driveway and head toward the blacktop.

He closed and locked the door, before he returned to Kate. "What did he want to know, honey?" He tried to keep his voice calm.

Dixie jumped on the bed, settling near Kate's feet.

Kate whispered, "What—they said, did."

"Did he scare you? When I walked in you looked relieved. Were you afraid?" He frowned.

"He knew." She had trouble forming words. "Said he—called me. No answer." She struggled to cough and moaned. "Thought—I changed—my mind. Didn't call—here or you."

"We believed you were going to Kansas City to stay with a friend. That's what your note to us said."

"Yes. Jamie Manville." She mumbled. "FBI—for protection."

"I know. She called me the day before we found you."

"He'd get you—Mom out." Her words garbled.

Cam rubbed his chin with a knuckle. "Did he say something to make you feel like he's not too sharp or do you think he's in the middle of it all?"

She shook her head. "Not certain. Phone's gone."

Cam's eyes brightened. "Ah, but phone records can be had on-line from your carrier."

Kate's face crinkled slightly, passing for a smile. She struggled for a deep breath.

"Hello?" Evangeline's silky voice summoned from a crack at the door.

"Come on in." Cam called back.

"I've come to see to my girl." She bustled into the room dressed in Winnie the Pooh scrubs, a stethoscope draped over her shoulder, a hot pink tote in her hand, matching her lipstick and nail polish. "How you feeling, sweetheart?" Evangeline leaned over Kate and kissed her clear cheek.

"Tired, hurt." Kate took Aunt Evie's hand.

Evie crooned, "I need to listen to your lungs and change a few dressings. Then I'll swap out the i.v. and give you a treat."

"Treat's nice—peach brandy." Kate countered.

"Too many narcotics just now, pet. We've gotta get you well quick for your wedding. Can't roll you down the aisle all black and blue." She began to remove bandages, cleaning wounds to redress them. "Your mom and I made Telulah's recipe of a healing salve, we used back home. Should heal most everything, at least on the surface."

"Thank you." Kate closed her eyes, submissive to her aunt's gentle directions.

"We set our charms around to bring you home, too, pet. My god how we missed you!" Evie dabbed her wet cheeks when she turned away with two handfuls of bandages, for the trash.

Cam looked at the list of incoming calls on Kate's phone number. *How many times did I call her? Thirty, forty? There're only three calls from me showing. Leo called twice. Ruth's calls are listed. The last call made to a number in Texas. Date and time match Skeet's phone.* He left Kate's laptop on the desk. He paced the old oak floor of the music room, studied the pattern of the ancient, worn Turkish rug in the center. *If I could, I'd grab a few clothes, my bride, our dogs, and head for…where would I go?*

He opened the bedroom door, eased through to peek around the corner. Kate seemed to be asleep. He leaned against the wall and pondered their future.

"What you thinking?" Kate mumbled, watching him through narrowed eyes.

"About running away." He chuckled. "I can't imagine where I'd take us, though. If you could be anywhere in the world you wanted, where would that be?" He crossed the room and sat in the wing-backed chair, by the bed, leaning his forearms on his thighs.

"Anywhere?" Kate asked.

"Your heart's desire, Katrina." He watched her ponder his question.

She croaked, "Your arms." A tear escaped, as she turned her face toward him.

He laughed. "I can handle that—with pleasure." He slipped to the other side of the bed and beneath the blanket, scooted to her side and propped on one elbow.

She placed her hand on his chest, her face raised slightly to see him. His scent of soap and shaving cream flirted with her nose and made her smile.

He arranged his arm across her, barely making contact with her body. His socked foot rested on the bottom of hers.

"Mmm." She relaxed and exhaled. "Thank you." She muttered wearily.

"You're welcome. It feels good to touch you." *Rips my heart open to see the bruises, burns and cuts on your lovely, soft skin.* He stroked her hair. "Kate, if you only knew how much I love you…"

Her dark eyes solemnly studied him. "You're—still here."

Cam replied, "I'll never leave you."

"It—may get—worse." Her voice broke.

"Then we'll ride that wave together, honey." He stroked her cheek, brushing one fingertip across a clear spot.

Kate's first night home was rough. Sleep was interrupted hourly with bad dreams. Camden turned on a closet and a bathroom light, set the mattress pad on low and lay beside his wife, barely touching her. She woke gasping for air a few times. She flailed trying to hit something. He caught her in his arms, talking her down until she woke up enough to be calmed.

Cam thought Kate's reactions to the dreams were horrifying. *She was terrorized, abused and god only knows how she was threatened. Being told she'd be buried alive, then locked in a box was inhuman. If I ever get my hands on any one of these monsters….*

Chapter Twenty-five
One week later

"Your first appointment with the psychiatrist is tomorrow morning. Are you good with that?" Cam led Kate toward the kitchen.

"No." She stopped, in the butler's pantry. when a coughing spell hit her. When the fit was over, she shuffled to the kitchen table, where her husband held her chair. "Call—Jamie, please."

"Leo Burnham said he called the Feds. They let Cracker out on bail to take care of family matters. He has to check in three times a day. Leo's just county sheriff's department. He can't control what the Feds do." Cam sat across from her.

She nodded. "Jamie can—check. Don't—believe Leo's a bad guy?"

Cam answered, "I don't know. When I think I've caught him in a lie, he comes up with a plausible answer. I'll let Jamie know you're okay and ask her to quietly investigate. Wish I could borrow your special talent."

"Thank you, I read only evil in that man." She closed her eyes and sighed. "Can't stay here. Need to sell. Mom?" Kate turned to Ruth, drying her hands, on a tea towel, by the sink.

Ruth answered, "Leroy and Evangeline are retiring to Florida, to be with Rickey. We can sell the cattle and be done. There's two year's work left on this place. For my part, let's put it up for auction. But, it's yours, so you make the final call."

"Cam?" Kate turned to meet his eyes.

"Ruth's got a point, but neither of us can decide what to do with your inheritance. You've poured a lot of money and sweat into rehabbing it. Do you really want to walk away?" He reached for her hand, massaging her fingertips.

"Call auctioneer?" Kate swallowed hard with a long blink. She opened her eyes to find her mother and husband watching her.

"We're not pushing you, honey." Cam brushed his hand over his beard and frowned. "If you want to stay, I'll finish the house. I'm about to have loads of spare time. Mark called. We have a buyer for the roofing company. They're also interested in the shop and land—where our house sat. We'll do alright out of it all."

Kate shook her head. "Not money. Plans changed." Her speech was laborious. "Never dreamed—you. Three months—of hell." She paused to rest.

"I'm not going anywhere." Cam reassured her.

"No chance to be your wife." She sipped warm water through a straw. "House consumes me. And this—battle. How to live here—and Texas?" She paused and inhaled, covering her mouth with a tissue in her hand, as she coughed a wad of phlegm.

Cam rubbed his hand down her back. "I've thought about that. Randy's near retirement. We can find another manager for the ranch, go down, when we can or find someone to run things here and live down there. I'll work with you on this, Kate."

"No. Sell." Kate's eyes brightened. "Auction." She leaned forward, resting her head in her hands propped on the table, exhausted.

Ruth turned to the window as a car pulled into the driveway. "Tere's here, Katie. Cam, get a chair for her to the mudroom. She's having her hair done, Mom's treat." Ruth leaned to kiss her daughter's right cheek, the clearest place on her face.

***

Two more weeks passed slowly as Kate healed in the solace and security of the Bailiwick. She and Ruth walked through the master bedroom with various colored sticky notes in hand. The auctioneer, Ben Brady, toured the property with Cam and Leroy.

Ruth said, "Take everything you want. Cam said Cooper's making great progress on your house. They should finish the foundation today and the limestone has been delivered. You'll need to furnish it, dear." Ruth gathered framed family photos, stacking the lot on a chair.

Kate answered, "Hopefully ready by auction. You sure we shouldn't turn our hand to wedding stuff?" Her hoarse whispered words still ran together.

"No, Elaine and I've had it planned for a while. We bought our dresses and shoes, on a shopping trip, a month before you moved back home. You only had to choose your cake and flowers." She paused, stretching. "I finished taking in your dress last night. Cam said as soon as boys arrive, we're leaving, to fly down. It'll be such fun, Kate. We all need a party, after the past three months."

Kate smiled. Her left eye had healed, but retained a bit of bruising. "Party will be nice. It's coming back I dread. I hate the feeling."

Ruth suddenly interjected, "Oh my gosh! I forgot about the lap harp. Isaac brought it, the day we had breakfast at Cam's house." She scurried toward the music room. In a moment, she returned with the instrument. "Let's pack this away right now. Can't have the auctioneer seeing it." She opened her suitcase and pushed the lap harp inside, snapping the lid definitively.

Ruth straightened and surveyed the bedroom, before saying, "I came here as a bride 50 years ago, Kate. There's a sense of freedom now, after all that time, tied down to this place. I've loved it and hated it in equal measure." She glanced at her child and said, "I only kept it for you, after Richard died. I could have sold up and moved into rental housing. Evie and I looked into it. But, I wanted you to have it, not as a burden, which I know it's become, but as a gift, left by your people for the past 200 years. Your daddy was proud of his family, but he wasn't around enough to teach you what he'd learned from grandparents and parents. Then you up and ran off to the city. He despaired of you ever coming home again."

Kate smiled at her father's memory and said, "I get that, but he wasn't here with us as I grew up. Sometimes, when he came back from Vietnam, I was frightened of him. He was a stranger until he stayed the last time, and we could learn a bit about each other. Right before I graduated high school, and moved to KC to uni."

Ruth agreed, "Yes, and that unwound him, too. I was so glad you married and had the boys quickly. Otherwise, they would never remember their grandpa. Asher reminds me of him sometimes, the way he cocks his head, when he's teasing, those broad shoulders…."

Kate nodded, "And when he smiles that crooked smile that we both inherited from Daddy. Isaac doesn't remember him well. He asks about things he *thinks* he recalls, wondering if it's true or the remnants of a story we told about Grampa. He's usually dead on, though. He's a very bright young man."

Ruth asked, "Shifting subjects, have you heard from your FBI friend?"

"Yes, she says Leo Burnham looks fine, so far." She shrugged. "We'll see. Ever get a sense about a person—like you don't feel right turning your back on them?"

"Occasionally, do you feel that way about him?" Ruth asked.

"First time we met, it was creepy. I can't put my finger on a specific action or words. I just felt…" She shuddered. "He was pleasant, respectful, polite. But, the way he looked at me was eerie."

Ruth studied her daughter for a moment. "I hadn't paid him a lot of attention, just took him at face value ,because of his rank in the sheriff's department. When Cam called for me to open the music room door, the day you came home from the hospital, I thought he was daft. Since then, I can't trust Leo alone with you again."

"Hope I'm wrong, Mom. I don't like feeling this way about anybody, much less someone who has so much authority over our lives." Kate put a green sticker on a framed print of "Master Bedroom" by Andrew Wyeth.

Ruth watched her for a moment, before responding. "You have that distinct DNA, girl. We have discernment to protect us. Our blood is full of conjures, brews, foresight and spells. Did you talk to Camden, about the way you felt, before you were abducted?"

"No, regrettably." She sighed and put a green sticker on the antique waterfall high-boy.

Chapter Twenty-six
The Wedding

Resplendent in black tuxedos, Camden, Isaac, and Asher stood at the front of a hundred-eighty-year-old stone church, a few miles from the Kendal ranch. The three of them watched as guests took their seats. Cam checked on two private security guards he'd hired, and one man who was obviously armed with a shoulder holster, under his suit coat. *Wonder who this dude is.*

"Y'all excuse me a minute." He left the boys and strode purposefully toward the man, who met him halfway, his hand out to shake.

Cam shook his hand and asked, "Who are you with?"

The man handed over his badge, introducing himself, "Mason Rodgers, FBI. Jaime said to tell you she had to fly home, her mom's sick. Ask me to cover this shindig for her. Since I owed her a favor," He shrugged. "here we are."

The groom nodded. "Good, we need all the help we can get. Did she tell you about the party later?"

Mason nodded. "She did. Got it covered." He turned and walked back to the corner, scanning the crowd, then the parking lot.

Cam turned to Asher and Isaac to point out folks they may be interested in knowing. "The gentleman in the gray suit about to sit down is our accountant, Jimmy Godwin. That pretty girl with him is his youngest daughter. I don't recall her name, but heard she started college at Baylor this past year."

Both young men brightened, but Isaac's interest was keen, as he studied the thin brunette.

"See the lady in the loud purple suit? Artie Foster owns the florist shop, downtown. She did all the flowers for the wedding and your mom's bouquet. Next to her, is one of her granddaughters." He turned to Asher. "You might want to dance with her. I hear she's a ballerina, so she's gotta be good on the dance floor.

"The couple seated by Leroy and Evangeline, is a plumbing contractor for my brother. Those are his twin girls beside him. Momma said they're both juniors at Texas Woman's University in Denton, this year, and beauties to boot."

Asher turned to Cam; his mouth open to respond. He froze in place. Cam and Isaac looked back, to see what captivated him.

Kate stood outside the bride's room. Her men headed her way.

She straightened the skirt of her dress and looked up. Her husband could have been on a *GQ Magazine* cover and her sons looked like handsome strangers. She spoke, "What? You guys never saw a girl before?"

A narrow-brimmed silk hat, wrapped in cream tulle and ribbon covered her short hair, perched at a jaunty angle. Her long-sleeved dress was antique lace overlaying raw silk, calf length in front, tea length in back, with a detachable train, that Tere puddled on the floor.

Tere stepped up beside Kate, in a rose silk tea length dress that set off her dark complexion and dark brown hair. She grinned at her best friend and said, "Marvelous, my sweet!" She spotted Cooper and waited until he reached her, with a smile.

Bouquet in hand, Tere met Cooper for the slow trip to the dais.

"Mom, you look wonderful!" Isaac muttered.

Kate smiled. "Thank you. Camden, breathe, you're turning blue."

Cam chuckled. "That's incredible! I saw you go in there in an old tee shirt and sweats not thirty minutes ago. Is that a magic closet?"

Asher watched her blush, before responding, "You're really beautiful. I'm proud you're my mom."

Kate said, "Thereza Diaz is the magician. Thank you, all. Love you too. Now, let's get this done. I'm hungry."

Cam lowered the short veil of her hat, over his bride's eyes and continued to devour her with his gaze.

Her sons preceded them into the church. The boys passed through ancient oak double doors, thrown wide. Kate took her place beside her husband, her hand resting inside the cleft of his left arm.

The first notes of a song began, accompanied by Elaine on the church's baby grand piano.

"Did you choose the music?" Kate asked Cam.

A saxophone sounded in the background, then a violin entered, as sharp and sweet as the first strawberry of summer.

"Yes, ma'am. I'll tell you about it later, okay?" Cam smiled at his bride.

Kate's eyes filled. She watched her mother-in-law playing the song chosen for that moment, as they strolled up the aisle, lined with friends and relatives.

Tere waited for Kate, on the left side, at the front; Cooper waited on Camden's right.

Asher and Isaac took their places on stage, opening a chuppah. Greta, Cam's aunt, and Han, his uncle, joined the boys to lift the poles to spread the sacred covering above the couple.

Kate's eyes widened, she turned to Cam. "What?"

"Happy wedding day, honey." He grinned and winked.

They took three steps, up to the top of the dais and stood beneath the blue silk.

Tere bent to straighten the bride's train. Cooper glanced her way and winked, when she met his admiring gaze.

Kate noticed movement behind the curtained entryway. Her mouth dropped open. "Sha'ul?"

The rabbi turned off his microphone, as he walked their way and leaned toward her, to kiss her cheek gently. He whispered, "Would I miss your wedding day? Am I that kind of friend?"

Tears escaped, as she dug for her hankie, stuffed up her sleeve. "You're a fine friend." She whispered back, sniffing.

Cam watched every movement; certain he had never been happier than that moment.

Rabbi turned his microphone on and addressed the audience, "Welcome! We're performing this formal ceremony for the families and friends, of the bride and the groom. Katrina and Camden have been married for three months already. But we need a party to celebrate these two. Thank you for coming to help us launch their married lives together.

"It isn't often that I'm asked to officiate, at a service in a Christian church. So, let us begin with a proper Jewish greeting, Shabbat Shalom!"

"Shabbat Shalom," most of the crowd responded.

The rabbi's eyes closed and he repeated the standard opening prayer. "Let us begin, Blessed are You, Adonai, Ruler of the Universe, Who is the source of all gladness and joy. Through Your grace we attain affection, companionship, love and peace. OMAIN!"

"Katrina Evangeline Bishop," his voice dropped to say, "my favorite bride today. You have sworn yourself to this man, Camden Bantz Fletcher, to be his faithful wife, in this place and time."

Kate sniffed before answering, hoping her voice wouldn't break, "I have."

Sha'ul turned to Cam, "And you, Camden Bantz Fletcher, have sworn yourself, to this beautiful woman, to be her faithful husband, protector and companion."

Cam cleared his throat and locked gazes with Kate. "I have."

The rabbi continued, "You have committed to live the rest of your lives as partners, lovers and friends. You have taken a sacred pledge, before all who hear these words."

Rabbi continued, "You may kiss your bride, sir, and we'll seal the pledges with our blessing. OMAIN!"

And some responded, "OMAIN!", others "Amen!"

Rabbi pointed to the walls on each side of the stage. "On the screens you'll find the Seven Wedding Blessings, Sheva B'ra-khot. We'll recite these together as the bride and groom share Kiddush, Communion." He nodded to Kate and Camden, who left their places for the communion cup, at a table beside the Rabbi.

Sha'ul began the incantation. "Blessed are You, Adonai our God, King of the universe, Who creates the fruit of the vine. Blessed are You, Adonai our God, King of the universe, Who has created all things in the universe to Your glory...."

Chapter Twenty-seven
The Reception

Pappy's Roadhouse filled with wedding revelers. Four buffet lines formed in the front room. The dance floor and surrounding area held a hundred additional tables and four hundred chairs. After dinner, the service crew removed them, as the band tuned their instruments.

Sha'ul, Asher, and Isaac gathered participants for the Mitzvah dance.

Cam, Mark, and Leroy joined them. Cam yelled to Coop. "Get up here! It's a line dance. You can do this." To his surprise and delight his Uncle Han accompanied Cooper, holding his arm. A quick glance beyond them, Cam noticed Jane heading for the exit, with her purse in hand.

Aunt Greta's husband, Reverend Warren Bales followed closely behind Han.

The men danced to the best middle eastern tune a Southern honkytonk band could strike and ended yelling, "Hey, hey, hey!" in unison.

Kate noticed that Han gravitated toward wherever Ruth happened to be, securing as much of her mother's notice as possible. They danced together frequently, sat beside each other and leaned in for private conversation in the noisy club.

At midnight Camden whispered into Kate's ear, "Wanna blow this joint?"

"I'm with you. Where're we going?" She asked.

"I booked a suite in Austin. The one we honeymooned in, a few months ago. Won't be like going home, but it'll do for the night." He held her gently in his arms.

"I won't break, you know." She squeezed his arm into her side.

He shook his head and grinned. "Guess I got used to handling you softly and can't get over it." He rubbed his chin with his thumb. "I'm tickled you're well enough to be doin' this, Kate."

"I know, me too. Are we saying goodbye or sneaking out?" Her gaze noted every move he made.

Cam answered, "One last dance and we'll let them know we're leaving."

"One more for the road." She glided toward the small crowd moving slowly, in time, to the music.

Cam pulled her closer to the stage and nodded at the guitarist.

Kate smiled as she melted into his arms. "This is the first song we danced to here."

"Yes, ma'am. Circumstances are a lot better, all things considered." He sang along with the music.

"There's that." She laughed.

After saying goodnight, the couple walked toward the entrance. Kate glanced back, as the processional song, played at the wedding, began. She yanked on Cam's arm. "They're playing the wedding song."

He glanced back and grinned, sending a thumbs up, to the band. He said, "Yeah, baby, they're studio musicians too." He held the door for Kate to pass through.

"Okay, what else?" She asked, stopping outside the door.

"I know a guy with a studio. I wrote the music, with my mother's professional help. She went to the studio and cut the tune, with the studio musicians backing her. She brought the recording to the church and played along with it, to sort of bolster the sound. It's awfully pretty, don't you think?"

Kate listened without interruption. She nodded, then asked, "What's it called?"

Cam studied the air between them for a moment, before answering, "*Sonata for Katrina.*" He risked a glance into her dark eyes. "It was why your photograph sat on the piano, in our house. It took me almost a year to get every note just right. Momma polished it up a bit and took care of the rest." He took her arm again.

Kate followed quietly, inhaling the fine, rain-washed air of the evening, trying to stem tears.

Cam loosened his tie as they walked out to the Jeep slowly. His cell phone rang. "Fletcher."

"You're clear here." A voice informed.

"Thanks." He rang off.

"Who was that?" Kate asked.

He shushed her, a fingertip over his lips. He whispered into her ear. "No talking."

He helped her into the Jeep and walked around to the driver's side. He scouted the parking lot for the man who made the call. He barely saw the salute, from the dark corner of the lot that hid him. Cam returned the salutation.

He climbed in and waited a moment before starting the engine. He reinforced silence to Kate with a finger to his lips. He let the vehicle warm for a moment. He turned the opposite direction from Austin.

Kate frowned and almost spoke.

Camden shook his head and pointed down the road. They turned right, out of Pappy's, and drove across the tiny burg. On the opposite side of town in a stand of hundred-year-old oaks stood a Greek revival, similar to the Kendal home. It was a bed and breakfast.

Cam parked the Jeep and reached for his cell, which rang again. "Fletcher."

"Got 'em, Cam. How'd you know?" The voice demanded.

"Didn't. Suspected." He listened to the particulars, nodding. "Thanks, I'll sleep a lot easier tonight." Cam turned on the radio and leaned to Kate's ear, "Darlin, you're buggy. Shh!" He pulled a sheet magnet and a roll of duct tape from the console and wrapped the magnet over her sleeve. He held it in place while he tacked it down with the tape.

"What?" She whispered back.

"We're gonna run down to the Naval Health Clinic in Corpus Christi tomorrow, to have the tat removed. A buddy of mine, in Naval Intelligence, will meet us there."

"I want to keep it." Kate argued.

"They implanted a listening device. Were you awake for that?" He asked.

She shook her head. "No, they put a mask on my face that reeked of ether. I'd supposed, so I would stop thrashing around. Then, of course, there were the drugs."

"I'm betting we'll find they used more than ink on your arm. I put in a call to someone who'd know. He said they exist, they're illegal and about the size of a grain of rice. That's gotta go."

"We're here, instead of flying out, because the bad guys have been workin' on the airplane for the last hour. We wouldn't have gotten far. They set it to blow up about five minutes after takeoff."

Kate's voice became shrill, "What? Who—Cam—do you know who's doing this?"

"Well, Mrs. Fletcher, they've picked up our friend, Leo Burnham, and a couple of junior execs workin' with him. Jamie Manville kept it all under wraps, but she and I've talked, out of your hearing range, about the possibility of another attempt. We both felt like they'd pull out all the stops this time. We were right. There's no way we'd have lived through the plane exploding." He pulled away from her ear to see her face

"I don't know what to say." Kate looked confused and relieved.

"There's your final wedding gift, my heart. It's over. Now, to get on with life." He left the Jeep, walked to her side, and opened the door. She slid down into his arms, laid her head on his chest.

She sighed and felt the load lighten. "That's the best present of all. Thank you."

"I'm gonna have to wrap your arm in the magnet when I get you undressed. Sorry, but there may still be somebody listening."

***

Cam propped on his pillow, watching his bride sleep. She rolled toward him and stretched, before opening her eyes. Daylight behind the blackout curtains of the room threw off enough light through a crack to see.

"How long have you been awake?" She whispered.

He whispered back, "I don't know. Love looking at you. For years I've longed for that special someone to be sleeping close enough to touch. Now you are. There aren't words for what I feel every morning. I thought maybe you'd have some."

She smiled, laid her hand on his jaw, leaned her forehead on his chest, nuzzling the curly hair. "Mmm...."

"That's good enough." He wrapped her in his arms.

Chapter Twenty-eight
A year later...

"Fletcher." Cam answered his cell on the second ring.

"Camden, this is Jamie Manville."

"Yes ma'am." He sat in his favorite chair, in the living room, of their home, in a field on Kendal Ranch. The humidity heightened the heady fragrance of freshly hewn cedar.

"I called to warn you…" She continued.

"I see." His thoughts were already spinning, as she covered the details.

***

Kate drove her car into the garage, of the house that Cooper and Camden built. The similarities to Cam's house, in Missouri, were evident in the design, only smaller, and built of limestone. She watched her husband walk out to the front porch and wave. She climbed out and studied his calm descent.

"Hey, you!" She smiled as he dipped to her lips for a kiss.

Cam apologized, "I'm sorry I was late getting home. Ruth said I missed you by fifteen minutes. I really wanted to go with you, to your last appointment. How'd you do?"

"Good. I've been released to follow up, as needed. Thank you for the grace you've given me to get through therapy." She rested her head against his chest.

"It's been good for both of us, honey. Let's celebrate, take a few days off."

"Mmm…where?" She asked.

"It's a surprise…." He answered.

Kate glanced up. "Really?"

"Yep, made the reservations, filed the flight plan. We're packed to go. We'll take the plane and pick up a car when we get there."

"Sounds like fun." Her face broke into a wreath of smiles.

"Let's grab our bags and get outta here." He turned to the house, taking her arm in his. He nervously chattered, "I took Dixie up to the inmates to mind while we're away. Mark and I came to an understanding about Buddy yesterday. His grandkids love the dog too much to bring him back to us. Figure with Suga and Cinnamon living in Florida with your aunt and uncle, Dixie would be starved for canine company, but she's sure taken to Zelda. They get along fine."

***

Camden taxied down the runway of the pasture landing strip and lifted off as smoothly as a summer breeze. He checked Kate's brilliant smile. His heart lurched.

They headed southeast, toward the water. He peeked over at his wife. The bright orange, of the automatic inflatable life jacket, tinged her rosy cheeks.

He reached for the radio knob on the dash and clicked it off. Kate watched the Gulf of Mexico came into view.

"This is your favorite part, isn't it, honey?" Cam asked.

She nodded gleefully. She hadn't stopped smiling, since he told her the lie.

He dropped altitude, closing in on the waves stirred by an offshore storm. The flip of a switch started the windshield wipers.

***

Cooper's desk and cell phones rang in sequence. "Yeah? Hold on." He reached for his cell in his briefcase. "Fletcher, hold on."

He returned to the desk phone. "Jane, can this wait a minute? I got another call."

"No." The tone of her voice caused a pang of alarm in the pit of his stomach. "Jeff called from the airport."

Cooper looked at caller id on his cell. "Yeah, got him on the other phone."

"I'll hold while you talk to him." Jane's voice tightened.

He snatched the cell phone. "Jeff, what's goin' on?"

"Camden filed a flight plan this afternoon, for Biloxi. He dropped off radar twenty minutes ago and we can't raise him on the radio. What'll we do?"

"Called the Coast Guard?" Cooper, slipped on his jacket as he stood. He gathered the contract paperwork, from his desk, to slide into his briefcase.

"Done it. They're nowhere near where they should be, if they'd stayed on course. A chopper went up ten minutes ago and they don't spot wreckage. Of course, there's a storm stirring the waters."

"Keep me informed, Jeffrey. I better get to the ranch." Cooper rang off and picked up the desk phone. "Jane, I've gotta go to Momma's. I'll call you back later." He cradled the phone, snagged his briefcase, and jogged through the office, past his secretary's desk. "Call me, only if you absolutely have to." He yelled in her general direction. He jogged to his truck and climbed in the driver's seat.

Kendal Ranch

Cooper sat at the round oak table in the kitchen. The inmates gathered, curious about the hastily called conference.

Cooper's voice gentled, "Momma, Ruth, Jeff called from the county airport. He said that Camden filed a flight plan for Biloxi."

Elaine interjected, "Yes, Kate's therapy sessions are complete. They flew to Biloxi, to spend a few days celebrating." She checked the clock. "They should be there by now."

Coop shook his head slowly. "Jeff said they dropped off radar, over the Gulf, more than an hour ago. He can't raise 'em on the radio. I checked in with him, as I pulled in the driveway. There's still no word from the Coast Guard spotters."

Elaine began to shake. Her eyes fastened on her husband's face. "Harry?"

A smile teased the corner of his mouth. "He's a very good pilot, Elaine."

Ruth slung an accusation across the table, near hysterics, "Harry Kendal, do you know somethin' you're not telling?"

Harry's eyes glued to the spot where Cooper sat. "You know good and well Camden can put that plane down on the edge of a dime, anytime he pleases."

"Yes, sir, but we all make mistakes." Cooper argued.

Harry shook his head.

Cooper's cell phone rang. "Fletcher." He listened. "Yeah, Jeff, got that." He sighed and surveyed the occupants of the table. "They've called off the search. There's nothin' out there."

Elaine reached for her husband's arm. "Harry, what're you not telling us?"

Harry sat back in his chair and pondered the ceiling. "Cam and I had a conversation, a few months ago. He said he wouldn't let Kate go through hell again. If the orchestrators didn't get life without parole, they'd go to ground. My son's an excellent pilot. He's run to safety, with his wife. That's all I'm sayin' for the moment." Reaching for his dog's halter, Harry rose.

He and Zelda left the room in stunned silence.

Cooper got up and followed. "Pop, hang on."

Harry paused in the foyer; his tone curt. "What?"

"What's the password?" Cooper asked.

Harry grinned. "Biloxi."

The old man headed to the office, "Come on, Cooper." Harry sat behind the desk.

Cooper awaited instructions.

"Open the safe and pull the bottom drawer all the way out and look in the very back, in a yellow envelope with G R O U N D on the front." Harry listened to his son follow instructions.

Cooper stood up, "Got it, Pop."

"Take and share the information with your mother and Ruth, swear them to silence and return it to the safe."

Chapter Twenty-nine
Landing

Cam taxied the plane along a dirt runway. A young dark-skinned man, in coveralls, waved a checkered flag, to guide them into the hangar. Cam parked and turned off the engine.

He opened the door and addressed the young man in Spanish.

Kate heard, 'blue' and 'the new numbers'.

Cam left the door ajar and squinted at Kate. "I need to tell you something, honey."

She frowned. "What?" She unlatched her seatbelt and loosened the buckles, on the life jacket, slipping out of it with her husband's help.

He sat quietly for a moment and studied the back wall of the steel building. "I don't quite know how to say this but—I sorta lied to you. We aren't here for a few days. We may be here a long time."

"Camden?" She gripped his arm.

He glanced over at her. "Jamie called, while you were gone, Kate. Leo Burnham made a deal, convinced a federal judge he worked undercover, with the neo-Nazi group. His superior backed him up. He's supposed to be going into a witness protection program."

"Oh!" She paled.

"Jamie warned me, when they had him in custody, that this may never be over. Mark and I bought two small places here in Mexico a few years ago and set up accounts, so we could just step out of our world into this one, without a hassle. We have new passports, driver's license, the works."

"I see. That's why you turned off the radar and radio." She closed her eyes for a long blink.

"Also, I disabled our cell phones before we left, so we couldn't be traced."

A tear slid down her cheek. She passed a shaky hand over her face and through her hair. "What about my boys?"

"Jamie's taking care of that." Cam paused. "Reggie's parents are with her."

She sat still and quiet as death, for a full five minutes. Cam waited.

She croaked through tears, "At least we're together."

He nodded. "There's that." He climbed out of the plane and circled to her side. He opened her door and gently tugged on her arm. "Come on, baby."

Kate inhaled the stifling dusty air ,of the hangar, and climbed down into his arms. "My boys!" Her voice broke.

"We'll see them when we can. Jamie can handle visits. You'll be there when they graduate college. We just have to watch from a secure room instead of in public."

She whispered. "Mom?"

"Knows by now. Pop's covering the family. The only folks with access to our location are Jamie, Mark and Coop, at this point. Pop has a secret hiding place, in the safe, that Momma doesn't even know about. That's where our info's hidden."

She looked up into his sad smile and beautiful green eyes, saying, "You've thought of everything."

"Not exactly. I haven't figured out how to stop this hell train and just live like normal people." He brushed a lock of hair from her face.

"This hell train's because of me, Cam." Kate replied.

He shook his head. "No, Kate. There's no sane explanation for bigotry. It's hatred gone mad and the more it's indulged the madder it gets."

She nodded, taking a shaky, deep breath of the gritty hot air. "There's that."

www.ingramcontent.com/pod-product-compliance
Lightning Source LLC
Chambersburg PA
CBHW060635260626
47161CB00008B/2896